A Daughter of the Philistines

Leonard Merrick

Contents

A DAUGHTER OF THE PHILISTINES...7
CHAPTER I. 7
CHAPTER II. 12
CHAPTER III. 19
CHAPTER IV. 26
CHAPTER V. 31
CHAPTER VI. 37
CHAPTER VII. 44
CHAPTER VIII. 51
CHAPTER IX. 58
CHAPTER X. 64
CHAPTER XI. 70
CHAPTER XII. 77
CHAPTER XIII. 83
CHAPTER XIV. 90
CHAPTER XV. 96
CHAPTER XVI. 102
CHAPTER XVII. 109
CHAPTER XVIII. 116
CHAPTER XIX. 129
CHAPTER XX. 135
CHAPTER XXI. 143
CHAPTER XXII. 149
CHAPTER XXIII. 162
CHAPTER XXIV. 176

A DAUGHTER OF
THE PHILISTINES

BY

Leonard Merrick

A DAUGHTER OF THE PHILISTINES.
CHAPTER I.

Two friends were sitting together outside the Café des Tribunaux in Dieppe. One of them was falling in love; the other, an untidy and morose little man, was wasting advice. It was the hour of coffee and liquors, on an August evening.

'You are,' said the adviser irritably, 'at the very beginning of a career. You have been surprisingly fortunate; there is scarcely a novelist in England who wouldn't be satisfied with such reviews as yours, and it's your first book. Think, twelve months ago you were a clerk in the city, and managed to place about three short stories a year at a guinea each. Then your aunt what-was-her-name left you the thousand pounds, and you chucked your berth and sat down to a novel. "Nothing happens but the unforeseen"—the result justified you. You sold your novel; you got a hundred quid for it; and the *Saturday,* and the *Spectator,* and every paper whose opinion is worth a rush, hails you as a coming light. For you to consider marrying now would be flying in the face of a special providence.'

'Why?' said Humphrey Kent.

' "Why!" Are you serious? Because your income is an unknown quantity. Because you've had a literary success, not a popular one. Because, if you keep single, you've a comfortable life in front of you. Because you'd be a damned fool.'

'The climax is comprehensive, if it isn't convincing. But the discussion is a trifle "previous," eh? I can't marry you, my pretty maid, et cetera.'

'You are with her all day,' said Turquand. 'I conclude she likes you. And the mother countenances it.'

'There is really nothing to countenance; and, remember, they haven't any idea of my position: they meet me in a fashionable hotel, they had read the book, and they saw the *Times* review. What do they know of literary earnings?—the father is on the Stock Exchange, I believe! I am an imposter.'

'You should have gone to the little show I recommended on the quay, then. I find it good enough.'

Kent laughed and stretched himself.

'I am rewarding industry,' he said. 'For once I wallow. I came into the money, and I put it in a bank, and by my pen, which is mightier than the sword, I've replaced all I drew to live during the year. Am I not entitled to a brief month's splash? Besides, I've never said I want to marry—I don't know what you're hacking at.'

'You haven't "said" it, but the danger is about as plain as pica to the average intelligence, all the same. My son, how old are you—twenty-seven, isn't it? Pack your bag, ask for your bill, and go back with me by the morning boat; and, if you are resolved to make an ass of yourself over a woman, go and live in gilded infamy, and buy sealskin jackets and jewelry while your legacy lasts. I'll forgive you that.'

'The prescription wouldn't be called orthodox?'

'You'd find it cheaper than matrimony in the long-run, I promise you. When now and again some men play ducks and drakes with a fortune for a cocotte there are shrieks enough to wake his ancestors; but marriage ruins a precious sight more men every year than the demi-monde, and the turf, and the tables put together, and nobody shrieks at all—except the irrepressible children. Did it never occur to you that the price paid for the virtuous woman is quite the most appalling one known in an expensive world?'

'No,' said Kent shortly, 'it never did.'

'And they call you "an acute observer"! Marriage is man's greatest extravagance.'

'The apothegm excepted. It sounds like a dissipated copybook.'

'It's a fact, upon my soul. I tell you, a sensible girl would shudder at the thought of entrusting her future to a man improvident enough to propose to her; a fellow capable of marrying a woman is the sport of a reckless and undiscipled nature she should beware of.'

'The end is curacoa-and-brandy,' said Kent, 'and in your best vein. What else? You'll contradict yourself with brilliance in a moment if you go on.'

The journalist dissembled a grin, and Kent, gazing down the sunny little street, inhaled his cigarette pleasurably. To suppose that Miss Walford would ever be his wife looked to him so chimerical that his companion's warnings did not disturb him, yet he was sufficiently attracted by her to find it exciting that a third person could think it likely. He was the son of a man who had once been very wealthy, and who, having attempted to repair injudicious investments by rasher speculation, had died owning little more than enough to defray the cost of his funeral. At the age of nineteen Humphrey realized that, with no stock-in-trade beyond an education and a bundle of rejected manuscripts, it was incumbent on him to fight the world unassisted, and, suppressing his literary ambitions as likely to tell against him, betook himself to some connections who throve in commerce and had been socially agreeable. To be annihilated by a sense of your own deficiencies, seek an appointment at the hands of relations. The boy registered the aphorism, and withdrew. When 'life' means merely a struggle to sustain existence, it is not calculated to foster optimism, and the optimistic point of view is desirable for the production of popular English fiction. His prospect of achieving many editions would have been greater if his father had been satisfied with five per cent. He shifted as best he could, and garnered various experiences which he would have been sorry to think would be cited by his biographer, if he ever had one. 'Poverty is no disgrace,' but there are few disgraces that cause such keen humiliations. Eventually he found regular employment in the office of a stranger, and, making Turquand's acquaintance in the lodging-house in which he obtained a bedroom, contemplated him with respect and envy. Turquand was subediting *The Outpost,* a hybrid periodical for which he wrote a very little of what he thought and much that he disapproved, in consideration of a modest salary. The difference in their years was not too great to preclude confidences. An intimacy grew between the pair over their evening pipes, in the arid enclosure to which the landlady's key gave them access, and was transplanted to joint quarters embellished with their several possessions, chiefly portmanteaus and photographs, equally battered. The elder man, perceiving there was distinction in the unsuccessful stories displayed to him, imparted a good deal of desultory advice, of which the most effectual part was not the assurance that the literary temperament was an affliction, and authorship a synonym for despair. The younger listened, sighed, and burned. Aching to be famous, and fettered to a clerk's stool, he tugged at his chains. He had begun to doubt his force to burst them, when he was apprised, to his unspeakable amazement, that a maternal aunt, whom he had not seen since he was a schoolboy had bequeathed him a thousand pounds.

Dieppe had dined, and the Grand Rue was astir. He watched the passers-by with interest. In the elation of his success he was equal to tackling another novel on the morrow, and he saw material in every thing: in the chattering party of American girls running down from the Plage to eat more ices at the pastrycook's; in the coquettish dealer in rosaries and Lives of the Saints, who had put up her shutters for the night, and was bound for the Opera; in the little boy-soldiers from the barracks, swaggering everywhere in uniforms a size and more too big for them. Sentences from the reviews he was still receiving bubbled through his consciousness deliciously, and he wished, swelling with gratitude, that the men who wrote them were beside him, that he might be introduced, and grip their hands, and try to express the inexpressible in words.

I should like to live here, Turk,' he remarked; 'the atmosphere is right. It's suggestive, stimulating. When I see a peasant leaning out of a window in France, I want to write verses about her; when I see the same thing at home, I only notice she is dirty.'

'Ah!' said Turquand, 'that's another reason why you had better go back with me to-morrow. The tendency to write verses leads to the casual ward. Let us go and watch the insolent opulence losing its francs.'

The Casino was beginning to refill, and the path and lawn were gay with the flutter of toilettes as they reached the gates. Two of the figures approaching the rooms were familiar to the novelist, and he discovered their presence with a distinct shock, though his gaze had been scanning the crowd in search of them.

'There are the Walfords,' he said.

The other grunted—he also had recognized a girl in mauve—and Kent watched her silently so long as she remained in view. He knew he had nerves when he saw Miss Walford. The sight of her aroused a feeling of restlessness in him latterly which demanded her society for its relief, and he had not denied to himself that when a stranger, sitting behind him yesterday in the salon de lecture, had withdrawn a handkerchief redolent of the 'Corylopsis' which Miss Walford affected, it had provided him with a sensation profoundly absurd.

If he had nerves, however, there was no occasion to parade the fact, and he repressed impatience laudably. It was half an hour before the ladies were encountered. Objecting to be foolish, he felt, nevertheless, that Cynthia Walford was an excuse for folly as she turned to him on the terrace with her faint smile of greeting; felt, with unreasoning gratification, that Turquand must acknowledge it.

She was a fair, slight girl, with dreamy blue eyes bewitchingly lashed, and lips so delicately modeled that the faint smile always appeared a great tribute upon them. She was no less beautiful for her manifest knowledge she was a beauty, and though she could not have been more than twenty-two, had the air of carrying her loveliness as indifferently as her frocks—which tempted a literary man to destruction. She accepted admiration like an entremet at a table d'hôte—something included in the menu, and arriving as a matter of course; but her acceptance was so graceful that it was delightful to bend to her and offer it.

Kent asked if they were going in to the concert, and Mrs. Walford said they were not. It was far too warm to sit indoors to listen to that kind of music! She found Dieppe insufferably hot, and ridiculously overrated. Now, Trouville was really lively; did he not think so?

He said he did not know Trouville.

'Don't you? Oh, it is ever so much better; very jolly—really most jolly! We were there last year, and enjoyed it immensely. We—we had such a time I' She giggled loudly. 'How long are you gentlemen remaining?'

'Mr. Turquand is "deserting "to-morrow,' he said. 'I? Oh, I shall have to leave in about a week, I am afraid.'

'You said that a week ago,' murmured Miss Walford.

'like the place,' he confessed; 'I find it very pleasant myself.'

Mrs. Walford threw up her hands with a scream of expostulation. Her face was elderly, despite her attentions to it; but in her manner she was often a great deal more youthful than her daughter; indeed, while the girl had already acquired something of the serenity of a woman, the woman was superficially reverting to the artlessness of a girl.

'What is there to like? Dieppe is the Casino, and the Casino is Dieppe!'

'But the Casino is very agreeable,' he said, his glance wandering from her.

And the charges are perfectly monstrous, though, of course, you extravagant young men don't mind that.'

A friend might call me young,' said Turquand gloomily; 'my worst enemy couldn't call me extravagant.'

'*I* plead innocent too,' returned Kent. 'I'm as little complacent under extortion as anybody.'

She was pleased to hear him say so. All she asked of a young man was that he should be well provided for, but for him to have the good feeling to exercise a nice economy until he became engaged was an additional recommendation. Her giggle was as violent as before, though.

'Oh, I dare say,' she exclaimed facetiously; 'I'm always being taken in; I don't believe those stories any longer. Do you remember Willy Holmes, Cynthia, and the tales he used to tell me? I used to think that young man was so steady, I was always quoting him. And it turned out he was a regular scapegrace; and everybody knew it all the time, and had been laughing at me. I've given up believing in anyone, Mr. Kent—in anyone, do you hear?' She shook the splendors of her bonnet at him, and gasped and gurgled archly.' 'I've no doubt you're every bit as bad as the rest!'

He answered with the sort of inanity required. Miss Walford asked him a question, and he took a seat beside her in replying. Turquand also found a chair. Twilight was falling, and a refreshing breeze began to make itself felt. A fashionable sea purled on the sand below with elegant decorum. In the building the concert commenced, and snatches of orchestration reached them through the chatter of American and English and French from the occupants of the tables behind. Presently Mrs. Walford wanted to go and play Petits Chevaux. The subeditor, involuntarily attached to the party, accompanied her, and Kent and the girl followed. The crowds round the miniature courses were large, but Turquand prevailed on the dame to perceive that there was still space for them all to stand together. She complimented him on his dexterity, but immediately afterwards became fatigued, and begged him to pilot her to a corner where she could sit down. The party was now necessarily divided into couples.

CHAPTER II.

HE had appreciated the manœuvres sufficiently to feel no surprise when the room was pronounced stifling ten minutes later, and she declared she must return to the terrace. She had hitherto, however, evinced such small desire for his companionship that he was momentarily undecided which tête-à-tête was the one she had been anxious to effect.

'Pouf!' she exclaimed, as they emerged into the air. 'It was unbearable. Where are the others? Didn't they come out too?'

'They have no idea we've gone,' said Turquand dryly.

She was greatly astonished, and had to turn before she could credit it.

'I thought they were behind us,' she repeated several times. 'I'm *sure* they saw us move. Oh, well, they'll find it out in a minute, I expect. Never mind.'

They strolled up and down among the promenaders.

'Sorry you're going, Mr. Turquand?' inquired the lady. 'Your friend will miss you very much.'

I don't think so,' he answered. 'He knew I was only running over for a few days.'

He tells me it is the first holiday he has taken for years,' she said. 'His profession seems to engross him. I suppose it is an engrossing one. But he oughtn't to exhaust his strength. I needn't ask you if you've read his novel. What do you think of it?'

'I think it extremely clever work,' replied Turquand.

'And it's been a great success, too, eh? "One of the books of the year," the *Times* called it.'

'It has certainly given him a literary position.'

'How splendid!' she said. 'Yes, that's what *I* thought it: "extremely clever," brilliant—most brilliant! His parents must be very proud of him?'

'They are dead,' said Turquand.

Mrs. Walford was surprised again. She had somehow taken it for granted they were living, and as she understood he had no brothers or sisters, it must be very lonely for him.

'He sees a good deal of *me,*' said her escort, 'and I'm quite a festive sort of person when you know me.'

Her giggle announced that she found this entertaining, but the approval did not loosen his tongue. She fanned herself strenuously, and decided that, besides being untidy, he was dense.

'Of course, in one way,' she pursued, 'his condition is an advantage to him. Literary people have to work so hard if they depend on their writing, don't they?'

'*I* do,' he assented, 'I'm sorry to say.'

His constant obstrusion of himself into the matter annoyed her singularly. She had neither inquired nor cared if he worked hard, and felt disposed to say so. Turquand, who realized now why honors had, been thrust upon him this evening, regretted that loyalty to Kent prevented his doing him what he felt would be the greatest service that could be rendered, and removing the temptation of the mauve girl permanently from his path.

'With talent and private means our author is fortunate.'

'I often tell him so,' he said.

'If it doesn't tempt him to rest on his oars,' she added delightedly. 'Wealth *has* its dangers. Young men *will* be young men.'

' "Wealth" is a big word,' said he. 'Kent is certainly not to be called "wealthy." '

'But he does not rely on his pen?' she cried with painful carelessness.

'He has some private means, I believe; in fact, I know it.'

'I am so glad—so glad for him. Now I have no misgivings about his future at all. . . . Have *you?*'

'I'm not sure that I follow you.'

She played with her fan airily.

'He is certain to succeed, I mean; he need not fear anything, since he has a competence. Oh, I know what these professions are,' she went on, laughing. 'My son is in the artistic world; we are quite behind the scenes. I know how hard-up some of the biggest professionals are when they have nothing but their vocation to depend on. A profession is so precarious—shocking—even when one has aptitude for it.'

'Kent has more than "aptitude," ' he said. 'He has power. Perhaps he'll always work too much for himself an the reviewers to attract the very widest public. Perhaps he is a trifle inclined to over-do the analytical element in his stuff; but that's the worst that can be said of it. And, then, it's a question of taste. For myself, I'm a believer in the introspective school, and I think his method's admirable.'

'Schools' and 'methods' were meaningless to the lady in such a connection. Novels were novels, and they were either 'good' or they were 'rubbish,' if she understood anything about them; and she had read them all her life. She looked perplexed, and reiterated the phrase she had used already.

'Oh, extremely clever, brilliant—most brilliant, really! I quite agree with you.'

'Your son writes, did you say, Mrs. Walford?'

'Oh no, not writes—no! He sings! He is—er—studying for the operatic stage.' Her tone could not have been more impressive if she had said he was De Reszke. 'His voice is quite magnificent.'

'Really!' he replied with interest. 'That is a great gift—a voice.'

'He is "coming out" soon,' she said. 'He—er—he could get an engagement at any moment, but—he is so conscientious. He feels he must do himself entire justice when he makes his début. In professional circles he is thought an immense amount of—immense!'

'Has he sung at any concerts?'

'In private,' she explained—'socially. He visits among musicians a great deal. And of course it makes it very lively for *us* He is quite—er—in the swim!'

'You are to be congratulated on your family,' said Turquand. 'With such a son, and a daughter like Miss Walford'

'Yes, she is very much admired,' she admitted—'very much; but a strange girl, Mr. Turquand. You couldn't believe how strange!'

He did not press her to put him to the test, but she afforded the particulars as if glad of the opportunity. He remarked that, in narrating matters of which she was proud, she adopted a breathless, jerky delivery, which provoked in the hearer the perhaps unfounded suspicion that she was inventing the facts as she went on.

'She is *most* peculiar,' she insisted. 'The matches she has refused! Appalling!'

'No?' he said.

'A Viscount!' she gasped. 'She refused a Viscount in Monte Carlo last year. A splendid fellow! Enormously wealthy. Perfectly wild about her. She wouldn't look at him.'

'You astonish me!' he murmured.

Mrs. Walford shook her head speechlessly, with closed eyes.

'And there were others,' she said in a reviving spasm—'dazzling positions! Treated them like dirt. She said, if she didn't care for a man, nothing would induce her. What can one do with such a romantic goose? Be grateful that you aren't a mother, Mr. Turquand.'

'Some day,' he opined, without returning thanks giving, 'the young lady will be induced.'

'Oh, and before long, if it comes to that.' She nodded confidentially. 'To tell you the truth, I expect somebody here next week. A young man rolling in riches, and with expectations that—oh, tremendous! He raves about her. She has refused him—er—seven times—seven times. He wanted to commit suicide after her last rejection. But she **respects** him immensely. A noble fellow he is—oh, a most noble fellow! And when he asks her again, I rather imagine that pity may make her accept him, after all.'

'She must have felt it a grave responsibility,' observed the journalist politely, 'that a young man said he wanted to commit suicide on her account.'

'That's just it; she feels it a terrible responsibility. Oh, she's not fond of him. Sorry for him, you understand—sorry. And, between ourselves, I'm sure I really don't know what to think would be for the best—I don't indeed! But I wouldn't mind wagering a pair of gloves that, if she doesn't meet Mr. Right soon, she'll end by giving in, and Mr. Somebody-else will have stolen the prize before he comes—hee, hee, hee!'

Turquand groaned in his soul. In his mental vision his friend already flopped helplessly in the web, and he derived small encouragement from the reflection that she was mistaken in the succulence of her fly.

'You are not smoking,' she said. 'Do! I don't mind it a bit.'

He scowled at her darkly, and was prepared to see betrothal in the eyes of the absent pair when they rejoined them.

As yet, however, they were still wedged in the crowd around the tables. On their right, a fat Frenchwoman cried 'Assez! assez!' imploringly, as her horse, leading by a foot, threatened at last to glide past the winning-post, and leave victory in the rear; to their left, an English girl, evidently on her honeymoon, was losing francs radiantly out of the bridegroom's purse. Kent had paid for sixteen tickets, and Miss Walford for five, before they perceived that the others had retired.

'We had better go and look for them,' she declared.

The well-bred sea shimmered in the moonlight now, and the terrace was so thronged that investigation could only be made in a saunter.

'I wonder where they have got to,' she murmured.

Her companion was too contented to be curious.

'We are sure to come upon them in a minute,' he said. 'Do you also abuse Dieppe, Miss Walford?'

'Not at all—no. It is mamma who is bored.'

'I should like to show you Arques,' he said. 'I'm sure your mother would be interested by that. Do you think we might drive over one afternoon?'

'I don't know,' she replied. 'Is it nice?'

'Well, "nice "isn't what you will call it when you are there. It's a ruined castle, you know; and you can almost "hear" the hush of the place. It's so solemn, and still, and Norman. If you're very imaginative, you presently hear men clanking about in armor as you dream in the old courtyard. You *would* hear the men in armor, I think.'

'Am I imaginative?' she smiled.

'Aren't you?' he asked.

'Perhaps I am; I don't know. What makes you think so?'

He was puzzled to adduce any reason except that she was so pretty. He did not pursue the subject.

'There are several things worth seeing here,' he said. 'Of course Dieppe "is only the Casino," if one never goes anywhere else. I suppose you haven't even heard of the Cave-dwellers?'

'The "Cave-dwellers"?' she repeated.

'Their homes are the caves in the cliffs. Have you never noticed there are holes? They are caves when you get inside—vast ones—one room leading out of another. The people are beggars, very dirty, and occasionally picturesque. They exist by what they can cadge, and, of course, they pay no rent; it's only when they come out that they see daylight.'

'How horrid!' she shivered. 'And you went to look at them?'

'Rather! They are very pleased to "receive." One of the inhabitants has lived there for twenty years. I don't think he has stirred abroad for ten; he sends his family. Many of the colony were born there. Don't you consider they were worth a visit?'

'I don't know,' she said; 'one might be robbed and murdered in such a place.'

'With the greatest ease in the world,' he agreed; 'some of the inner rooms are so black that you literally can't see your hand before you. It would be a beautiful place for a murder! The next-of-kin lures the juvenile heiress there, and bribes the beggars to make away with her. Unknown to him, they spare her life because—because—Why do they spare her life?—but keep her prisoner, and bring her up as one of themselves. Twenty years later—I believe I could write a sensational novel, after all.'

What nonsense!' laughed Miss Walford daintily.

Do you like that kind of story?' he inquired.

'I like plots about real life best,' she said. 'Don't you?'

He found this an exposition of the keenest literary sympathies, and regarded her adoringly. She preferred analysis to adventure, and realism to romance. What work he might accomplish, inspired by the companionship of such a girl!

'Wherever have you been, Cynthia? We thought you were lost,' he heard Mrs. Walford say discordantly, and the next moment the party was united.

'It's where have *you* been, mamma, isn't it?'

"Well, I like that! We didn't stop a minute; I made certain you saw us get up. We've been hunting for you everywhere. Mr. Turquand and I have been out here ever so long, haven't we, Mr. Turquand? Looking at the moon, too, if you want to know, and—hee, hee, hee!—talking sentiment.'

Turquand, who was staring at Kent, allowed an eyelid to droop for an instant at the conclusion, and the latter stroked his moustache and smiled.

'Such a time we've been having, all by ourselves!' she persisted uproariously. 'Mr. Kent, are you shocked? Oh, I've shocked Mr. Kent! He'll always remember it—I can see it in his face.'

'shall always remember *you,* Mrs. Walford,' he said, trying to make the enforced fatuity sound graceful.

'We were left by ourselves, and we had to get on as we could,' she cried. 'Hadn't we, Mr. Turquand? I say we had to amuse ourselves as we could. Now Cynthia's glowering at me. Oh—hee, hee, hee!—you two young people are too respectable for *us.* We don't ask any questions, but—but I dare say Mr. Turquand and I aren't the *only* ones—hee, hee, hee!—who have been "looking at the moon."'

'Shall we find chairs again?' said Kent quickly, perceiving the frown that darkened the girl's brow. 'It's rather an awkward spot to stand still, isn't it?'

She agreed that it was, and a waiter brought them ices, and Mrs. Walford was giddy over a liquor. They remained at the table until the ladies asserted it was time to return to their hotel. Parting from them at its gates, the two men turned away together. Both felt in their pockets, filled their pipes, and, smoking silently, drifted through the rugged little streets, back to the café where they had had their conversation after dinner.

' "Thank you for a very pleasant evening," ' said Turquand, breaking a long pause.

It was the only criticism he permitted himself, and Kent did not care to inquire if it was to be regarded as ironical.

CHAPTER III.

AFTER his friend's departure, the mother and daughter became the pivot round which the author'? movements revolved. Primarily his own companionship and the novelty of Dieppe had been enough; but now he found it dreary to roam about the harbor, or sit sipping mazagrins, alone. Reviewing the weeks before Turquand joined him, he wondered what he had done with himself in various hours of the day, and solitude hung so unfamiliarly on his hands that Miss Walford's society was indispensable.

Soon after the matutinal chocolate, he accompanied the ladies to the Casino, and spent the morning beside them under the awning. Mrs. Walford did not bathe—while people could have comfortable baths in the vicinity of their toilet-tables, she considered the recourse to tents and the sea making an unnecessary confidence—and she disliked Cynthia to do so, 'with a lot of Frenchmen in the water.' Whether it was their sex, or only their nationality, that was the objection was not clear. She usually destroyed a novel while Mr. Kent and her daughter conversed. Considering the speed with which she read it, indeed, it was constant food for astonishment to him that she could contrive to do a book so much damage. In the evening they strolled out again, and but for the afternoon he would have had small cause for complaint. Even this gained a spice of excitement, however, from the fact that it was uncertain how long Miss Walford's siesta would last, and there was always the chance, as he lounged about the hotel, smoking to support the tedium, that a door would open and cause heart-leaps.

Mrs. Walford declared that the visit to Arques would be 'very jolly,' and the excursion was made about a week later. Kent found the girl's concurrence in his enthusiasm as pretty as he had promised himself it would be, and when they had escaped from the information of the gardien, and wandered where they chose to go, the chaperon was the only blot upon perfection.

Perhaps she realized the influence of the scene, though her choice of adjectives was not happy, for the explorations fatigued her before long, and, since the others were so indefatigable, they might continue them while she sat down.

It was, as Kent had said, intensely still. The practical obtruding itself for a moment, he thought how blessed it would be to work here, where doors could never slam and the yells of children were unknown. They mounted a hillock, and looked across the endless landscape silently. In the dungeons under their feet lay dead men's bones, but such facts concerned him little now. Far away some cattle—or were they deer?—browsed sleepily under the ponderous trees. Of what consequence if they were cattle or deer? Still further, where the blue sky dipped and the woodland rose, a line of light glinted like water. Perhaps it *was* water, and if not, what matter? It was the Kingdom of Imagination; deer, water, fame, or love—the Earth was what he pleased! Among the crumbling walls the girl's frock fluttered charmingly; his eyes left the landscape and sought her face.

'It is divine !' she said.

He did not disguise from himself that life without her would be unendurable.

'I knew it would please you,' he said unsteadily.

She again regarded the questionable cattle; his tone had said much more.

Kent stood beside her in a pause in which he believed he struggled. He felt that she was unattainable; but there was an intoxication in the moment he was not strong enough to resist. He touched her hand, and, his heart pounding, met her gaze as she turned.

'Cynthia,' he said in his throat. The color left her cheeks, and her head drooped. 'Are you angry with me?' She was eminently, graceful in the attitude. 'I love you,' he said—'I love you. What shall I say besides? I love you.'

She looked slowly up, and blinded him with a smile. Its newness jumped and quivered through his nerves.

Cynthia! Can you care for me?'

Perhaps,' she whispered.

He was alone with her in Elysium; Adam and Eve were not more secure from human observation when they kissed under the apple-tree. He drew nearer to her— her eyes permitted. In a miracle he had clasped a goddess, and he would not have been aware of it had all the pins of Birmingham been concealed about her toilette to protest.

Presently she said:

'We must go back to mamma!'

He had forgotten she had one, and the recollection was a descent.

'What will she say?' he asked. 'I'm not a millionaire, dearest; I am afraid she won't be pleased.'

'I will tell her when we get home. Oh, mamma likes you!'

'And you have a father?' he added, feeling vaguely that the ideal marriage would be one between orphans, whose surviving relatives were abroad and afraid of a voyage. 'Do you think they will give you to me?'

'After I have spoken to them,' she said deliciously. 'Yes—oh, they will be nice, I am sure, Mr. Kent! . . . There, then! But one can't shorten it, and it sounds a dis-agreeable sort of person.'

'Not as you said it.'

'It was very wrong of you to *make* me say it so soon. Are you a tyrant? . . . We must really go back to mamma!'

'Did you know I was fond of you?' asked Kent.

'I—wondered.'

'Why?'

'Why did I wonder?'

'Yes.'

'I don't know.'

'No; tell me ! Was it because—you liked me?'

'You are vain enough already.'

'Haven't I an excuse for vanity?'

'*Am* I?'

Language failed him.

Tell me why you wondered,' he begged.

Because You are wickedly persistent!'

'I am everything that is awful. Cynthia?'

'Yes?'

'Because you liked me?'

'Perhaps; the weeniest scrap in the world. Oh, you are horrid! What things you make me say! And we are only just'

'Engaged! It's a glorious word; don't be afraid of it.'

'I shall be afraid of you in a minute. How do you think of your—your proposals in your books?'

'have only written one book.'

'Did you make it up? He didn't talk as *you* talk to *me?*'

'He wasn't so madly in love with her.'

'But he said the very sweetest things!'

'That's why.'

'You are horrid!' she declared again. 'I don't know what you mean a bit . . . Mr. Kent!'

'Who is *he*?'

'Humphrey.'

'Yes—sweetheart?'

'Now you've put it out of my head.' She laughed softly. 'I was going to say something.'

'Let me look at you till you think what it was.'

'Perhaps that wouldn't help me.'

'Oh, you are an angel!' he exclaimed. 'Cynthia, we shall always remember Arques?'

She breathed assent.

'Was this Joan of Arc's Arques?

'No; Noah's.'

'*Whose*' she said.

He smiled.

'Not the Maid of Orleans; it is spelled differently, besides.'

'I believe you're being silly,' she said, in a puzzled tone. 'I don't understand. Oh, we **must** go back to mamma; she'll think we're lost!'

Mrs. Walford did not evince any signs of perturbation, however, when they rejoined her, nor did she ask for particulars of what they had seen. She seemed to think it likely they might not feel talkative. She said she had 'enjoyed it all immensely,' sitting there in the shade, and that the gardien, who had come back to her, had imparted the most romantic facts about the château. Upon some of them she was convinced that Mr. Kent could easily write an historical novel, which she was sure would be deeply interesting, though she never read historical novels herself. Had Mr. Kent and Cynthia any idea of the quanity of pippins grown in the immediate neighborhood every summer? The gardien had told her that too. No; it had nothing to do with the château; but it was simyly extraordinary, and the bulk of the fruit was converted into cider, and the peasantry obtained it quite for nothing, which was a perfect godsend for them when they could not afford the wine, and she had no doubt much more wholesome besides, though, personally, she had only tasted cider once, and then it had made her ill.

They drove back down the dusty hill listening to her. The girl spoke scarcely at all, and the onus of appearing entertained devolved upon Kent opposite. When the fly deposited them at the hotel door at last, he drew a sigh in which relief and apprehension were blended. Cynthia followed her mother upstairs, and he caught a glance from her, and smiled his gratitude; but he questioned inwardly what would be the upshot of the announcement she was about to make. He perceived with some amusement that he was on the verge of an experience of whose terrors he had often read without realizing them. He was a candidate for a young lady's hand. Yes; it made one nervous. He asked himself for the twentieth time in the past few days if he had been mistaken in supposing Mrs. Walford overestimated his eligibility; perhaps he was no worse off than she thought him. But even then he quaked, for he had seen too little society since he was a boy to be versed in such matters, and he was by no means ready to make an affidavit that she had extended him encouragement.

A signal at the entrance to the dining-room was exciting but obscure, and there was no opportunity for inquiries before the ladies took their seats. He anathematized an épergne which to-night seemed more than usually obstructive. Cynthia was in white. He did not recollect having seen her in the gown before, and the glimpse of her queenliness shook him. No mother would accord him so peerless a treasure. He had been mad.

It was interminable, this procession of courses, relieved by glances at a profile down the table. His mouth was dry, and he ordered champagne to raise his pluck. It heated him, without steadying his nerves. The room was like a Turkish bath; yet the curve of cheek he descried was as pale as the corsage. How could she manage it? He himself was bedewed with perspiration.

He could wait no longer. He went on to the veranda and lit a cigar. He saw Mrs. Walford come out, and, dropping it, rose to meet her. She was alone. Where was Cynthia? Seeking him? or was her absence designed?

'I hope our excursion hasn't tired you, Mrs. Walford?'

'Oh dear no,' she assured him. She hesitated, but her manner was blithesome. His courage mounted.

'Shall we take a turn?' she suggested.'

'Mrs. Walford, your daughter has told you what I . . . of our conversation this afternoon, perhaps? I haven't many pretensions, but I am devoted to her. *She* is good enough to care a little for *me.* Will you give her to me, and let me spend my life in making her happy?'

She made a gesture of sudden artlessness.

'I was perfectly astonished!' she exclaimed. 'To tell you the truth, Mr. Kent, I was perfectly dum-founded when Cynthia spoke to me. I hadn't an idea of it. I-er—I don't know whether I'm particularly obtuse in these affairs—hee ! hee! hee!—but I hadn't a suspicion.'

'But you do not refuse your consent?' he begged. 'You do not disapprove?'

She waved her hands about afresh, and went on jerkily, with a wide, fixed smile:

'I never was more astounded in my life. Of course, I—er—from what we've seen of you . . . most desirable—most desirable in many ways. At the same time—er—Cynthia's a delicate girl; always been used to every luxury. So few young men are really in a position to justify their marrying.'

'*My* position is this,' he said. 'I've my profession and a little money—not much; a thousand pounds, left me by a relative last year. Assisted by that money, I reckon that my profession would certainly enable us to live in a comfortable fashion until I could support a wife by my pen alone.' Her jaw dropped. He felt it before he turned, and shivered.

'I'm afraid you do not think it very excellent?' he murmured.

She was breathing agitatedly. 'It . . . I must say—er—I fear her father would never sanction Oh no; I am sure. It is out of the question.'

A man may keep a wife on less, Mrs. Walford, without her suffering. My God! if I thought that Cynthia would ever know privation or distress, do you suppose I would'

'A wife!' she said, 'a wife I My dear Mr. Kent, a man must be prepared to provide for a family as well. Have you—er—any expectations?'

'I expect to succeed,' said Kent; 'I've the right to expect it. No others.'

'May I ask how much your profession brings you in?'

'I sold my novel for a hundred pounds,' he answered. 'It was my first,' he added, as he heard her gasp; 'it was my first . . . Mrs. Walford, I love her. At least think it over. Let me speak to her again; let me *ask* her if she is afraid. Don't refuse to consider.'

The pain in his voice was not without an effect on her disgust. She was mercenary, though she did not know it; she was not good-natured, though she had good impulses; she was ludicrously artificial; but she was a woman, and he was a young man. She did not think of her own courtship, for she had only been sentimental when her parents approved—she had not 'married for money,' but her heart had been providentially warmed toward the one young gentleman of her acquaintance who was 'comfortably off.' She thought, however, of Cynthia, who had displayed considerable feeling in the bedroom an hour ago.

'I must write to her father,' she said, in a worried voice. 'I really can't promise you anything; I am very vexed at this sort of thing going on without my knowledge—*very* vexed. I shall write to her father to-night. I must ask to consider the whole matter entirely indefinite until he comes. Immense responsibility . . . immense! I can't say any more, Mr. Kent.'

She left him on the veranda, and reëntered the house. His sensation was that the world had been shattered about him, and a weighty portion of the ruin was lying on his chest.

CHAPTER IV.

WHEN Sam Walford ran over to Dieppe, in obedience to his wife's summons, he said:

'Well, what's this dam nonsense, Louisa, eh? There's nothing in this, you know—this won't do.'

'Cynthia is very cut up,' she averred; 'you had better tell her so. I'm sure I wish we had waited, and gone to Brighton later. . . . A lot of bother.'

'An author,' he said, with amusement; 'what do you do with authors? You do "find 'em," my dear.'

'I don't know what you mean,' she returned tartly. 'I can't help a young man taking a fancy to her, can I? If you're so clever, it's a pity you didn't stop here with her yourself. If you don't think it's good enough, you must say so, and finish the matter, that's all. You're her father.'

'I'll talk to her,' he declared. 'Where is she now? Let us go and see. And where's Mr.—what d'ye call him? what's he like?'

'Mr. Kent. He is a very nice fellow. If he had been in a different position, it would have been most satisfactory. There's no doubt he's very clever—highly talented—the newspapers are most complimentary to him. And—er—of course a novelist is socially—er—he has a certain '

'Damn it! he can't keep a family on compliments can he? I suppose he's a bull of himself, eh? Thinks he ought to be snapped at?'

'Nothing of the sort; you always jump to such extraordinary conclusions,' she said. 'He is a perfect gentleman, and proposed for her beautifully. After all, there aren't many young men who've got so much as a thousand pounds in ready money.'

'But he isn't making anything, you tell me,' objected Mr. Walford; 'they'll eat up a thousand pounds before they know where they are. He wouldn't expect anything with her, I suppose?'

She shook her head violently.

'*No* earthly *occasion. Oh* dear no!'

'Let me go and see Cynthia,' he said again. 'It's a funny thing a girl like that hasn't ever had a good offer—upon my soul it is!'

'You ask home such twopenny-halfpenny men,' retorted his wife. 'She is in her room; I'll let her know you're here.'

Cynthia *was* 'cut up.' She liked Humphrey Kent very much—and everything is relative; she felt herself a Juliet. She considered it very unkind of mamma to oppose their marriage, and said as much to her father, with tears on her lashes and pathetic little sobs. Sam Walford was sorry for her; his affection for his children was his best attribute. He said 'Damn it!' several times more, and then patted her on the cheek, and told her not to cry, and went out on the Plage to commune with tobacco.

After his cigar, he explored for a coiffeur's—there is a very excellent one in Dieppe; and he was shaved—an operation which freshened him extremely—and had his thin hair anointed with various liquids of agreeable fragrance and most attractive hues, and submitted his moustache to the curling-irons. The French barber will play with you nearly as long as the American, and when Mr. Walford had acquired a carnation for his buttonhole, and sipped a vermouth over the pages of *Gil Blas,* it was time to think of returning to the hotel. A pretty woman, who had looked so demure in approaching that the impropriety was a sensation, lifted her eyes to him, and smiled as she passed. He momentarily hesitated, but remembered it was near the dinner-hour, and that he was a father with a daughter's love-affair upon his hands. But he reëntered the hotel in a good humor.

Cynthia went to bed radiantly happy that night, and kissed a bundle of lilies that had cost fifty francs, for the Capulets had relented.

The two men had had a long conversation on the terrace over their coffee, and the senior, who was favorably impressed, had ended by being jovial, and calling Kent "my boy,' and smacking him on the shoulder.

Nor was Mrs. Walford displeased by the decision, since it could never be said that she had advocated it. 'My daughter's fiancé, Mr. Kent, the novelist, you know,' sounded very well, and she foresaw herself expatiating on his importance, and determined what his income would be in her confidences with intimate friends. Really, if the house were nice, he might be making anything she liked—who could dispute her assertions?

The Capulets had relented, and the sun shone—especially in Paris, where Kent went in haste to procure the engagement-ring, and the thirsty trees were shuddering in the glare, and the asphalt steamed. But he could not wait, although the stay in Dieppe was drawing to a close now, and they would all be back in London soon. It seemed to him that it would be as the signing of the agreement when Cynthia put her finger through his ting; and he was resolved that it should be a better one than any of those her mother wore with such complacence. Poor devil of an author though he was, her acquaintances should not tell that Cynthia was marrying badly by the very emblem of his devotion!

In the Rue de la Paix he spent upwards of an hour scrutinizing all the jewelers' windows before he permitted himself to enter a shop. He chose finally a pearl and diamonds—one big white pearl, and a diamond flashing on either side of it. It was in a pale blue velvet case, lined with white satin. He was satisfied with his purchase, and so was the salesman.

Cynthia's flush of delight as he disclosed it repaid him superabundantly, and when the girl proudly displayed it to them, it was gratifying to observe her parents' surprise. The expressions of admiration into which Mrs. Walford broke were fervent, and she felt instantaneously she could increase the income she had decided he should possess by fully a third, in view of so magnificent a substantiation of her truthfulness.

His days were now delicious to Kent. A magic haze enwrapped their stereotyped incidents, so that the terrace of the Casino, the veranda of the hotel, Nature, and the polyglot lounging crowd itself, were all beatified. They were as familiar things viewed in a charming dream—'the pleasant fields traversed so oft,' which were still more pleasant as they appeared to the sleeping soldier. A tenderness overflowing from his own emotions was diffused over the scenes, and he found it almost impossible to realize sometimes that the goddess beside him, who had been so unapproachable a month ago, was actually going to belong to him directly. It dazzled him, and seemed incredible.

He had once sat down in the salon de lecture with the intention of apprising Turquand of his felicity; but the knowledge that the news he had to give entailed a defence, if he did not wish to write formally, had resulted in his destroying the preparatory lines he had achieved. Delicacy demanded that he should excuse his action by word of mouth if excuses were required at all. To do such a thing in permanent pen-strokes looked to him profanation of an angel, and an insult to the bounty of God.

Mr. Walford was unable to remain in Dieppe so long as the day fixed for the others' return; nor, he said genially, was there any occasion for him to put himself out now that he had a prospective son-in-law to take his place. Humphrey was well content. He understood that the elder lady was a bad sailor, and clung obstinately to the saloon, while Cynthia found the passage enjoyable, and he anticipated several golden hours to which the paternal presence would have proved alloy.

He was not disappointed. Sustained by Heidsieck and the stewardess, Mrs. Walford stayed below, as usual, and he tasted the responsibility of having the girl in his charge. He let the flavor dissolve on his palate slowly. It was as if they were already on the honeymoon, he thought, as they paced the deck together, or he made her comfortable in a chair, and brought her strawberries, and watched her eat them with amused interest, vaguely conscious that he found it wonderful to see her mouth unclose, and a delicate forefinger and thumb get pinky.

'You are sure you have the address right?' she asked once. 'Humphrey, fancy if you lost it, and could never find us again after we said "Good-bye" to-day! Wouldn't it be awful?'

'Awful,' he assented, smiling.

'Such a thing might happen,' she declared. 'You try and try your hardest to remember where we told you we lived, but you can't. It is terrible I You go mad '

'Or to a post office,' he said.

She laughed gaily.

'How could you write to me when you'd forgotten the address? You foolish fellow! There, I was brighter than you that time.'

He felt it would be prolix to explain that he was thinking of a directory, and not of stamps.

'Come, after that, I must really hear if you've learnt your lesson. What is it? Quick!'

You live in one of the seven—seven thousand three hundred and forty-nine houses in the suburbs that are called The Hawthorns,' he said. 'You would have called it The Cedars, only that name was appropriated by the house next door. I take the train to Streatham Hill—I must be very particular to say "Hill," or catastrophes will happen. To begin with, I shall lose an hour of your society'

'And dinner—dinner will certainly be over.'

'Dinner will certainly be over. When I come out, I turn to the right, pass the estate agent's, take the first to the left, and recollect that I'm looking for a bow-window and a white balcony, and a fence which makes it impossible to see them. Do I know it?'

'Not impossible. But—yes, I'll trust you.'

He parted from the ladies at Victoria, and, getting into a hansom, gave himself up to reflection. The rooms he shared with Turquand were in the convenient, if unfashionable, neighborhood of Soho, and an all-pervading odor of jam reminded him presently that he was nearing his destination. He was not sure of finding Turquand in at this hour. He opened the door with his latchkey, and, dragging his portmanteaus into the passage, ran upstairs. The journalist, in his shirt sleeves, was reading an evening paper, with his slippered feet crossed upon the window-sill.

'Hallo!' he said; 'you've got back?'

'Yes,' said Humphrey. 'How the jam smells!'

'It's raspberry to-day. I've decided the rasp berry's the most penetrating. How are you?'

'Dry, and hungry too. Is there anything to drink in the place?'

'There's a very fine brand of water on the landing, and there's the remainder of a roll, extra sec, in the cupboard, I believe. I finished the whisky last night. We can go and have some dinner at the Suisse. Madame is desolée; she's asked after you most tenderly.'

'Good old Madame! And her moustache?'

'More luxuriant.'

There was a pause, in which Humphrey considered how best to impart his tidings. The other shifted his feet, and contemplated the smoke-dried wall—the only view from the window attainable. Kent stared at him. It was displayed to him clearly for the first time that his marriage would mean severance from Turquand, and the Restaurant Suisse, and all that had been his life hitherto, and that Turquand might feel it more sorely than he expressed. He was sorry for Turquand. He lounged over to the mantelpiece and dipped his hand in the familiar tobacco-jar, and filled a pipe before he spoke.

'Well,' he said, with an elaborate effort to sound careless, 'I suppose you'll hardly be astonished, old chap—I am engaged.'

CHAPTER V.

TURQUAND did not answer immediately.

'No,' he rejoined at last; 'I'm not astonished. Nothing could astonish me but good news. When is the event to take place?'

'That's not settled. Soon. . . . We shall always be pals, Turk?'

'I'll come and see you sometimes—oh yes. Father consented?'

'Things are quite smooth all round.'

'H'mph!'

He looked at the wall hard and pulled his beard.

'You said it would happen, didn't you? I didn't see a glimmer of a possibility myself.'

'Love's blind, you know.'

'You said, too, it—er—it wouldn't be altogether a wise step. You'll change your mind about that one day, Turk.'

'Hope so,' said Turquand. 'Can't to-night.'

'You still believe I shall regret it?'

'What need is there to discuss it now?'

'Why shouldn't we?'

'Why *should* we? Why argue with a chap whether the ice will bear after he has made a hole in it?'

'We shan't be extravagant, and I shall work like blazes. I've a plot simmering already.'

'Happy ending this time?'

'I don't quite see it to be consistent; no.'

'you must manage it. They like happy endings, consistent or not.'

'Damn it, I mean to be true! I *won't* sell my birthright for a third edition! I shall work like blazes, and we shall live quite quietly somewhere in a little house'

'That's impossible,' said Turquand. 'You may live in a little house, or you may live quietly, but you can't do both things simultaneously.'

'In the suburbs—in Streatham, probably. Her people live in Streatham, and of course she would like to be near them.'

'And you will have a general servant, eh, with large and fiery hands—like Cornelia downstairs? Only she will look worse than Cornelia, because your wife will dress her up in muslins and streamers, and try to disguise the **generality** If you work in the front of your pretty little house, your nervous system will be shattered by the shrieks of your neighbors' children swinging on the gates—forty-pound-a-year houses in the suburbs are infested with children; nothing seems to exterminate them, and the inevitable gates groan like souls in hell—and if you choose the back, you'll be assisted by the arrival of the joint, and the vegetables, and the slap of the milk-cans, and Cornelia the Second's altercations with the errand-boys. A general servant with a tin pail alone is warranted to make herself heard for eleven hundred and sixty yards.'

'Life hasn't made an optimist of you,' observed Kent, less cheerfully,' that you talk about "happy endings." '

'The optimist is like the poet—he's born, he *isn't* made. Apropos of life, I suppose you'll assure yours when you marry?'

'Yes,' said Kent meditatively; 'yes, that's a good idea. I shall. . . . But your suggestions are none exhilarating,' he added; 'let's go to dinner.'

The subeditor put on his jacket and sought his boots.

'I'm ready,' he affirmed. 'By the way, I never thought to inquire. Mrs. Walford hasn't a large family, has she?'

'A son as well, that's all. Why?'

'I congratulate you,' said Turquand; it was the first time the word had passed his lips. 'It's a banality to say a man should never marry anybody; but if he must blunder with someone, let him choose an only child, if possible. Marrying into a large family's more expensive still. His wife has for ever got a sister having a wedding, or a christening, or a birthday, and wanting a present; or a brother asking for a loan, or dying, and plunging her into costly crape. Yes, I congratulate you.'

Humphrey did not express any thanks, and he determined that his engagement was a subject he would avoid as much as he could in their conversations together henceforward.

He was due at The Hawthorns the following afternoon at five o'clock, and his impatience to see the girl again was intensified by the knowledge that he was about to see her in her home. The day was tedious. In the morning it was showery, and he was chagrined to think that he was doomed to enter the drawing-room in muddy shoes; but after lunch the sky cleared, and when he reached Victoria the pavements were dry. The train started late, and traveled slowly; but he heard a porter bawling 'Stretta Mill!' on the welcome platform at last, and, making the station's acquaintance with affectionate eyes, he hastened up the steps, and in the direction of the house.

He was prepossessed by its exterior, and his anticipations were confirmed on entering the hall.

Mrs. Walford was in the garden, he was told, and the parlormaid conducted him there. It was an extremely charming garden. It was well designed, and it had a cedar and a tennis-court, which was pleasant to look at, though tennis was not an accomplishment his life had furnished opportunities for mastering; and it contained a tea-table under the cedar's boughs, and Cynthia in a deck-chair and a ravishing frock.

He was welcomed with effusion, and presented his bonbons. Mr. Walford, already returned from town, was quite parental in his greeting. Tea was very nice and English in the cedar's shade and Cynthia's presence. It was very nice, too, to be made so much of under the circumstances. Really they were very delightful people I

The son was in Germany, he learnt.

'We could have given you a treat else, my boy,' exclaimed the stockjobber, 'if you are fond of music. You will hear a voice when he comes back. That's luck for a fellow, to be born with an organ like Cæsar's! He'll be making five hundred a week in twelve months. I tell you it's wonderful.'

'."Five hundred a week"'! echoed Mrs. Walford. 'He'll be getting more than five hundred a week, I hope, before long. They get two or three hundred a night—***not*** voices as fine as Cæsar's—and won't go on the stage till they have had their money, either. You talk such nonsense, Sam. . . . absurd!'

'I said "in twelvemonths," ' murmured her husband deprecatingly. I said "in twelvemonths," my dear.' He turned to Kent, and added confidentially, 'There isn't a bass in existence to compare with him. You'll say so when you hear. Ah, let me introduce you to another member of the family—my wife's sister.'

Kent saw that they had been joined by a spare little woman with a thin, pursed mouth and a nose slightly pink. She was evidently a maiden lady, and his hostess's senior. Her tones were tart, and when she said she was pleased to meet him, he permitted himself no illusion that she spoke the truth.

Miss Wix, as a matter of fact, was not particularly pleased to meet anybody. She lived with the Wal-fords because she had no means of her own, and it was essential for her to live somewhere; but she accepted her dependence with mental indignation, and fate had soured her. Under a chilly demeanor she often burned secretly with the consciousness that she was not wanted, and the knowledge found expression at long intervals in an emotional outbreak, in which she quarreled with Louisa violently, and proclaimed an immediate intention of 'taking a situation.' What kind of situation she thought she was competent to fill nobody attempted to conjecture, neither did the 'threat' ever impose on anyone, nor did she take more than a preliminary step toward fulfilling it. She nursed the 'Wanted' columns of the *Telegraph* ostentatiously for a day or two, and waited for the olive-branch. The household were aware she must be persuaded to forgive them, and she always was, and relapsed into the acidulated person, in whom hysteria looked impossible, again. But the outbreak would be repeated a year or so later, and she then threatened to 'take a situation' quite as vehemently as before.

'Tea, Aunt Emily?'

'Yes, please, if it hasn't got cold.'

Humphrey bore it to her. She stirred the cup briskly, and eyed him with critical disfavor.

'I've read your book, Mr. Kent.'

'Oh,' he responded, as she did not say any more. 'Have you, Miss Wix?'

'Very good, I'm sure,' she brought out, after a further silence. He would not have imagined the simple words could convey so clearly that she thought it very small beer indeed. 'I suppose you're in the middle of another?'

'No,' he replied, 'not yet.'

'Really!'

She obviously considered that he ought to be.

'You should call her "aunt,"' exclaimed Sam Walford. 'You'll have to call her "Aunt Emily." We don't go in for formality, you'll find, my boy. Rough diamonds! Take us or leave us as what we are—eh, Emily?'

'Perhaps Mr. Kent thinks it would be rather premature,' suggested Miss Wix. He talked to Cynthia.

Fruit and fowls might be admired if he liked, and she and papa took him on a tour of inspection. There were moments when he was alone with Cynthia, while her father discovered that there were not any eggs.

'He is very good-looking,' said Mrs. Walford; 'don't you think so?'

' I can't say he struck me as being remarkable for beauty,' said the spinster.

'I did not say he was "remarkable for beauty," but he has—er—distinction— decided *distinction.* I'm surprised you don't see it. And he has very fine eyes.'

'His eyes won't give 'em any carriage-and-pair,' opined Miss Wix. '*I* used to have fine eyes, my dear, but I've stared at hard times so long.'

'I don't know where the "hard times" come in, I'm sure,' replied Mrs. Walford sharply. 'And he wanted to give her a carriage directly they married, but Sam's forbidden it/'

The maiden sniffed.

'He is most modest for his position. I tell you, he was chased in Dieppe; the women *ran* after him. A baroness in the hotel positively threw her daughter at his head. . . . He wouldn't look at anybody but Cynthia. . . . The Baroness was *miserable* the day the engagement was known.'

'Cynthia should be very proud,' returned her sister dryly.

'Oh, of course the girl is making a wonderful match—no doubt about it! He sold his novel for an extraordinary sum—quite extraordinary!—and the publishers have implored him to let them have another at his own terms; I saw the telegrams. . . . Astonishing position for such a young man!'

'She's very lucky!'

'She's a very taking girl. Her smile is so sweet, and her teeth are quite perfect.'

'She was in luck to meet such a "catch"—some people didn't have the opportunity. . . . I once had a beautiful set of teeth,' added Miss Wix morosely; 'but you can't pick rich husbands off gooseberry bushes.'

On the white balcony, after dinner, Kent begged Cynthia to fix the wedding-day. After she had named one in May, it was agreed that, subject to her parents' approval, they should be married two months hence. He made his way to the station at eleven, with a flower in his coat and rapture in his soul.

The first weeks of the period were interminable.

He went to The Hawthorns daily, and Mrs. Walford was so good as to look about for a house for them in the neighborhood. He was in love, but he was not a fool; he was determined that he would not cripple himself at the outset by assuming unjustifiable responsibilities, and in conference with the fiancée he intimated that it would be preposterous for them to think of paying a higher rent than fifty pounds. Cynthia was a little disappointed, for mamma had just seen a villa at sixty-five that was a picturesque duck. He strangled an impulse to say, 'We'll take it,' and repeated that as soon as their circumstances brightened they could remove. She did not argue the point, though the **rara avis** evidently allured her, and Kent felt her acquiescence to be very gracious, and trusted she did not consider him mean.

If he was resolved to avoid burdening himself with a heavy rental, however, he was not deeply concerned about the extent of the outlay made on furniture. As Mrs. Walford pointed out, the things would always be there, and once they were bought, they were bought. In her company they visited the Tottenham Court Road every morning for a week, and this one sped more quickly to him than any yet. It was a foretaste of life with Cynthia to choose armchairs, and etchings, and ornaments, and the rest, for their home together. They had now selected one at the desirable fifty pounds; it was about ten minutes' walk from The Hawthorns, a semi-detached erection in red brick, with nice wide windows, and electric bells, and rose-trees on either side of the tessellated path. They wanted to be able to drive up to it when they returned from the honeymoon and find it ready for them. Mrs. Walford would procure the kitchen utensils and engage a servant during their absence, and all they had to do themselves was to buy the articles of interest, and settle the wall papers, and have little intermediate lunches, and go back to the shop, and sip tea while rolls of carpet were displayed. It was great fun.

The pictures in the catalogues, though, never seemed quite realized by the originals, and it was generally necessary to purchase something of a more expensive description than they had proposed. But, again, 'once it was bought, it was bought.' The recollection was sustaining. If Kent felt blank when he contemplated the total of what they had spent, and remembered that the kitchen clamored still, he reflected that to kiss Cynthia in such a jolly little ménage would certainly be charming, and the girl averred ecstatically that the dessert-service 'looked better than mamma's!' He estimated that they could live with perfect comfort at the rate of two hundred and fifty per annum—for the first year, at all events, and by then he would have completed a novel which, in view of the press notices he had obtained, he believed he could dispose of for quite as much. Even if he did not, there would be a substantial sum remaining of his capital, and with the third book—No, he had no cause for dismay, he thought; and, indeed, he had not.

They had decided upon Mentone for the wedding trip—a fortnight. It was quite enough, and they would rather be somewhere like that for a fortnight than in Bournemouth or Ventnor for a month. It would amount to the same thing pecuniarily, and be much more pleasant.

'The morning after we come back, darling,' said Kent, 'I shall go straight to my desk after breakfast, and you know you'll see scarcely more of me till evening than if I were a business man, and had to go to the City.'

'Y-e-s,' concurred Cynthia meekly. 'Of course; I understand.'

CHAPTER VI.

MR. and MRS. WALFORD'S offering was to be a grand piano—or a semi-grand possibly, since the drawing-room was not extensive—and with a son being educated for the musical profession, it was natural they should wait till he returned before selecting it, so that they might have the advantage of his judgment.

He was traveling on the Continent with Pincocca, the master under whom he studied. On hearing of his sister's engagement, he had at once despatched affectionate letters, and now he was expected home in two or three days to make Mr. Kent's acquaintance, and tender his felicitations in person.

The better Kent learned to know the Walfords, the more clearly he perceived how inordinately proud they were of their son. Cæsar's arrival and Cæsar's approaching début were topics discussed' with a frequency he found tedious. Even Cynthia was so excited by the prospect of reunion that a tête-à-tête with her lost a little of its fascination, and he occasionally feared, if his prospective brother-in-law did not arrive without delay, he would have been bored into a cordial dislike for him by the time they met. He foresaw himself telling him so at a distant date, when they were intimate, and that they would joke over the matter together. Miss Wix alone appeared untainted by the prevailing enthusiasm, and the first ray of friendliness for the spinster of which he had been conscious was when he caught a glance of comprehension from her little eyes one afternoon after the subject had been discussed energetically for upwards of half an hour. It struck him there was even a gleam of ironical humor in her gaze.

'Enthralling, isn't it?' she seemed to say. 'What do you think of 'em?'

He said to Cynthia later:

'They do talk about your brother and his voice an awful lot, dearest, don't they?'

She looked somewhat startled.

'Well, I suppose we do,' she answered slowly, 'now you point it out. But I didn't know. You see, ever since his voice was discovered, Cæsar's been brought up for the profession. When you've heard it, you'll understand.'

'Is it really so magnificent?' he asked respectfully.

'Oh, I'm sure you'll say so. Signor Pincocca told mamma it would be a *crime* if she didn't let him study seriously for the career. And Cæsar has been under him years since then. Pincocca says when he "comes out" people will rave about him. If he had only had just a "fine voice," he would have gone on the Stock Exchange, you know, with papa; but—but there could be no question about it with a gift like that.'

Kent acknowledged it was natural that they should be profoundly interested by the young fellow's promise, and privately wished that a literary man could also leap into fame and fortune with his début.

The next afternoon when he reached The Hawthorns he heard that Cæsar had already come—indeed, he had divined as much by Mrs. Walford's jubilant air in greeting. At the moment the traveler was not in the room, however, and Cynthia ran in haste to summon him. Humphrey awaited his entrance with considerable curiosity, heightened by the fact that the mother kept looking toward the door as impatiently as a child toward the curtain that is to disclose the glories of a pantomime.

'I don't know what is keeping him,' she said in her most staccato tones. 'He just went to the balcony to fetch my book. Oh, he'll be here in a minute—or shall we sit out there ourselves? Perhaps he's gone down to the garden, and Cynthia can't find him. What do you say?'

'Just as you please,' said Kent.

But as he spoke the girl returned, to announce that her brother was following her, and the next moment there was an atmosphere of a barber-shop, and Humphrey found his finger-tips being gently pressed in a large, soft palm.

'I am charmed!' said Cæsar Walford with a sweet, lingering smile. 'Charmed!'

Kent saw a fat young man of six or seven and twenty, with an enormous chest development, and a waist that suggested he wore stays, and was already wrestling with his figure. His hair, which had been grown long, was arranged on his forehead in negligent curls, and his shirt-collar, low in the neck, lay back over a flowing bow.

'I'm very pleased to meet you' said the author with disgust.

I am charmed!' repeated Cæsar tenderly. 'It is quite a delight! And it's you who are going to take Cynthia away from us, eh?' He glanced from one to the other, and shook a playful forefinger. 'You bad man! . . . O wicked puss!'

Mrs. Walford viewed these ponderous antics beamingly.

'There's grace!' her expression cried. "There's dramatic gesture for you!'

Again Humphrey's gaze sought the sour spinster's, and—yes, her own was eloquent.

He sipped his tea abstractedly. So this was the gifted being of whom he had heard so much—this dreadful creature who bulged out of his frock-coat, and minced, and posed, and was alternately frisky and pompous. What a connection to have! Was it possible his voice was so wonderful as they all declared, or would that be a disappointment too? In any case, his self-complacence made a stranger sick.

It was about two hours after dinner when the young man was begged to oblige the company, and Humphrey, who was now truly eager to hear him, feared for a long while that the persuasions would not succeed, for the coming bass objected in turn to Wagner and Verdi, and all the songs in his répertoire. He shrugged his shoulders pityingly at this one, had forgotten that, and was not equal this evening to a third. At length, however, Cynthia rose, and declared that he should give them 'Infelice.' ***Ernani*** was ' intolerable,' but, since they would not let him alone, he crossed languidly to her side.

A hush of suspense settled upon the long drawing-room. Sam Walford fixed Kent with a stare as if he meant to watch the admiration forming in him. Louisa, the hilarious and untruthful, appeared to be experiencing some divine emotion even before the song began. Miss Wix closed her eyes, with her mouth to one side. Then the young man languished at the gasalier, and roared.

It was a marvelous roar. No one could dispute that he possessed a voice of really phenomenal power, if it were once conceded that it was a voice, in the musical sense, at all. It seemed as if he must burst his corsets, and shift the furniture—that the very ceiling itself must crack with the noise he sent up. The perspiration broke out on him, and rolled down his face as he writhed at the gas-globes. His large body was contorted with exertion, but he never faltered. Bellow upon bellow he emitted to the welcome end, till Cynthia struck the final chord, and he bowed.

'A performance?' said Mr. Walford to Kent proudly. Kent said indeed it was.

The compliments were effusive. It was discussed whether he was, or was not, 'in voice' to-night. He averred that to 'lose himself' when he sang he need Pincocca at the piano, and sank into his chair again and mopped his brow.

'The amateur accompaniment is very painful,' he said winningly.

Kent made his adieux earlier than was his habit, explaining that he had work to do.

The momentous date was now close at hand, and Turquand, who had not refused to be best man, had made a present which was indubitably handsome in view of his chronic impecuniosity and his opinions. In the days that intervened Humphrey and he alike found it impracticable to banish the important subject from their colloquies, and it was arranged that on the eve of the ceremony they should have a 'bachelor dinner' by themselves, and subsequently smoke a few cigars together in a music-hall. Neither wanted anybody else, nor, in point of fact, did Humphrey know many men to invite. For the time to attend the wedding the journalist had characteristically applied on the grounds of 'a bereavement,' and, though he had not confessed it to Kent, he was more than ever convinced, as he watched him collect his possessions, and pore over a Continental Bradshaw, and fondle the sacred ring, that he had used the right term.

It was a wet evening—the eve of the wedding-day. A yellow mist hung over Soho, and a light rain had fallen doggedly since noon, turning the grease of the pavements to slush. On the moist air the smell of the jam clung persistently, and along the narrow streets fewer children played tip-cat than was usual in the neighborhood.

Kent's impedimenta were packed and labelled, and among the litter a brown-paper parcel contained the costume of the groomsman. The coat would be creased by to-morrow, and he knew it; but he had had a repugnance to undoing the parcel earlier than was compulsory, and once, when Kent had not been looking, he had kicked it.

The two men put up their collars, and made their way across the square.

'Are you sure we'll go to the Suisse?' asked Kent. 'It isn't festive, Turk.'

'Yes, let's go to the Suisse,' said Turquand grumpily. 'It's close.'

Both were aware that its proximity was not the reason it had been chosen, but the pretence was desirable.

'We'll have champagne, of course,' said Humphrey, as they passed in, and took their seats at their customary little table, with its half-yard of crusty bread and damp serviettes. 'We'll have champagne, and—and be lively. For heaven's sake don't look t as if you were at a funeral, Turk! This is to be an enjoyable evening. Where's the wine-list?'

'don't suppose there's such a thing as champagne in the show,' said Turquand. 'Auguste will think you're getting at him.'

Auguste was prevailed upon to believe that the demand was made in sober earnest. Monsieur really desired champagne. Monsieur also considered that he had better run out for it, as he did for the 'bittare' when it was wanted—voilà! Madame, at the semicircular counter, waved her fat hand in their direction gaily. Monsieur had inherited a fortune, it was evident—oh hè ! la, la, la!

'Well,' said Turquand, when the waiter returned and the cork had popped, 'here's luck. Wish you lots of happiness, old chap, I'm sure.'

'Same to you,' murmured Kent. 'God knows I do. It's awful muck, this stuff, isn't it? What's he brought?'

'It's what you ordered. Your mouth's out of taste. Eat some more kidneys.'

Humphrey shook his head.

'I suppose you'll come here to-morrow evening—the same as usual, eh?'

'May as well, I suppose. One's got to feed somewhere. *You'll* be all rice and rapture then. I'll think of you.'

'Do. I don't know how it is; but—but just now, somehow, between ourselves—But perhaps I oughtn't to say that. . . . I say, don't think I was going to—to—I wouldn't have you think I meant I wasn't fond of her, old boy, for the world. You don't think *that,* do you? She—oh, heaven !—she's a perfect angel, Turk ! . . . Fill up your glass, for goodness' sake, man, and do look jolly! Turk, next time we dine together it'll be at Streatham, and there'll be a little hostess to make you welcome; and—and there'll always be a bottle of Irish, old man, and we'll keep a pipe in the rack with the biggest bowl we can find, and call it yours. By God, we will!'

'Yes,' said Turquand huskily. . . . 'Going to have any more of this stew?'

'I've had enough; help yourself.'

'No, I'm not ravenous either—smoked too much, perhaps. I say, Madame doesn't know yet; better tell her.'

She was induced to join them presently, and to drink a glass of champagne, enchanted by the invitation; Monsieur Kent was always très gentil; but champagne! was it that he celebrated already another romance? Comment! he was going to be married—*nevare?* But yes—and to-morrow! Oh, mon Dieu! She rocked herself to and fro, and screamed the intelligence down the dinner-lift to her husband in the kitchen. Allors, they must drink a chartreuse with her—she insisted. Yes, and she would have one of Monsieur Kent's cigarettes. Oh hè ! la, la, la! again.

Outside the rain was still falling as they left the Restaurant Suisse, and tramped to a music-hall. Here their entrance was unfortunately timed. Some capital turns appeared earlier in the programme, some excellent ones figured lower down; but during the half-hour that they remained the monotony of the material which the average music-hall 'comedian' regards as humorous struck Kent more forcibly than ever. Wives eloped with the lodgers, or husbands beat their wives and got drunk with 'the boys.' There seemed nothing else—nothing but conjugal infelicity; it was rang-tang-tang on the one vulgar discordant note.

'I've had enough of this,' he said; 'let's go. What time is it?'

'Time for a quiet pipe at home, and then to turn in early. Let's cab it.'

They were glad to get off their wet boots, and to find themselves once more in their own shabby chairs. But Cornelia had let the fire out, and the dismantled room was chilly. Turquand produced the whisky and the glasses, and, blowing a cloud, they drew up to the cold hearth, remarking that there had been a change in the weather, and a fire would have been out of place on such a night.

"It looks bare without my things, doesn't it?" observed Kent. 'One wouldn't have believed they made so much difference.'

'Yes,' assented Turquand.

'You'll have to get some books for that shelf there, you know; it's horful empty.'

Turquand shivered, and said he should.

'You aren't cold?'

'Cold? Not a bit—no. You were saying'

'I don't know; I wasn't saying anything particular. I'll write you from Mentone, old fellow—not at once, but you shall have a line.'

'Thanks,' answered Turquand; 'be glad to hear from you.'

Not that there'll be anything to say.'

'No, of course not. Still, you may just as well twaddle a bit, if you will.'

There was a pause, while the pair smoked slowly, each busy with his thoughts, and considering if anything of what he felt could be said without its sounding sentimental. Both were remembering that they would never be sitting at home together in the room again, and though it had many faults, it assumed to the one who was leaving it a 'tender grace' now. He had written his novel at that table; his first review had come to him here. Associations crept out and trailed across the floor; he felt that this room must always contain an integral portion of his life. And Turquand would miss him.

'Be dull for you to-morrow evening, rather, I'm afraid, won't it?' he said in a burst.

'Oh, I was alone while you were in Dieppe, you know. I shall jog along all right. . . . You've bought a desk for yourself, haven't you?'

'Yes. Swagger, eh?'

'You "won't know where yer are." . . . What's that—you feel a draught?'

'No—I—well, perhaps there is a draught now you mention it. Yes, I shall work in style when we come back. Strange feeling, going to be married, Turk.'

'Is it?' said Turquand. 'Haven't had the experience. Hope Mrs. Kent will like me—they never do in fiction. You . . . you might tell her I'm not a bad sort of a damned fool, will you? And—er—I want to say, don't have the funks about asking me to your house once in a way, old chap, when I shan't be a nuisance; take my oath I'll never shock your wife, Humphrey . . . too fond of you. . . . Be as careful as—as *you* can, I give you my word.'

His teeth closed round his pipe tightly. Neither man looked at the other; Humphrey put out his hand without speaking, and Turquand gripped it. There was a silence again. Both stared at the dead ashes. The clock of St. Giles-in-the-Fields tolled twelve, and neither commented on it, though they simultaneously reflected that it was now the marriage morning.

"Strikes me we were nearly making bally asses of ourselves,' said Turquand at last, in a shaky voice. 'Finish your whisky, and let's to bed.'

CHAPTER VII.

As the wheels began to revolve, he looked at the girl with thanksgiving. Perhaps the top thought in the tangle of his consciousness was that he was relieved. The worry and publicity of the day were over. They were married. For good or for ill—for always—whether things went well or went badly with him, she was his wife now! He realized the fact much more clearly here while the train rushed forward, than he had done when making his responses at the altar; indeed, at the altar he had realized little but the awkwardness of his attitude, and that Cynthia was very nervous. And he was glad; but, knowing that he was glad, he wondered vaguely why he did not feel more exhilaration.

They were alone in the compartment, and he took her hand and spoke to her. She answered by an obvious effort, and both sat gazing from the window over the flying fields. She thought of her home, and that 'everything was very strange,' and that she would have liked to cry' properly,' without having Humphrey's eyes upon her. *He* speculated whether she would like to cry while he affected to be unaware of it behind a paper, or if she would imagine he wanted to read, and consider him unfeeling. He thought that a wedding-day was a very exhausting experience for a girl, and that her evident desire to avoid conversation was fortunate, since, to save his soul, he could not think of anything to say that was not stupid. He thought, also, though his palate did not crave tobacco, that a cigar would have assisted him tremendously, and that it was really extraordinary to reflect that 'Cynthia Walford' and he were man and wife.

Next, he questioned inwardly what *she* was thinking, and attempted, in a mental metamorphosis, to put himself in her place. It made him feel horribly sorry for her. He pitied her hotly, though he could not say so; and by a sudden impulse he squeezed her gloved fingers again, with remorseful compassion. At the moment that he was moved to the demonstration, however, she was really wishing that the dressmaker had cut the corsage of her blue theatre frock square, instead of in a 'V.' The engine screamed. Both spoke perfunctorily. He congratulated himself on his character, boasting a feminine side, which had made such insight into her mind possible. Some men would have failed to comprehend. She felt that the tears with which she was fighting had made her nose red, and longed for an opportunity to use her powder-puff. The train sped on.

As he sat by her side before the sun-wrapt sea, he looked, not at the girl, but within him. He thought of the book that had formed in his head, and perhaps his paramount feeling was impatience, and the desire to find the first chapter already shaping into words. They were married. The unconscious pretences of the betrothal period were over in both. To him, as well as to her, the magic, the subtile enchantment, was past. She was still Cynthia—more than ever Cynthia, he understood; but there had been a fascination when 'Cynthia' was a goddess to him, which an acquaintance with strings and buttons had destroyed. The 'Corylopsis' stood in a squat little bottle with a silver lid among brushes and hairpins on a toilet-table, and his senses swam no more when he detected its faintness on her gown.

Companionship, and not worship, was required now, and neither found the other quite as companionable as had been expected. This the girl in her heart excused less readily than the man. Primarily, indeed, the latter refused to acknowledge it. It was preposterous to suppose, if they did not possess much in common, that he would not have perceived the disparity during the engagement. Then he reminded himself that his life might have rendered him a shade intolerant; he must remember that the subject of literary work, all-engrossing to his own mind, made on hers unaccustomed demands. To try to phrase a sensation, the attempt to seize a fleeting impression so delicately that it would survive the process, and not expire on the pen's point, were instinctive habits with himself; to her they appeared motiveless and wearisome games.

He had endeavored, in the novels they read together during the honeymoon, to cultivate her appreciation of what was fine, for she had told him some of her favorite authoresses, and he had shuddered. She had obtained a book for herself one day, and offered it to him. He thanked her, but said he was sure by the title that he should not care for it. She answered that it was very silly and unliterary—she had acquired that word—to judge a book by what it was called. She was surprised at him! If *she* had done such a thing, he would have ridiculed her. And, apart from that, she did not see that 'Winsome Winnie' *was* a bad title. What was the matter with it?

Kent said he could not explain. She declared with a little triumphant laugh that that just showed how wrong he was.

He made his endeavor very tenderly. To be looked upon as the schoolmaster abroad was a constant dread with him when he discovered that, if a similarity of taste were to subsist between them, she would have to advance or he must regress. Sometimes—very occasionally—he handed her a passage with an air of taking it for granted the pleasure would be mutual, but her assent was always so constrained that he was forced to realize that the cleverness of expression was lost upon her, that the word-painting had to her painted nothing at all.

He wondered if his wife's blindness fairly represented the eyes with which the novel-reading public read, and if it was folly to spend an hour revising a paragraph in which the majority would, after all, see no more artistry than if it had been allowed to remain as it was written first. He knew that it *was,* in a man like himself, with whom literature was a profession, and not a luxury, though he was aware at the same time that he would never be able to help it; that to the end there would be nights when he went up to bed having written no more than a hundred words all day, and yet with elation, because, rightly and wrongly, he felt the hundred words to have been admirably said. He knew there would be evenings in the future, as there had been in the past, when, after reading a page of somebody else's novel with physical delight, he would go and tear up five sheets of his own manuscript with misery and disgust; and he knew already—though he shrank from admitting this—that when it happened he would never be able to confess it to Cynthia, as he had done to Turquand, because Cynthia would find it incredible and absurd.

The fortnight was near its conclusion, and both looked forward to the return to England with eagerness. He would plunge into his work; she would be near The Hawthorns, and have friends to come to see her. Neither of the pair regretted the step they had taken; each loved the other; but a honeymoon was a trying institution, viewed as a whole.

Presently, where they sat, she turned and put some questions to him about his projected book. Her intentions were praiseworthy; she was a good girl, and having married an author, she understood that it was incumbent on her to take an interest in his vocation, though perhaps, she had fancied once or twice, it might really have been nicer if he had been a stock-jobber, and not cared to discuss his business at home. Papa never had, she knew. Discussing an author's work did not seem so simple as she had assumed it would be. There seemed so many tedious details that did not matter to the story.

'When do you think it will be finished, Humphrey?' she said.

'In nine months, I hope, if I stick to it.'

'So long as nine months?' she exclaimed with surprise. 'Why, I've read—let me see—two, three new ones of Mrs. St. Julian's this year! Will it **really** take so long as nine months?'

'Quite, sweetheart; perhaps longer. I don't write quickly, I'm sorry to say. Still, it won't be bad if Cousins pay the two hundred and fifty that I expect. I think they ought to, after the way the last has been received.'

'Some people get much more, don't they?'

'Just a trifle,' he said. 'Yes; but I'm not a popular writer, you see. Wait a bit, though; we'll astonish your mother with our grandeurs yet. You shall have a victoria, **and** two men on the box with powdered hair, and drive out on a wet day, and splash mud at your enemies.'

'I don't think I have enemies,' she laughed.

'You will when you have the victoria and pair, be easy. Some poor beggar of an author who's hoping to get two hundred and fifty pounds for nine months' toil will look at you from a bus and cuss you.'

'Suppose you can't get two hundred and fifty?' she inquired. 'You can't be sure.'

'Oh, well, if it were only a couple of hundred, we shouldn't have to go to the workhouse, you know. If it comes to that, a hundred, the same as I got for the other, would see us through, though of course I wouldn't accept such a price. Don't begin to worry your little head about ways and means on your honeymoon, darling; there's time enough for arithmetic. And it's going to be good work. I've been practical, too. I can end it happily, and retain a conscience. It's almost a different plot from what it was when I commenced to think, and it's better. It ends well, and it's better. The thing's a Koh-i-noor.'

'Tell me all about it,' she suggested.

He complied enthusiastically. She was being very sympathetic, and he felt with perfect momentary content how jolly it was to have a lovely wife and talk these things over with her. Just what he had pictured.

'But wouldn't it be more exciting if you kept that a mystery till the third volume?' she said, at the end of five minutes.

It was as if she had thrown a bucket of ice-water on his animation.

'I don't want it to be a mystery,' he said, speaking more difficultly. 'That isn't the aim at all. What I mean to do is to analyze the woman's sensations when she learns it. I want to show how she feels and suffers; yes, and the temptation that she wrestles with, and loathes herself for being too weak to put aside. Don't you see—don't you see?'

She was chiefly sensible that his pleasure had vanished, and that the note of interest in his voice had died. She, however, repeated her suggestion; if she was to be a critic, she must be prepared to maintain her literary views.

'I think all that would be much duller than if you had the surprise,' she declared.

He did not argue—he did not attempt to demonstrate that her suggestion amounted to proposing he should write quite another story than the one he was talking about; he felt hopelessly that argument would be waste of time.

'Perhaps you are right,' he said; 'but one does what one can.'

'But you should say, "What one *will,*" dear; it can be done whichever way you like.'

'There is only one way possible to *me,* I assure you,' he answered; 'for once "the wrong way" is the more difficult.'

'That which you *think* is the wrong way,' said Cynthia, with gentle firmness.

He looked at her a moment incredulously.

'Good Lord!' he said; 'let me know something about my own business! I don't want to pose on the strength of a solitary novel—I'm not arrogant—but let me know *something*—at all events, more than you! Heavens above! a novelist devotes his life to trying to learn the technique of an art which it wants three lifetimes to acquire, and Mr. Jones, who is a solicitor, and Mr. Smith the shoe manufacturer, and little Miss Pugh of Putney, who don't know the first laws of fiction—who aren't even aware there are any laws to know—are all prepared to tell him how his books should be written.'

'I am not Miss Pugh of Putney,' she said. 'And if I were, we all know whether we like a book or whether we don't.'

' "Like !" ' he echoed. 'To "like" and to "criticise"—Men are *paid* to criticise books when they can do it; it's thought to be worth payment. Editors, who don't exactly bubble over with generosity, sign checks for reviews. *I* don't pretend to teach Mr. Smith how to make his shoes; I've sense enough to understand he knows the way better than I. Nor do these people think they can teach a painter how to compose his pictures, or that they can give a musician lessons in orchestration. Why on earth should they imagine they're competent to instruct a novelist? It is absurd!'

'Your comparisons are far-fetched,' she said. 'A painter and a musician, we all know, have to study; they—'

'They're entitled to the consideration due to a certain amount of money sunk—eh? That is really it. There are thousands upon thousands of families belonging to the upper middle classes in England to whom fiction will never be an art, because the novelist hasn't been to an academy and paid fees. As a matter of fact, it is only in artistic and professional circles—and, one believes, in "Society," as it is called—that a novelist in England is regarded with any other feeling than good-humored contempt, unless he is publicly known to be making a large income. The commercial majority smile at him. They've a shibboleth—I'm sure it will be familiar to you: "You can't improve your mind by reading novels." They are persuaded it's true. They have heard it since they were children, in these families where no artist or no professional man of any kind has ever let in a little light. "You can't improve your mind by reading novels "is one of the stock phrases of middle-class English Philistia. Ask them if they improve their minds by looking at pictures in the National Gallery, or even in the New, and they know it is essential they should answer, "Certainly." Ask them how they do it, and they are "done." Of course, they don't really improve their minds either way, because, before the contemplation of art in any form can be anything more than a vague amusement, a very much higher standard of education than they have reached is necessary; only they have learnt to pretend about pictures. It's an odd thing—or, perhaps, a natural one—that an author of the sort of book that they are impressed by, a scientist, a brain-worker of any description, literary or not, talks and thinks of a novelist with respect, while these people themselves find him beneath him.'

There was a silence, in which both stared again at the sea. His irritation subsiding, it occurred to him that he might have expressed his opinions less freely, considering that Philistia was his wife's birthplace. He was beginning to excuse himself, when she interrupted him.

'Don't let us discuss it any more, Humphrey,' she said, in a grieved voice, 'please! I am sorry I said so much.'

'I was wrong,' said Kent; 'I have vexed you.

'No; I am not vexed,' she replied, in a tone that intimated she was only hurt.

'Cynthia, don't be angry! . . . Make it up!'

She turned instantly, touching him with her hand with a quick, pleased smile, and he set himself to efface the effect of his ill-humor upon her mood with entirely successful results. As they strolled back to the hotel side by side, he felt her to be a long way from him—there was even a sense of physical remoteness. Mentally, she did not seem so near as in the days of their earliest acquaintance. He caught himself wishing he could debate a certain point in construction with Turquand, and from that it was the merest step to perceiving that Mentone would be jollier if Turquand were with him instead. He was appalled to think that such a fancy should have crossed his brain, and strove guiltily to believe it had not; but once again he felt spiritless and blank, and it was a labor to maintain the necessary disguise. He observed forlornly that Cynthia always appeared happiest in their intercourse when the ineptitude of it was weighing most heavily upon himself.

CHAPTER VIII.

MRS. KENT placed few obstacles in the way of her husband's industry, and installed in Leamington Road, Streatham, he commenced his novel, and deleted, and destroyed, and rewrote, until at the expiration of three weeks he had accomplished Chapter I. Primarily he did not experience so many domestic discomforts to impede him as Turquand had once predicted. Mrs. Walford had obtained a very respectable and nice-looking servant, whose only drawback was having a father in a lunatic asylum, and the frequently expressed misgiving that, if she were harassed by a multitude of orders, she might be overtaken by a similar fate. Ann was so 'superior,' Mrs. Walford explained, and a 'general' had really proved so difficult to procure, that she had not allowed the thought of a hereditary taint to disqualify her, and both the bride and bridegroom declared she had been quite right. Cynthia confessed later to finding it a little awkward when a duty was neglected, since she was deterred from remonstrating by the fear 'the girl might go mad at her'; but apart from this Ann was an acquisition.

The author's working hours were supposed to be from ten o'clock till seven, with an interval for lunch; but the irregular habits of bachelorhood made it hard for him to accustom himself to them, and it was often agreed that he should take his leisure in the afternoon, and reseat himself at his desk in the alluring hours of lamplight, when the neighbors' children were at rest, and the scales ceased from troubling. To these neighbors he found he was an object of considerable curiosity. He had never lived in a suburb hitherto, and he discovered that for a man to remain at home all day offered much food for conjecture there. Subsequently, in some inexplicable manner, his vocation was ascertained, and then, when Cynthia and he strolled out, people whispered behind their window-curtains, and stared at them with smiles which suggested that they were not thought very respectable.

Of his wife's family he saw a good deal, both at The Hawthorns and at No. 64,

Leamington Road, and his liking for his brother-in-law did not increase. There was an air of condescension in Mr. Cæsar Walford's self-sufficiency that he found highly exasperating. The bass's début had been fixed during their absence for the coming season, and he repeated the newest compliments paid him by his master with the languid assurance of an artist whose supremacy was already acknowledged by all the world. The latest burst of admiration into which Pincocca had been betrayed had always to be dragged by his parents from reluctant lips, but he never forgot any of it.

Humphrey was sure the artist thought even less of him than the neighbors. Fiction he rarely read, he said. He said it with an elevation of his eyebrows, as if novels were far beneath his attention. His eyebrows were, in fact, singularly expressive, and he could dismiss an author's claim to consideration, or ridicule a masterpiece, without uttering a word. There had been more truth than is usual in such statements when Humphrey had averred that he was not conceited on the score of his unprofitable spurs, but when he contemplated the complacent sneer by which this affected young man pronounced a novelist of reputation to be entirely fatuous, he was galled.

Cynthia had told her mother how hard he was working, and once, when they were spending an evening at The Hawthorns some weeks after their return, the subject was mentioned.

'Well,' exclaimed the stock-jobber tolerantly, 'and how's the story?—getting along, heh?'

'Yes,' said Kent, 'I'm plodding on with it fairly well, sir.'

He was aware his father-in-law did not take fiction seriously, either, and he always felt a certain restraint in speaking of his profession here.

'And what's it about?' asked Mrs. Walford, much in the indulgent tone in which one puts such a question to a child. 'Have you made Cynthia your lovely heroine, and are you flirting with her at Dieppe again? *I* know what it'll be—ha! ha! ha! I'm sure you meant yourself by the hero in your last book; you know I told you so long ago.'

He was convinced also that she would say it with equal perspicacity about every book he wrote.

'N-no,' he said, 'I shouldn't quite care to try to make "copy" out of my wife. It wouldn't be easy, and it wouldn't be congenial.'

'You ought to know her faults better than anybody else's, I should think, by this time,' said Miss Wix tartly.

'And her virtues,' answered Humphrey.

'Oh,' said Miss Wix, with acidulated humor, 'he says two months are quite long enough to find out all Cynthia's virtues, Louisa.'

'didn't hear him say anything of the sort,' said Mrs. Walford crossly. 'Well, what is it about? Tell us.'

He felt awkard and embarrassed.

'I can't explain a plot; I'm very stupid at it,' he said. 'You shall have a copy the moment it is published, mater, and read the thing.'

'I do wish he'd call me "mamma"!' she cried. 'He makes me feel a hundred years old.'

To divert the conversation, he inquired if she had read the last of Henry James's.

'I don't know,' she said. 'Oh yes, they sent it me from the library this week. It isn't bad; I didn't like it much. Did *you* read it, Cæsar?'

Cæsar became conscious that people talked.

'Read?' he echoed wearily. 'Read what?'

'James's last. I forget what it was called—er—something. I saw you with it the other day. A red book.'

'I looked through it. I had nothing to do.'

'Quite amusing,' she said, 'wasn't it?'

I forget,' he murmured; ' I never do remember these things.'

'It took a clever man some time to write,' said Kent; 'it might have been worth your attention for a whole afternoon.'

The other was not disturbed. Neither his confidence nor his amiability was shaken.

Do you think so?' he said with gentleness. 'I *can't* read these things any more. There's nothing to be gained. What does one acquire—whether Angelina marries Edwin, or whether she marries Charles?' He shook his head and smiled compassionately. Sam Walford guffawed. 'When I feel that my mind's been at too great a tension, I sometimes *glance* at a novel; but I'm afraid—I'm really afraid—I can't concede that I should be justified in giving an afternoon to one.'

'Cæsar has his work to think of, you know,' put in Cynthia; 'he is not like us women.'

'You'll find it a tough job to get the best of Cæsar in an argument,' added Walford good-humoredly.

'Oh, I don't deny that I *have* read novels in my time. There was a time when I could read a yellowback.' He made this admission in the evident belief that a book was far more frivolous in cardboard covers than while it was in its first edition of cloth. 'But I can't do it to-day.'

Well,' cried Mrs. Walford, '*I* must say I agree with Humphrey. I must say I think it's—it's really very clever to write a good novel, *I* couldn't write one; I'm sure I couldn't. I haven't the patience.'

Oh! 'exclaimed Cæsar, with charming confusion; 'it's Humphrey's own line— of course it is. I always forget.' He turned to Kent deprecatingly: 'Do you know, I never think of you as going in for that; it's a surprise every time I recollect it.'

Kent said it was really of no consequence whatever.

'Well, well, well,' said Walford, 'everybody to his trade. We can't all be born with a fortune in our throats. Wish we could—eh, Humphrey, my boy? Did you hear what Lassalle said about his voice the otter day? Cæsar, just tell Humphrey what Lassalle said about your voice the other day.'

'Oh, Humphrey doesn't want to listen to that long story,' declared Mrs. Walford, 'I'm sure.'

He could do no less after this than express curiosity.

'Well then, Cæsar, tell us what it was.'

'Do, Cæsar,' entreated his sister; '*I* haven't heard, either.'

'A trifle,' he demurred, 'not interesting. I didn't know I'd mentioned it.'

'Oh yes,' said Miss Wix. 'Don't you remember you told us the story at tea, and then you told it again to your father at dinner? But do tell Cynthia and Humphrey.'

'I—er—dined with Pincocca last night at his rooms,' he drawled. 'One or two men came in afterward. He introduced me. I didn't pay much attention to the names—you know what it is—and by-and-by Pincocca pressed me to sing. He said I was "a pupil," and I could see one of the men was pre-pared to be bored. . . . This really is so *very* personal that'

'No, no, no! go on. What nonsense I' said his mother.

'I could see he was prepared to be bored; so I made up my mind to—*sing*! I was nettled—very childish, I admit it—but I was nettled. I didn't watch him while I sang—I couldn't. I did better than I expected. I—"

'You forgot *everything*,' said Sam Walford, '*I* know.'

'I did, yes. I didn't think of Pincocca, of him, of anybody in the room. When I had finished, he came up to me, and said, "Mr. Walford, I am sick with envy. Ah, heaven! if *I* could command such a career!" The man was Lassalle!'

'Flattering?' said his father to Kent. 'Flattering? "If *I* could command such a career!" Eh?'

Kent asked himself speechlessly if this thing could be.

"If *I* could command such a career!" ' reiterated Mr. Walford. 'What do you think of that! He's coming out in the spring, you know.'

'Yes, so I've heard,' said Humphrey. 'Where?'

'That's not settled; here in town, probably, at the Opera House. He sang to the manager last week. The man was—was altogether staggered.'

'Ha!' said Kent perfunctorily.

'There's never been anything heard like it. I tell you, he'll take London by storm.'

'What *I* can't understand,' said Miss Wix, her mouth pursed to a buttonhole, 'is how you didn't know Lassalle directly he came in. Is he the only musical celebrity you aren't intimate with?'

Her nephew looked momentarily disconcerted.

One doesn't know everybody,' he said feebly; 'Lassalle happened to be a man I'd not met.'

'What do you mean, Emily?' flared Mrs. Walford. 'You don't imagine that Cæsar made the story up, I suppose?"

"Mean"?' said Miss Wix with wonder. " 'Make it up"? Why *should* he make it up? I said I did not understand, that is all. Quite a simple observation.'

She rose, and seated herself stiffly on a distant couch. Mrs. Walford panted, and turned to Humphrey, who she was afraid had overheard.

'How very absurd,' she said jerkily—how very absurd of her to make such a remark! So liable to misconstruction. By the way, do you see anything of that Mr. Turkey—Turquand—what was he called?—now? Has he—er—er—any influence on the press?'

'He knows a good many people of a kind. Why do you ask?'

'We shall be very pleased to see him,' she said; 'I liked him very much. He might dine with us one night—when there's nobody particular here. . . . I was thinking he might be useful to Cæsar. The press can be so spiteful, can't it—so very spiteful? Of course, Cæsar will really be independent of criticism, but still—'

'Still, you'll give Turquand a dinner.'

'Oh, you satirical villain!' she said playfully. 'Hee! hee! hee! You're all alike, you writing men; you'll even lash your mamma-in-law. Aren't you going to have anything to drink? Sam, Humphrey has nothing to drink. Cynthia, a glass of wine?'

The servant had entered with a salver and the tantalus, and Sam Walford proposed the toast of his son's début. They prepared to drink it, and it was noticed then that Miss Wix sat alone in her distant corner.

'Emily, aren't you going to join us?'

'I beg your pardon, Emily,' exclaimed Walford; 'I didn't know you were with us any longer, upon my word I didn't.'

' "The poor are always with us," 'said Miss Wix, in a low and bitter voice. 'If it can be spared, a modicum of whisky.'

'Then, you'll tell Mr. Turquand we shall be happy to see him?' said Mrs. Walford to Kent. 'Don't forget it. You might bring him in with you one evening—I dare say he'll be very glad of the invitation—and he can hear Cæsar sing. What's your hurry? I want to talk to Cynthia. You aren't going to write any more when you get back, I suppose?'

He acknowledged that he was—that he had taken his wife to a matineé with the understanding—but it was past twelve when they left her mother's house and turned homeward through the silent suburb, to which the railway had just yielded back a few theatre-goers, weary and incongruous-looking. In the cold clearness of the winter night the women's long-cloaked figures and flimsy headgears drooped dejectedly, and the men, with their dress-trousers flapping thinly as they walked by their side, appeared already oppressed by the thought of the early breakfast to which the maid-servant's knock would summon them in time to hurry to the station again. The prosperous residences lying back behind spruce, trim shrubberies and curves of carriage-drive finished abruptly, and then began borders in which fifty pounds was already a distinguished rental. The monotonous rows of villas, with their little hackneyed gables and their little hackneyed gates, their painful grandiloquence of nomenclature, seemed to Kent a pathetic expression of lives which had for the most part reached the limit of their potentialities, and now passed without ambition and without hope. Some doubtless looked forward or looked back from the red brick maze, but to the majority the race was run, and this was conquest. He was about to comment on it, but the girl was unusually quiet, and the remark upon his lips was not one that would have been productive of more than a monosyllabic assent under any circumstances.

Their front-garden slept. He unlocked the door, and, saying that she was very tired, Cynthia held up her face immediately and went upstairs. After he had extinguished the gas, Kent mounted to the little room where he worked, and lit the lamp. Beyond the window, over the bare trees, the moon was shining whitely. He stood for a few moments staring out, and thinking he scarcely knew of what; then he seated himself, and began to re-read the last page of the manuscript that lay on the desk. He had just commenced to write, when Cynthia stole in and joined him.

'Are you busy?' she asked.

'No, dearest,' he said, surprised. 'What is it?'

She came forward, and hung beside him, fingering the pen he had laid down. She had put on her dressing-gown, and her hair was loose. She was very lovely, very youthful, so; she looked like a child playing at being a woman. The sleeves fell away, giving a glimpse of the delicate forearms, and he thought the softness of the neck she displayed seemed made for a parent's kisses.

'How cold it is!' she murmured; 'don't you feel it?'

'You shouldn't have come in,' he said; 'you'll take a chill. You'd be better off in bed, Baby.'

She shook her head.

'I want to stop.'

'Then, let me get you a rug and wrap you up.' He rose, but she stayed him petulantly.

'I don't want you to go away; I want to speak to you. . . . Humphrey'

'Is anything the matter?'

'I've something to tell you.' She pricked the paper nervously with the pen-point. 'Something . . . can't you guess what it is, Humphrey? Think—it's about *me*.'

A tear splashed on the paper between them. Kent's heart gave one loud throb of comprehension, and then yearned over her with the truest emotion that she had wakened in him yet. He caught her close and caressed her, while she clung to him sobbing spasmodically.

'Oh, you do love me? You do love me, don't you?' she gasped. 'I'm not a disappointment, *am* I?'

She slipped on to the hassock at his feet, resting her head on his leg, with the tumbled fairness of her hair across his trouser; as she crouched there she looked more like a child than ever, a penitent child begging forgiveness for some fault. He swore she had fulfilled and exceeded his most ardent dreams, that she was sweeter in reality than his imagination had promised him; and he pitied her vehemently and remorsefully as he spoke, because in such a moment she was answered by a lie. The lamp, which the servant had neglected, flickered and expired, and on a sudden the room, and the two bent figures before the desk, were lit only by the pallor of the moon. Cynthia turned herself, and looked up in his face deprecatingly:

'Oh, I am so sorry; I meant to remind her. See, I'm punished—I'm left in the dark myself.'

He stooped and kissed her. The fondness he felt for her normally, intensified by compassion, assumed in this ephemeral circumscription of idea the quality of love, and he rejoiced to think that, after all, he was deceived, and their union was indeed, indeed, the mental companionship to which he had looked forward. He did not withdraw his lips; her month lay beneath them like a flower, and, his arms enclosing her, she nestled to him voicelessly, pervaded by a deep sense of restfulness and content. In a transient ecstasy of illusive union their spirits met, and life seemed to him divine.

CHAPTER IX.

As, chapter by chapter, the novel grew under his hand, Kent saw, from the little back-window, the snow disappear and the bare trees grow green, till at last a fire was no longer necessary in the room, and the waving fields that he overlooked were yellow with buttercups.

He rose at six now, and accomplished about three hours' work before Cynthia went down. Then they breakfasted, and, with an effort to throw some interest into her voice, she would inquire how he had been getting on. He probably felt that he had not been 'getting on' at all, and his response was not encouraging. Afterwards he would make an attempt to read the newspaper, with his thoughts wandering back to his manuscript, and Cynthia had an interview with Ann. This interview, ostensibly concluded before he returned to his desk, was generally reopened as soon as he took his seat, and for some unexplained reason the sequel usually occurred on the stairs. 'Oh, what from the grocer's, ma'am?' 'So and so, and so and so.' 'Yes, ma'am.' 'Oh, and—Ann!' 'What do you say, ma'am?' More instructions, interrupted by a prolonged summons at the tradesman's door, and the girl's rush to open it. 'What is it, Ann?' 'The fishmonger, ma'am.' 'Nothing this morning.' 'Nothing this morning,' echoed by Ann; the boy's departing whistle. 'Ann!' 'Yes, ma'am.' 'Ask him how much a pound the salmon is to-day.' 'Hi! how much a pound's the salmon?' While Kent beat his fists on the desk, and swore. Once he had pitched his pen at the wall in a frenzy, and dashed on to the landing to remonstrate; but he felt such a brute when Cynthia cried, and declared he had insulted her before the servant, and it had wasted so much of his morning, kissing her into serenity again, that he decided it would hinder him less on the whole to bear the nuisance without complaint.

The ink-splashes on the wall paper testified to his having raged in private on more than the one occasion, however, and the superior person's feet appeared to him to grow heavier every week. The domestic machinery was in his ears from morning till nightfall—from the time she began to bang about the house for cleaning purposes to the hour that heard her rattle the last of the dinner things in the scullery and go to bed. It often seemed to him that it could not take much longer washing the plates and dishes supplied for a Lord Mayor's banquet than Ann took to wash those used for his and Cynthia's simple meals, and when, like the report of a cannon, she slammed the oven door, he yearned for his relinquished apartment in Soho as for a lost paradise.

Nor was this all. His wife was less companionable to him daily. Fifty times he had registered a mental oath that he would abandon his hope of cultivating her, and resign himself to her remaining what she was; but he had too much affection for her to succeed in doing it yet, and with every fresh endeavor and failure that he made his dissatisfaction was intensified. He burned to talk about his work, about other men's work, to speak of his ambitions, to laugh with someone over a witty article; instead, their conversation was of Cæsar, whose début had been postponed till the autumn; of the engagement of Dolly Brown, whom he did not know, to young Styles, of Norwood, whom he had not met; of the laundress, who had formerly charged fourpence for a blouse, and who now asked fivepence. When he pretended to be entertained, she spoke of such things with animation. When he dropped the mask, her manner as well as her topics was dull, for she was as sensitive as she was uninteresting. Her wistful question, whether she had proved a disappointment, frequently recurred to him, and to avoid wounding her he affected good spirits more often than he yawned; but the strain was awful, and when he escaped from it at length, and sank into a chair alone, it was with the sense of exhaustion one feels after having been saddled for an afternoon with a talkative child. The oases in his desert were Turquand's visits, but Turquand never came without a definite invitation. Streatham was a long distance from Soho, and there was always the risk of finding that they had gone to the Walfords'. It was necessary to book to Streatham Hill, besides, from the West End, and the service was appalling, with the delays at the stations and the stoppages between them, especially on the return journey, when the train staggered to a standstill at almost every hundred yards.

One evening when he dined them, Humphrey gave him some sheets of his manuscript to read. He did not expect eulogies from Turquand, but he would rather have had to listen to intelligent disapproval than refrain from discussing the book any longer, and when the other praised the work he was delighted.

'You really think it good?' he asked. 'Better than the last? You don't think they'll say I haven't fulfilled its promise? Honest Injun, you know.'

'Seems very strong,' said Turquand, sucking his pipe. 'No, I don't think you need tremble if these pages aren't the top strawberries. Rather Meredithian, that line about her eyes in the pause, isn't it? You remember the one I mean, of course?'

Kent laughed gaily.

'It came like that,' he said. 'Fact! Does it look like a deliberate imitation? Would you alter it? Oh, I say, talking of lines, I'm ill with envy. "Occasionally a girl kissed from behind as she stretched to reach a honeysuckle, rent with a scream the sickly-colored, airless evening." The "sickly-colored, airless evening." Isn't it admirable? What do you think of that for atmosphere? And he's got it with the two adjectives. But the "honeysuckle"—the "honeysuckle" in conjunction with that "sickly-colored, airless"—it's perfect!'

'Whose?'

'Moore's. I opened the book the other day, and it was the first thing I saw. I had been hammering out a lane and summer evening paragraph myself, and when I read that I knew there wasn't an "impression" in all my two hundred words.'

'You shouldn't allow him to read, Mrs. Kent, while he has work on the stocks,' said the journalist. 'I know this sort of phase in your husband of old.'

'Yes, and you used to be very rude,' put in Kent perfunctorily. 'My wife isn't. I can be depressed now without being abused.'

Cynthia laughed. She was very pretty where she lay back in the rocker by the window. Her face was a trifle drawn now, but she looked girlish and graceful still. She looked a wife whom any man might be proud to possess.

'You didn't mention it,' she said; c I didn't know. But I don't see anything wonderful in what you quoted, I must say. Do you, Mr. Turquand? I'm sure "sickly-colored" doesn't mean anything at all.'

'It means a good deal to me,' answered Kent. 'I'd give a fiver to have found that line.'

'Cousins wouldn't give you any more for your book if you had,' said Turquand. 'Put money in thy purse! I suppose you'll stick to Cousins?'

'Why not? Life's too short to find a publisher who'll pay you what you think you're worth; and they were affable. Affability covers a multitude of sins, and there's a lot of compensation in a compliment. Cousins senior told me I'd a "great gift." '

'Perhaps he was referring to his hundred pounds.'

'He was referring to my talent, though I says it as shouldn't. That was your turn, Cynthia!'

'Yes,' said Turquand; 'a wife's very valuable at those moments, isn't she, Mrs. Kent?'

'How do you mean?' said Cynthia, who found the conversational pace inconveniently rapid.

'I shall send it to Cousins,' pursued Humphrey hastily; 'and I want two hundred and fifty this time.'

'They won't give it you.'

'Why not?'

'Partly because you'll accept less. And you haven't got into a second edition, remember.'

'Look at the reviews!'

'Cousins's will look at the sale. The thing will have to be precious good for you to get as much as that.'

'It *will* be precious good,' said Kent seriously. 'I'm doing all I know! You shall wade right through it when it's finished, if you will, and tell me your honest opinion. I won't say it's going to "live," or any rot like that; but it's the best work it is in me to do, and it will be an advance on the other, that I'll swear.'

'Mrs. St. Julian's last goes into a fourth edition next week,' observed Turquand grimly, 'if that is any encouragement to you.'

'Good Lord,' said Kent, 'it only came out in January! Is that a fact?'

'One of Life's Little Ironies! Hers is the kind of stuff to sell, my boy! The largest public don't want nature and style; they want a pooty story and virtue rewarded. The poor "companion" rambles in the moonlight and book-muslin, and has love passages in the grounds at midnight, which wouldn't be respectable, only she's so innocent. The heiress sighs for a title and an establishment in Park Lane; and the poor "companion" says, "Give *me* a cottage, with the man I love," making eyes at the biggest catch in the room, no doubt, though the writer doesn't tell you that, and hooks him. Blessed is the "companion" whose situation is in a lady-novelists's story, for she shall be called the wife of the lord. Sonny, the first mission of a novel is to be a pecuniary success—you are an idiot! Excuse me, Mrs. Kent.'

'You may give him all the good advice you can,' she responded. 'I've said before that I like Mrs. St. Julian's stories, but Humphrey has made up his mind not to. That's firmness, I suppose, as he is a man.'

She laughed.

'Mr. Turquand scarcely implied that he liked them either,' replied Kent. 'Isn't it painful, though, to think of the following a woman like that can command? What a world to write for—it breaks one's heart!'

'It's an overrated place,' said Turquand; 'it's a fat-headed, misguided, beast of a world!'

'It isn't the world,' said Cynthia brightly; 'it's the people in it!'

A ghastly silence followed her comment, a pause in which the journalist stared at the stove ornament, affecting not to have heard her, and Kent felt the sickness of death in his soul. Shame that his wife should show herself so stupid in Turquand's presence paralyzed his tongue, and the latter, pitying his embarrassment, turned to the girl with an inquiry about her relatives. Humphrey had taken him to The Hawthorns, as requested, and Turquand, with characteristic perversity, professed to have discovered a congenial spirit in Miss Wix. It was about Miss Wix that he asked now.

Cynthia laughed again.

'Yes, your favorite is quite well,' she answered—'as cheerful as ever.'

'Fate hasn't been kind to Miss Wix,' said Turquand; 'she's been chastened and chidden too much. Under other circumstances—'

'Skittles!' said Humphrey.

'Under other circumstances, she might have been sweeter, and less amusing. Personally, I am grateful that there were not other circumstances. I like Miss Wix as she is; she refreshes me.'

'I wish she had that effect on *me,*' said Kent, as the other rose to go, and he reflected gloomily that he would hear nothing refreshing until the next time they met. He begged him to remain a little longer, and, when Turquand withstood his persuasions, insisted on accompanying him to the station, and parted from him on the platform with almost sentimental regret.

Only his interest in his book sustained him. He had got deep enough into it to feel the fascination of it on him now, and, though there were still days when he did not produce more than a single page, there were others on which composition was spontaneous and delightful, and happy sentences seemed to fall off his pen's point of their own accord. He wrote under difficulties when the summer came, for Cynthia required more and more attention; but while he often devoted whole mornings or afternoons to her, he made up for it by working on the novel half through the night. More than once he worked through it entirely, merely forsaking his desk to splash in a bath before joining her at breakfast. On such occasions, he was in a very good humor, and, to have completed his felicity, it was only necessary for him to have breakfasted with a woman to whom he could have reported his progress, and cried, 'I've come to such a point,' or, 'That difficulty we foresaw, you know, is overcome—a grand idea!' His exhilaration speedily evaporated at breakfast, and, if he returned to his room an hour later, he did so feeling far less fresh than when he had left it.

Yes, Cynthia demanded many attentions through the summer months; she was petulant, capricious, and dissolved in tears at the smallest provocation. There was much for Kent to consider besides the novel, and also there were anticipations in which they momentarily united, and he felt her to be as close to him as she was dear. But these moments could not make a life, and despite the fact that the date when their child was expected to be born was rapidly approaching, he was living more and more within himself. Cynthia had no complaint to make against him; if marriage was not altogether the elysium she had imagined it would prove, she did not hold that to be Humphrey's fault. She found him, if eccentric, tender and considerate on the whole, but he was bored and weary. His feeling for her was the affection of a man for a child, tinged more or less consciously by compassion, since he knew that she would sob her heart out if she suspected how tedious she appeared to him. Though she would have been a happier woman with a different man, the cost of the mistake they had made was far more heavy to him than to her. He realized what a mistake it had been, while she was unconscious of it, and for this, at least, he was glad.

CHAPTER X.

She was very ill after her confinement, and for several weeks it was doubtful if she would recover. The boy throve, but the mother seemed sinking. The local doctor came three times a day, and a physician was summoned for consultation, and then other consultations were held between the physician and a specialist, and it appeared to Kent that he was never remembered by Mrs. Walford or the nurse during this period, excepting when he was required to write a check. 'You shall see her for a moment by-and-by,' one or the other of them would say; 'she is to be kept very quiet this afternoon. Yes, yes, now you're not to worry; go and work, and you shall be sent for later on.' Then he would wander round the neglected little sitting-room, and note drearily, and without its striking him he might attend to them, that the ferns in the dusty majolica pots were dying for want of water, or go to his desk, and compose, by a dogged effort, at the rate of a word a minute, asking himself more anxiously than he had done hitherto what sum he might safely expect from Messrs. Cousins. His banking account was diminishing rapidly under the demands made upon it at this period, and he found it almost as hard to write a chapter of a novel now as a man who had never attempted such a thing before. He returned thanks to Heaven that he was not a journalist, to whom the necessity for covering a certain number of pages by a stated hour daily was unavoidable, and wished himself a mechanic or a petty tradesman, whose avocations, he presumed, could be fulfilled independently of their moods.

It was not until the crisis was past, and Cynthia was downstairs again in a wrapper on the sofa, that he began to feel he was within measurable distance of the conclusion. The nine months in which he had anticipated completing the task had long gone by, but that it would have taken him a year did not trouble him, for he knew the work to be good. He told her so on an afternoon when they were alone together again, she with her couch drawn to the fire, and he sitting at the edge, holding her hand.

'I'm satisfied,' he declared. 'When I say "satisfied," you know what I mean, of course; it's as well done as I expected to do it. Another week, darling, will see it finished.'

She patted his arm.

'Poor old boy! it hasn't been a happy time for him either, has it?'

'I've known jollier. But you're all right again now, thank God! and I'm going to pack you off to Bournemouth or somewhere soon, to bring your color back. I was speaking to Dr. Roberts about it this morning. He said it was just what you needed.'

'I've been very expensive, Humphrey,' she said wistfully. 'How much? We didn't think it would cost so much as it has, did we? You should have married a big, strong woman, Humphrey, or—'

'Or what?'

'Or nobody,' she murmured.

The eyes she fixed upon the fire glittered. He squeezed her hand, and laughed constrainedly.

'I'm quite contented, thank you,' he said, in as light a tone as he could manage. 'What are you crying for? Your nurse will look daggers at me, and think I've been bullying you. Tell me—was she kind to you? I've been haunted by the idea she was treating you badly, and you were too frightened of her to let anyone know. You're such a kid, little woman, in some things—such an awful kid.'

'Not such a kid as you imagine,' she said. 'I've been thinking; I've thought of many things since baby was born. Often when they believed I was asleep, I used to lie and think and think, till I was wretched.'

'What did you think of?' asked Kent indulgently.

'You mustn't be vexed with me if I tell you. I've thought that, perhaps, although you don't feel it yet—though you don't suppose you ever *will* feel it—that it might have been best for you, seriously and really, if you had married nobody, Humphrey; if you had had nothing to interfere with your work, and had lived on with Mr. Turquand just as you were. There, now you *are* vexed. Bend down, and let me smooth that frown away.'

'Whatever put such a stupid idea into your head?' said Kent, wishing pityingly that he had not felt it quite so often. 'Don't be a goose, sweetheart! What nonsense! I should be perfectly lost without you.'

'I think I suit you better than any other woman would,' she said, with pathetic confidence; 'but if you had kept single—that's what I've doubted: if you wouldn't be better off without a wife at all. Oh, you should hear some of the stories nurse has told me of places she has been in! I didn't think there could be such awfulness in the world. And in the first confinement, too! It makes one fear that no woman can ever expect to understand any man.'

'Hang your nurse!' responded Humphrey. 'Cackling old fool! I suppose in every situation she is in she talks scandal about the last, and where there wasn't any, she makes it up. When does she go?'

'She can't leave baby until we get another, you know. At least, I hope she won't have to.'

'Another?' said Kent.

'Another nurse. Mamma is going to advertise in the **Morning Post** for us at once. We want a thoroughly experienced woman, don't we, dear? We don't know anything about babies ourselves, and—'

Oh, an experienced one by all means,' he answered. 'Poor little soul! we owe him as much as that. Life is the cost of the parents' pleasure defrayed by the child. We'll make the world as desirable to him as we can.'

He paused for her to comment on his impromptu definition of life, by which he was agreeably conscious he had said something brilliant; but it passed by her unheeded. He reflected that Turquand would either have accorded it approval, or picked it to pieces, and that for it to go unnoticed altogether was hard.

She looked at him tenderly.

'I knew you would say so.' she replied. 'It doesn't really make much difference to our expenses whether we pay twenty pounds a year or twenty-five, and to the kind of nurse we shall get it makes all the difference on earth. What shall we call him?'

'Him! You're not going to get a man?'

'Baby, you silly! Have you thought of a name? *I* have.'

He was still wishing she had a sense of humor, and occasionally made a witty remark.

'What?' he inquired.

'Yours. I want to call him Humphrey. What do you say to it?'

'What for? It's ugly. You said so the first time you jerked it out. I think we might choose something better than that.'

'But it's yours,' she persisted. 'I want him called by your name—I do, I do!' She held his hand tightly, and her lips trembled. 'If . . . if I were ever to lose you, Humphrey, I should like our child to be called by your name. Don't laugh at me; I can't help feeling that. That night when he was born—oh, that night! shall I ever forget it?—and Dr. Roberts looked across me and said, "Well, you have a little son come to see you, Mrs. Kent," the first thing I thought was, "We can call him Humphrey." I wanted to say it to you when they let you in, but I couldn't, I was so tired; I thought it instead. When nurse brought him over to me, or he cried, or I could see him moving under the blanket in the bassinet, I thought, "There's my other Humphrey." '

He kissed her, and sat staring at the fire, his conscience clamorous. He had not realized that he had grown so dear to her, and the discovery made his own dissatisfaction crueller. He felt a thankless brute, a beast. It seemed to him momentarily that the situation would be much less painful if the disappointment were mutual— if she, too, were discontented with the bargain she had made. To listen to her speaking in such a fashion, and accept her devotion, knowing how little devotion she inspired in return, stabbed him. He asked himself what he had done that she should love him so fondly. He had not openly neglected her, but secretly he had done it often, and with relief. Had she missed him when he had shut himself in his room, not to write, but to wish he had never met her? His mind smote him.

The question obtruded itself into his reveries during the following days, but now at least his plea of being busy was always genuine enough, and he was writing fiercely. The pile of manuscript to which he added sheet after sheet was heavy and thick, and then there came a morning when he went to bed at three, and rose again at eight, to begin his final chapter, having told the servant he should not go down for luncheon, but that she was to bring a sandwich and a glass of claret into the room. When one o'clock struck, and she entered, tobacco had left him with no appetite and a furred tongue. He threw a 'thank you' at her, and remained in the same bent attitude, his pen traversing the paper steadily. He was working with an exaltation which rarely seized him, and with which the novelist of fiction is depicted as working all the time. In his aspect he was untidy enough to have served as an admirable model for that personage. He had not shaved for three days, and a growth of stubbly beard intensified his look of weariness, due to the want of sufficient sleep.

The wind was causing the fire to be more a nuisance than a comfort, and every now and again a gust of smoke shot out of the narrow stove, obscuring the page before him, and making him cough and swear. The atmosphere was villainous, but, saving in these moments, he was unconscious of it. He was near the closing lines. His empty pipe was gripped between his teeth, and he wanted to refill it, but was averse to take his eyes from the paper while he stretched for his pouch and the matches. He was instinctively aware that he should refill it the instant he had written the last words, but now an access of uncertainty assailed him, and he could not decide upon them. He stared at the paper without daring to set a sentence down, and drew at the empty bowl mechanically, his palate craving for the taste of tobacco, while bis sight was magnetized by the pen's point hovering under his hand. He sat so for a quarter of an hour. Then he wrote with supreme satisfaction what he had thought of first, and rejected as impossible. His pen was dropped. He drew a breath of thanksgiving and relief, and lit his pipe. His novel was done.

Unlike the novelist of fiction whom he resembled exteriorly, he did not weep that the characters who had peopled his solitude for the past twelvemonths, and whom he loved, were about to leave him for the harsher criticism of the world. He was profoundly glad. He felt exhilaration leap in his jaded veins as he picked up his pen again and added 'The End.' He felt that he was free of an enormous load, a tremendous responsibility, of which he had acquitted himself well. Every morning, with rare exceptions, for a year he had, so to speak, awakened with this unfinished novel staring him in the face; every night during a year he had gone up the stairs to the bedroom remembering what a lump of writing remained to be added to it still. And now it was finished; nor could he do it better. Blessed thought! If he recast it chapter by chapter and phrase by phrase, he could not handle the idea more carefully or strongly than he had handled it in the bulky package that lay in front of him—the story told!

He was anxious to forward it to the publishers without delay, but Turquand had so recently referred to his expectation of reading in the manuscript, that he despatched it to Soho first. 'Send it back quickly,' he begged, and the journalist's answer in returning the parcel reached him on the next evening but one. He showed it to Cynthia delightedly. Turquand wrote very warmly. The manuscript was sent to Messrs. Cousins with a note, requesting them to give it their early consideration; and now Kent was asked constantly by the Walfords if they had written yet, and what terms he had obtained. Cynthia had not regained enough strength to care to travel at present, and her parents and brother generally spent the evening at No. 64, where, truth to tell, Kent found the interest his wife's parents manifested in the matter rather a nuisance. His father-in-law evidently held that it was derogatory for him to be kept waiting a fortnight for his publishers' offer, and Mrs. Walford made so many foolish inquiries and ridiculous suggestions that he was sometimes in danger of being rude. Cæsar alone displayed no curiosity in a matter so frivolous, but listened with his superior air, which tried Kent's patience even more. The fat young man's début had been postponed again. Now he was to appear for certain in the spring, and he explained, in a tone implying that he could, if he might, impart esoteric and extraordinary facts, that the delay had been politic.

'No outsider can have any idea,' he said languidly, 'what wheels within wheels there are in our world.' (He meant the operatic world, into which he was ambitious to squeeze a foot.) 'This last season it would have been madness for a new bass to sing in London; he was doomed before he opened his mouth—doomed!' He looked at the ceiling with a meditative smile, as if dwelling upon curiously amusing circumstances. '*Very* funny!' he added.

Excepting his master, he did not know a professional singer in England, and, whenever a benefit concert was to be given, would chase the organizer all over the town in hansoms, and telegraph him for an appointment 'on urgent business,' in the hope of prevailing upon him to let him appear at it; but his assurance was so consummate that—albeit one was aware he had not yet done anything at all—he almost persuaded one while he talked that he was the pivot round which the musical world revolved. Cæsar excepted, Kent had really no grounds for complaint against the Walfords. The others' queries might worry him, but their cordiality was extreme; and they made Cynthia relate Turquand's opinion of the book—for which no title had been found—again and again. Even the stock-jobber's view that a fortnight's silence was surprising was due to an exaggerated estimate of the author's importance, and Mrs. Walford, when she refrained from giving him advice, appeared to think him a good deal cleverer now that the manuscript was in Messrs. Cousins' hands than she had done while it was lying on his desk. Indeed, there were moments at this stage when his mother-in-law gushed at him with an ardor that reminded him of the early days of his acquaintance with her in Dieppe

CHAPTER XI.

'Well, have those publishers of yours made you an offer yet?"

' No, sir; I haven't heard from them.'

'You should drop them a line,' said Walford irritably. 'Dam nonsense! How long have they had the thing now?'

'About three weeks.'

'Drop 'em a line! They may keep you waiting a month if you don't wake them up. Don't you think so, Cynthia? He ought to write.'

'I dare say we shall have a letter in a day or two, papa. We were afraid you weren't coming round this evening; you're late. How d'ye do, mamma? How d'ye do, Aunt Emily?'

'And how are you?' asked Mrs. Walford. 'Have you made up your mind about Bournemouth yet? She is quite fit to go now, Humphrey. You ought to pack her off at once; there's nothing to wait for now you've got your nurse. How does she suit you?'

'She seems all right,' said Cynthia, rather doubtfully. 'A little consequential, perhaps—that is all.'

'Oh, you mustn't stand any airs and graces; put her in her place at the start. What has she done?'

'She hasn't done anything, only—'

'She's our first,' explained Kent, 'and we're somewhat in awe of her. She was surprised to find that there weren't two nurseries—she is frequently "surprised," and then we apologize to her.'

'Don't be so absurd!' murmured his wife; 'he does exaggerate so, mamma! No; but, of course, she has always been in better situations, with people richer than us. . . . "Us?"' she repeated questioningly, looking at Kent with a smile.

He laughed a negative.

'Than *we,* then! And she is the least bit in the world too self-important.'

'Than "we"?' echoed Mrs. Walford. 'Than "we"? Nonsense! "Than *us*"!'

Kent pulled his moustache silently, and there was a moment's pause.

'Than *us!*' said the lady again defiantly. 'Unquestionably it is "than *us*"!'

'Very well,' he replied; 'I'm not arguing about it, mater.'

'*I* always say "than us,"' said Sam Walford good-humoredly. 'Ain't it right?'

'No,' said Miss Wix; 'of course it isn't, Sam.'

'Ridiculous!' declared Mrs. Walford, with asperity. ' "Than we" is quite wrong—quite ungrammatical. I don't care who says it isn't—I say it *is.*'

'A literary man might have been supposed to know,' said Miss Wix ironically. 'But Humphrey is mistaken too, then?'

'What is the difference—what does it matter?' put in Cynthia. 'There is nothing to get excited about, mamma.'

'I'm not in the least excited,' said her mother, with a white face; 'but I don't accept anybody's contradiction on such a point. I'm not to be convinced to the contrary when I'm sure I'm correct.'

'Well, let's return to our muttons,' said Kent. 'Once upon a time there was a nurse, and—'

'Oh, you are very funny!' she exclaimed. 'Let me tell you, you don't know anything about it. And as to Emily, I don't take any notice of her at all. She may say what she likes.'

'What I like is the Queen's English,' said Miss Wix, 'since you don't mind. This lively conversation must be very good for Cynthia. Humphrey, you're quite a member of the family, you see. We are rude to one another in front of you. Isn't it nice?'

'I shouldn't come to you to learn politeness, either,' retorted Mrs. Walford hotly. 'I shouldn't come to you to learn politeness or grammar, either. You are most rude yourself—most ill-bred!'

'That'll do—that'll do,' said the stock-jobber; 'we don't want a row. Damn it! let everybody say what they choose; it ain't a hanging matter, I suppose, if they're wrong.'

'I'm *not* wrong, Sam. Humphrey, just tell me this: Do you say "than whom" or "than who"? Now, then!'

'You say "than whom," but it's the one instance where the comparative does govern the objective in English. And Angus, or Morell, or somebody august, even denies that it ought to govern it there.'

She looked momentarily disconcerted. Then she said:

'All I maintain is that "than we" is very pedantic in ordinary conversation—very pedantic indeed; and I shall stick to my opinion if you argue for ever. "Than us" is much more usual, and much more euphonious. I consider it's much more *euphonious* than the other. I prefer it altogether.'

Miss Wix emitted a little tart laugh.

'You may consider it more euphonious to say "heggs" and "happles,"' she observed; 'but I suppose you don't do it.'

Her sister turned to her wrathfully, and the ensuing passage at arms was terminated by the spinster putting her handkerchief to her eyes and beginning to cry.

'I am not to be spoken to so,' she faltered—'I am not! Oh, I quite understand—I know what it means; but this is the last time I will be trampled on and insulted—the last time, Sam'.

'Don't be a fool, Emily; nobody wants to "trample" on you. You can give as good as you get, too. What an infernal rumpus about nothing, anyhow! 'Pon my soul! I think you have both gone crazy.'

'I am in the way—yes; and I am shown every hour that I'm in the way!' she sobbed, in crescendo. 'Humphrey is a witness how I am treated. I will not stop where I'm not wanted. This is the end of it, I will go—I will take a situation!'

Everybody excepting the offender endeavored to pacify her. Cynthia put an arm about her waist, and spoke consolingly, while Walford patted her on the back. Humphrey brought her whisky-and-water, but she waved it aside violently, reiterating her resolve.

'I will take a situation; I have made up my mind. Thank Heaven! I'm not quite dependent on a sister and a brother-in-law yet. Thank Heaven! I have the health to work for my living. I would rather live in one room on a pound a week than remain with you. I shall leave your house the moment I can get something to do. I will be a paid "companion"—I will go into a shop!' And she went into hysterics.

When she recovered from the attack, she drank the whisky-and-water tearfully, and begged Kent to escort her back to The Hawthorns at once. He complied amiably, and attempted on the way to dissuade her from the determination she had expressed. It was his first experience of this phase of Miss Wix, and he was a good deal surprised by the valor she displayed. Her weakness had passed, and the light of resolution shone in the little woman's eye. Her nostrils were expanded; her carriage was firm and erect. He felt it was no empty boast when she asserted stoutly that she should go to a registry-office on the morrow—nor was it; she probably would do as much as that. She was quite sincere. But the prospect of employment was as the martyr's stake or an arena full of lions, to her mind; and, after the office had been visited, the decision of her manner would perceptibly decrease, and the heroism in her eye subside, until at last she trembled in a cold perspiration lest her relatives meant to take her at her word.

'It will be a small household if you go,' he said; 'I suppose Cæsar won't live at home after he "comes out," and your sister and brother-in-law will be left by themselves.'

Miss Wix sniffed.

'**When** he "comes out."'

'Yes; he seems to have been rather a long while doing it,' answered Kent. 'But there can't be any doubt about it this time; the agreement for the spring is drawn up, and signed, I hear.'

They were passing a lamp-post. Miss Wix's mouth was the size of a sixpence, and her eyebrows had entirely disappeared under her bonnet.

'It always is,' she said. 'The agreements are always drawn up, and signed, and written in invisible ink. I don't seem to remember the time when that young man **wasn't** coming out "next spring," and I knew him in his cradle. He was an affected horror then.'

Kent laughed to himself in walking home; he had suspected the accuracy of the proud parents' statements before, just as he suspected when he had been invited to meet an operatic celebrity at dinner at The Hawthorns, who sent the telegram of excuse which was shown him to explain the non-arrival of the star. He wondered how much the Walfords' foolishness and his pupil's vanity had been worth to the Italian singing-master, who gesticulated about the drawing and foretold such triumphs.

When he reentered No. 64, he was relieved to find the company quite cheerful again; they even seemed to be in high spirits, and the cause was promptly ascertained. Cynthia pointed radiantly to a letter that was lying on the table.

'For you,' she cried, 'from "Cousins." Read it quickly; we're all dying of impatience, but I wouldn't open it. How did you leave Aunt Emily?'

'She is going to bed,' he said, tearing the envelope apart.

His heart had leapt, and he only trusted he was not destined to be damped by the suggested price. The others sat eagerly regarding him, waiting for him to speak. Cynthia tried to guess the amount by his expression.

'Well,' said Mrs. Walford at last—'well? What do they say?'

Kent put the note down slowly with a face from which all the color had gone. His lips shook, and his voice was not under control as he answered.

'They haven't accepted it,' he said huskily; 'they are returning it to me. They don't think it's good.'

'What?' she ejaculated.

'Oh, Humphrey!' she heard Cynthia gasp; and then there was some seconds in which he was conscious that everyone was staring at him, and would have given a five-pound note to be in the room alone, That Messrs. Cousins might refuse the book after such reviews as had been written upon his last was a calamity that he had never contemplated, and he felt absolutely paralyzed and speechless. When he had been despondent he had imagined the publishers proposing to pay a couple of hundred pounds for it; when he had been gloomier still, he had fancied the sum would be a hundred and fifty; in moments of profound depression he had even groaned, 'I shan't obtain a shilling more for it than I did for the other one.' But to be rejected, 'declined with thanks,' was a shock for which he was totally unprepared. It almost dazed him.

'What do you mean?' demanded Sam Walford, breaking the silence angrily. 'Not accepting it? But—but—this is a fine sort of thing! It takes you a year to write, and then they don't accept it. A dam good business you're in, upon my word!'

'Hush, Sam!' said Mrs. Walford. 'What do they say? what reason do they give? Let me look.'

Kent handed her the letter mutely, his wife watching him with startled, compassionate eyes, and she read it aloud:

' "Dear Sir,

' "We are obliged for the kind offer of your MS., to which our most careful consideration has been given." '

('Been better if they'd considered it a little less,' remarked Walford.)

' "We regret to say, however, that, in view of our reader's report, we are reluctantly forced to decide that the construction of the story precludes any hope of its succeeding. The faults seem inherent to the story, and irremediable, and we are therefore returning the MS. to you to-day, with our compliments and thanks." '

'Ha, ha!' said Kent wildly; 'they return it with their compliments!'

'I don't see anything to laugh at,' said his mother-in-law with temper; 'I call it dreadful! Anything but funny, I'm sure.'

'Do you think so?' he said. '*I* call it very funny. There's a touch of humor about their "compliments" that would be hard to beat.'

'Ah,' said Walford disagreeably, 'your mother-in-law's sense of humor isn't so keen and "literary" as yours. She only sees that your year's work isn't worth a tinker's curse!'

'Papa!' murmured Cynthia, wincing.

Kent's mouth closed viciously.

'Against your judgment on such a matter, sir,' he said, 'of course there can be no appeal.'

'It ain't my judgment,' answered Walford; 'it's your own publishers'. It's no good putting on the sarcastic, my boy. Here'—he caught up the letter as he spoke, and slapped it—' here you've got the opinion of a practical man, and he tells you the thing's valueless. There's no getting away from facts.'

'And I say the thing's strong, sound work,' exclaimed Kent, 'and the reader's an ass! Oh, what's the use of arguing with you! You see it rejected, and so to you it's rubbish; and when you see it paid for, to you it will be very good. I want some whisky—has "Aunt Emily" drunk it all?' He helped himself liberally, and invited his father-in-law to follow his example. Walford shook his head with a grunt. 'You won't have a drink? *I will;* I want to return thanks for Messrs. Cousins' compliments. It's very flattering to receive compliments from one's publishers. I'm afraid you none of you appreciate it as much as you ought. We are having a very jolly evening, aren't we, with hysterics and rejections? And whisky's good for both. Well, sir, what have you got to say next?'

'I think we'll say "good-night,"' said Mrs. Walford coldly; 'I will be round in the morning, Cynthia. Come, Sam, it's past ten.'

She rose, and put on her cape, Kent assisting her. The stock-jobber took leave of him with a scowl; and when the last adieu had been exchanged, Cynthia and the unfortunate author stood on the hearth vis-à-vis. The girl was relieved that her parents were gone. The atmosphere had been electric, and made her nervous of what might happen next. She had been looking forward, besides, to consoling him when the door closed—to his lying in her arms under her kisses, while she smoothed away his mortification. She could enter into his mood to-night better than she had entered into any of them yet, and she ached with pity fox him. To turn to his wife on any matters connected with his work, however, never entered his head any more, so that when she murmured deprecatingly, 'Papa didn't mean anything by what he said, darling, I know; you mustn't be vexed with him,' all he did was to reply, 'Oh, he hasn't made an enemy for life, my dear! If you are going up to your room now, I think I'll take a stroll.'

She said, 'Do, and—and cheer up;' but her heart sank miserably. He dropped a kiss on her cheek with a response as feeble as her own, and went out. A woman may have little comprehension of her husband's work, and yet feel the tenderest sympathies for disappointments that it brings him, but of this platitude the novelist had shown himself ignorant.

Cynthia did not go up to her room at once. She sat down beside the dying fire and ruminated. She asked herself—in the hour in which she had come mentally nearest to him—if, after all, Humphrey and she were united so closely as she had supposed.

CHAPTER XII.

She loved him. When they married, perhaps neither had literally loved the other, but the girl had aroused much stronger feelings in the man than the man had wakened in the girl; to-day the position was reversed, and it was the inception of a struggle to render herself a companion to him, this perception that he did not find her so companionable as she had dreamed.

If she had been a woman of keener intuitions, she must have perceived it long ago, but her intuitions were not keen. She was not so dull as he thought her, nor was she so dull as when she became his wife, but a woman of the most rapid intelligence she would never be. Her heart was greater than her mind—much greater; her heart entitled her to a devotion she was far from receiving. To her mind marriage had made a trifling difference; her sensibilities it had developed enormously. Her husband overlooked the latter, and chafed at the former. Fortunately for her peace, her tardy perception of their relations did not embrace quite so much as that.

She stayed in Bournemouth a fortnight, and when she came home her efforts to acquire the quickness that she lacked, to talk in the same strain as Kent, to utter the kind of extravagance which seemed to be his idea of wit, were labored and pathetic. Especially as he did not notice them. She read the books he admired, and was bored by them more frequently than she was moved. She attempted, in fact, to mould herself upon him, and she attempted it with such scanty encouragement, and with so little apparent result, that, if her imitation had not become instinctive by degrees, she would have been destined to formally renounce it in despair.

He was not at this time the most agreeable of models; he was too humiliated and anxious. Though Mr. and Mrs. Walford were superficially affable again, he felt a difference that he could not define in their manner, and was always uncomfortable in their presence. He had called the book 'The Eye of the Beholder,' and submitted it to Messrs. Percival and King, but February waned without any communication arriving from the firm, and once more his wife's parents asked him almost every day if he had 'any news.' His only prop was Turquand, whom he often went to town to see now. Turquand had been genuinely dismayed by Messrs. Cousins' refusal, and it was by his advice that the author had selected Percival and King to try next. Kent awaited their verdict feverishly. Not only was his humiliation bad to bear, but his pecuniary position was beginning to be serious, and the Walfords' knowledge of the fact aggravated the unpleasantness of it.

Messrs. Percival sent the manuscript back at the end of April. They did not offer any criticism upon the work, as the others had done; they regretted merely that in the present state of the book market they could not undertake the publication of 'The Eye of the Beholder.'

Then the novelist packed it up again, and despatched it to Fendall and Green. Messrs. Fendall and Green were longer in replying, and the fact of the second rejection could not be withheld from the Walfords. After they had heard of it, the change in their manner toward him was more marked. They obviously regarded him as a poor pretender in literature, and her mother admitted as much to Cynthia once.

'Well, mamma,' said Cynthia valiantly, 'I don't see how you can speak like that. It is terribly unfortunate, and he is very worried, but you know what Humphrey's reviews have been—nothing can take away the success he has *had*.'

'Oh, "reviews"!' said Mrs. Walford, with impatience. 'He musn't talk to us about "reviews"! Of course all those were "worked" for him by Cousins. We are behind the scenes, you know; we are aware what such things are worth.'

This conviction of hers, that his publishers had paid a few pounds for various columns in praise of him in the leading London papers, was not to be shaken. Cynthia did not repeat it to him, and Kent did not divine it, but Miss Wix—who had consented to remain at The Hawthorns—appeared quite a lovable person to him now in comparison with his wife's mother. Of intention Louisa did not snub him, the stock-jobber was not rude to him deliberately, but both felt that their girl had done badly indeed for herself, and their very tones in addressing him were new and resentful.

In secret they were passionately mortified on another score. Their prodigy, the coming bass, had once more failed to secure a debut, and at last there was no help for it but to admit that the thought of a musical career for him must be abandoned. The circumstances surrounding this final failure were veiled in mystery, even from Cynthia, but the fact was sufficiently damning in itself. The wily Pincocca was paid fees no longer, and Caesar took a trip to Berlin with a company-promoter his father knew, and who did not speak German, while his mother invented an explanation.

Yes, it was a trying time for the Walfords, their swans turning out to be ganders both together, and that one of them had been acquired, not hatched, was more than they could forgive themselves or him. There were occasions, too, when Kent was more than slighted now, when there was no disguise made at all. One day in July Walford said to him:

'I tell you what it is, Humphrey: this can't go on. You'll have to give your profession up and look for a berth, my boy. How's your account now?'

'Pretty low,' confessed his son-in-law, feeling like a lad being rebuked for a misdemeanor.

Walford looked at him indignantly.

'Ha!' he said. 'It's a nice position, 'pon my word! And no news, I suppose—nothing fresh?'

'Nothing, sir.'

'You'll have to chuck it all. You'll have to chuck this folly of yours, and put your shoulder to the wheel, and work.'

'I thought I did work,' said Kent doggedly. 'Do you think literature is a game?'

'I think it is an infernal rotten game—yes!'

'Ah, well, there,' said Kent, 'many literary men have agreed with you.'

'You'll have to put your mind to something serious. If you only earn thirty bob a week, it's more than your novels bring you in. What your wife and child will do, God knows—have to come to us, I suppose. A fine thing for a girl married eighteen months!'

'She hasn't arrived at it yet,' answered Kent, very white, 'and I don't fancy she will. Many thanks for the invitation.'

Walford stopped short—they had met in the highroad—and cocked his head at him, his legs apart.

'Will you take a berth in the City for a couple of quid, if I can get you one?' he demanded sharply.

'No,' said Kent, 'I'll be damned if I will! I'll stick to my pen, whatever happens, and I'll stick to my wife and kid, too!'

The other did not pursue the conversation, but on the next occasion that Humphrey saw Louisa she told him that his father-in-law was very incensed against him for his ingratitude.

'It is sometimes advisable for a man to change his business,' she said. 'A man goes into one business, and if it doesn't pay he tries another. Your father-in-law is much older than you, and—er—naturally more experienced. I think you ought to listen to his opinion with more respect. Especially under the circumstances.'

'Oh!' he remarked. 'Have you said that to Cynthia?'

'No; it is not necessary to say it to anybody but you. And it might make her unhappy. She is troubled enough without.'

She had, as a matter of fact, said it to her with much eloquence the afternoon before.

'And another thing,' she continued, 'I am bound to say: I don't see any grounds for your believing—er—er—that your profession has any prizes in store for you, even if you could afford to remain in it. You mustn't mind my speaking plainly, Humphrey. You are a young man, and—er—you have no one to advise you, and you may thank me for it one day.'

'Let me thank you now,' he murmured, fighting to conceal his rage.

'If you can,' she said, 'if you feel it, I am very glad. You see what you have done. You wrote a book, which you got very little for—some nice reviews'—she smiled meaningly—'which we needn't talk about. And then you spend a year on another, which nobody wants. To succeed as a novelist, one must have a very strong gift;

there is no doubt about it. A novelist must be very brilliant to do any good to-day—very brilliant! He wants—er—to know the world—to know the world, and—er—oh, he must be very polished—very smart!'

'I see,' he said shakily, as she paused. 'You don't think I've the necessary qualifications?'

'You have aptitude,' she said; 'you have a certain aptitude, of course, but to make it your profession—So many young men, who have been educated, could write a novel. *You* happen to have done it; others haven't the time. They go into an office, or on the Stock Exchange, or perhaps they haven't the patience. I'm afraid your publishers did you a mistaken kindness by those unfortunate reviews.'

'How do you mean?' he asked. 'Yes, the reviewers didn't agree with you, did they?'

She smiled again, and spread her hands abroad expressively.

'Oh, they were very pretty, very nice to have; but—er—newspaper notices do not take *us* in. Naturally, those were paid for. Cousins and Co. arranged with the papers for all that.'

'With—'

He looked at her opened-mouthed, as the names of some of the journals in which he had been eulogized recurred to him.

'With them all,' she said. 'Oh yes! You must remember, we are quite behind the scenes.'

'Pincocca,' he said musingly. 'Yes, you knew Pincocca! But he was a singing-master, and he doesn't come here now.'

'Oh, Pincocca was one of many—one of very many.' She giggled nervously, 'How very laughable that you should suppose I meant Pinoocca! You mustn't forget that Cæsar knows everybody. I'm almost glad he isn't going in for the stage on that account. He brought such crowds to the house at one time that really we lived in a whirl. I believe—between ourselves—that this man he has gone to Berlin with is at the bottom of his throwing up his career. A financier. A Mr. McCullough. One of the greatest powers in the City. And—er—Cæsar was always wonderfully shrewd in these things. Don't say anything, but I believe McCullough wants to keep him.'

'1 won't say a word,' he said.

'McCullough controls millions,' she gasped; 'and your father-in-law thinks, from certain rumors he has heard, that he's persuaded Cæsar to join him in some negotiations he has with the German Government. Of course, we mustn't breathe a whisper—hush! What were we saying? Oh yes, I'm afraid those unfortunate reviews have done you more harm than good. Nothing great in the City can be got for you, because you haven't the commercial experience, but a clerkship would be better than doing nothing. You must really think about it, Humphrey, if you can't do anything for yourself. As your father-in-law says, you are sitting down with your hands in your pockets, eating up your last few pounds.' It occurred to her that a clerkship and the ease with which her son was obtaining a partnership in millions formed a contrast. 'Of course,' she added, 'Cæsar always did have a head for finance. And—er—he's a way with him. He has aplomb and address, that make him immensely valuable for negotiations with a government. It's different in his case.'

Kent left her, and cursed aloud. He went the same evening to Turquand's, partly as a relief to his feelings, and partly to ask his friend's opinion of the feasibility of his procuring any journalistic work.

'For Heaven's sake, talk!' he exclaimed, as he went in and flung himself down in the rickety chair that used to be his own. 'Say anything you like, but talk. I've just had an hour and a half of my mother-in-law neat! Take the taste out of my mouth. Turk, I wish I were dead! What the devil is to be the end of it? The Walfords say "a clerkship"! Oh, my God, you should hear the Walfords! I've "a little aptitude," but I mustn't be conceited. I mustn't seriously call myself a novelist. I've frivolled away a year on "The Eye of the Beholder," and Cousins' squared the reviewers for me on the *Spectator* and the *Saturday*! Look here, I must get something to do. Don't you know of any thing? can't you introduce me to an editor who wants a genius? isn't there anything stirring at all? I'm buried; I live in a red-brick tomb in Streatham; I hear nothing, and see nobody, except my blasted parents-in-law. But you're in the thick of it; you sniff the mud of Fleet Street every day; you're the salaried sub of a paper that's going to put a cover on itself, and "throw it in" at the penny; you—'

' " 'Ave flung ray tharsands gily ter the benefit of tride And gin'rally (they tells me) done the grand," '

said Turquand.

'Yes; I know all about that; but surely you can advise me of a chance? I don't say an opening, but a chance of an opening. Man alive, the outlook's as dark as the devil! I shall be stony directly. You must!'

'Fendall's have still not written, eh?'

'No; Fendall's regrets haven't come yet. How about short stories?'

'You didn't find 'em particularly lucrative, did you?'

'A guinea each; one in six months. No; but I want to be invited to contribute: "Can you let us have anything this month, Mr. Kent?"'

'My dear chap! should I have stuck to *The Outpost* all these years if I had such advice to give away? I did'—he coughed, and spat out an invisible shred of tobacco—'I did stick to it.'

'You weren't going to say that. You were going to say, "I did advise you once, but you would marry." Well, I don't complain that I married. The only fault I have to find with my wife is that she's the Walfords' daughter. She's not literary, but she's a very good girl. Don't blind facts, Turk; my money would have lasted longer if I hadn't married, but I shouldn't have got my novel taken because I was single. The point of this situation is that, after being lauded to the skies by every paper of importance in England, I can't place the book I write next at any price at all, nor find a way to earn bread and cheese by my pen! If a musician had got such criticisms on a composition, he would be a made man. If an artist had had them on a picture, the ball would be at his feet. If an actor had got them on a performance, he would be offered engagements at a hundred a week. In literature alone such an anomalous and damnable condition of affairs as mine is possible. You can't deny it.'

'I don't,' said Turquand.

CHAPTER XIII.

NOR did the conference, which was protracted until a late hour, provide an outlet to the dilemma; it I was agreeable, but it did not lead anywhere. If he should hear of anything, he would certainly let the other know; that was the most the subeditor could say. Authors are not offered salaries to write their novels, and Kent was not a journalist by temperament, nor possessed of any journalistic experience. As to tales or articles for *The Outpost,* that periodical did not publish feuilletons, and their rate for other matter was seven and sixpence a column. However, some attempt had to be made, and Kent went to town every day, and Cynthia saw less of him than when he had been writing 'The Eye of the Beholder.' He hunted up his few acquaintances, and haunted the literary club that he had joined in the flush of his success. He applied for various posts that he saw were vacant by the ***Daily News,*** and inserted a skilfully-framed advertisement in the Athenœum. No answer ever arrived, and the tradesmen's bills, and the poor rates, and the gas notices, and the very competent nurse's wages, continued to fall due in the meanwhile. When the competent nurse's were not due, the incipient lunatic's were. Dr. Roberts' account came in, and the sight of his pass book now literally terrified the young man.

They had not been married quite two years yet, and he asked himself if they had been extravagant, in view of this evidence of the rapidity with which money had melted; but, excepting the style in which they had furnished, he could not perceive any cause for such self-reproach. They had lived comfortably, of course, but if the novel had been placed when it was finished, they could have continued to live just as comfortably while he wrote the next. He feared they would have to take a bill of sale on the too expensive furniture, and that way lay destitution. Cynthia's composure under the circumstances surprised him. He told her so.

'It will all come right,' she said. 'You are sure to get something soon, and perhaps Fendall and Green will accept "The Eye of the Beholder" fulsomely.'

This was an improvement, for a few months since she would have been unable to recollect the firm's name, and referred to them vaguely as the publishers. He felt the sense of intimacy deepen as Fendall and Green dropped glibly from her lips, and the 'fulsomely' made him feel quite warm toward her.

'Have you told your people how low we are?' he asked.

She shook her head.

'Why should I? That is our affair.'

'So it is,' he assented. 'Poor little girl! it's awful rough on you, though. I wonder you aren't playing with straws. You didn't know what economy meant when we married'

Praise from him was nectar and ambrosia to her. She wanted to embrace him, but felt that if she embraced the opportunity to give a happy definition of economy it would be appreciated better. She perched herself on the arm of his chair, and struggled to evolve an epigram. As she could not think of one, she said:

'What nonsense!'

'I wish you had read the book, and liked it,' said Kent, speaking spontaneously.

'Say you wish I'd read it?' replied his wife.

'Oh, you'd like it, because it was mine. But I mean I wish—'

'What?'

'1 don't know.'

She twisted a piece of his hair round her finger.

'My taste is much maturer than it was,' she averred, with satisfaction. 'Somehow, I can't stand the sort of things that used to please me; I don't know how I was able to read them. They bore me now.'

He smiled. As she had often done to him before, she seemed a child masquerading in a woman's robes.

'You're getting quite a critic!'

'Well,' she said happily, 'you'll laugh, but I got "A Peacock's Tail" from the library, and when the review in the ***Chronicle*** came out, the reviewer said just what I'd felt about it. He did. I'm not such a silly as you think, you see.'

'My dear!' he cried, 'I never thought you were a "silly." '

'Not very wise, though. Oh, I know what I lack, Humphrey; but I ***am*** better than I was—I am really! Remember, I never heard Literature talked about until I met you; it was all new to me when we married, and—if you've noticed it— you aren't very, ***very*** interested in anything else. The longer we live together, the more—the nicer I shall be.'

He answered lightly:

'You are nice enough now.'

But he was touched.

After a long pause, and as if uttering the conclusion of a train of thought aloud, she murmured:

'Baby's got ***your*** shaped head.'

'1 hope to God it'll be worth more to him than mine to me!' he exclaimed.

She was silent again.

'What are you so serious for, all of a sudden?' he said, looking round.

Cynthia bent over him quickly with a caress, and sprang up.

'It was you who wanted the *t's* crossed for once,' she said tremulously. 'There, now I must go and knock at the nursery door, and ask if I'm allowed to go in.'

The man of acute perceptions wondered what she meant, and in what way he had shown himself dull at comprehending so transparent a girl.

It was in October, when less than twenty pounds remained to them, that something at last turned up. Turquand had learnt that a subeditor was required on *The World and his Wife,* a weekly journal recently started for the benefit of the English and Americans in Paris. The editor was familiarly known as 'Billy' Beaufort, and the backer was a sporting Baronet who had reduced his income from fourteen thousand per annum to eight by financing, and providing with the diamonds, which were the brightest feature of her performances, a lady who fancied she was an actress. Beaufort had been the one dramatic critic who did not say she was painful, and it was Beaufort who had latterly assured the Baronet that *The World and his Wife* would realize a fortune. He had gone about London assuring people that various enterprises would realize a fortune for thirteen years—that was his business—but the Baronet was the first person who believed him. Then Billy Beaufort took his watch, and his scarf-pin, and his sleeve-links away from Attenborough's—when in funds he could always pawn himself for a considerable amount—and turned up at the club, whose secretary had been writing him unkind letters on the subject of his subscription, resplendent again. The only alloy to his complacence, though it did not diminish it to any appreciable degree, was that he was scarcely more qualified to edit a paper than was a landsman to navigate a ship. He described himself as a journalist, and the description was probably as accurate as any other he could have furnished of a definite order; but he was a journalist whose attainments were limited to puffing a prospectus and serving up a réchauffé from *Truth.* He was never attached to a paper for longer than two or three months, but while he was so he was usually attached to a woman too. He drove in hansoms every day of the year; always appeared to have bought his hat half an hour ago; affected a big picotee as a buttonhole, and lived heaven alone knew how. While he was ridiculed in Fleet Street as a penman, he was treated with deference there on account of his reputed smartness in the City, and—while the City laughed at his business pretensions—there he was respected for his supposed abilities in Fleet Street. So he beamed out of the hansoms perkily, and drove from one atmosphere of esteem to another, waving a gloved hand to clever men who envied him en route.

In days gone by he had tasted a spell of actual prosperity. By what coup he had made the money, and how he had lost it, are details, but he had now developed the fatal symptom of loving to dwell upon that period when he had been so lucky, and so courted, and so rich. There is hope for the man who boasts of the thousands he means to make in the future; there is hope for the bore who proses ever so mendaciously about his successes in the present. But the man whose passion it is to brag about his past is doomed; he is a man who will succeed no more. If the sporting Baronet had observed this fact, ***The World and his Wife*** would never have been started, and Billy Beaufort would not have been looking for a subeditor to do the work of it.

Kent obtained the post. Beaufort believed in Turquand's opinion, and had always thought him a fool for being so shabby, knowing him to have ten times the brain-power he possessed himself, and Turquand had blown Humphrey's trumpet sturdily. He did more than merely recommend him; he declared—with a recollection of the nurse and baby—that Kent was ***the*** man to get, but he was afraid it would not be worth his while to accept less than seven pounds a week. When the matter was settled, Humphrey sought his friend again, and, wringing his hand, exclaimed:

'You're a pal; but—but, I say, what are a subeditor's duties?'

Exhilaration and misgiving were mixed in equal parts in his breast.

Turquand laughed, as nearly as he could be said to ever approach a laugh.

'The sub on ***The World and his Wife*** will have to cut "pars" out of the English society journals and the Paris "dailies," and "put 'em all in different language—the more indifferent, the better." He must handle the scissors without fatigue, and arrange with someone on this side to supply a column of London theatrical news every week—out of the previous Saturday's ***Telegraph***. Say with ***me***. It's worth a guinea, and I may as well have it as anybody else.'

'You are appointed our London dramatic critic,' said Kent. 'Won't you have thirty bob?'

'A guinea's the market price; and I can have some cards printed, and go to the theatres for nothing, you see, when I feel like it. They don't take any stock in ***The Outpost***. He must attend the représentations générales himself, and make all the acquaintances he can, "against the time" when the rag "busts." '

' "Busts!" ' echoed Kent. 'Is it going to bust?'

'Oh, it won't live, my boy. If it had been a permanent job, I shouldn't have handed it over to you. I'm not a philanthropist. But it will give you a chance to turn round, and an enlightened publisher may discern the merits of "The Eye of the Beholder" in the meanwhile. You'd better go on looking for something while you are on the thing; perhaps you'll be able to get the Paris Correspondence for a paper, if you try.'

'What more? What besides the scissors—nothing?'

'There's the paste; I don't imagine you'll need much else.'

'You're a trump!' repeated Kent gratefully. 'I feel an awful fraud taking such a berth, Turk; but in this world one has to do what one—'

'Can't!'

'Exactly; and, by George! it seems a better-paid line than what one can, though I should have thought it was more overcrowded.'

'There is always room at the top, you know,' said Turquand. 'When you rise in what you can't do, the emolument is dazzling!'

Beaufort was returning to Paris the same day, and he was anxious for Kent to join him there with all possible speed. Kent's first intention was to go alone, and let Cynthia follow him at her leisure; but when he reached home and cried, 'Mary, you shall ride in your carriage, and Charles "shall go to Eton," ' she would not hear of it.

'I can be ready by Wednesday or Thursday at the latest,' she exclaimed delightedly, when the explanation was forthcoming. 'What did you mean by "Charles" and "Mary"? Oh, Humphrey, didn't I tell you it would all come all right! How lovely! and how astonished mamma and papa will be!'

'Yes, I fancy it will surprise 'em a trifle,' he said. 'We'll go round there this evening, shall we? And we'll put the salary in francs—it sounds more.' He hesitated. 'I say, do you think nurse will mind living in Paris?'

Cynthia paled.

'I must ask her; I hadn't thought of that. Oh . . . oh, I dare say I shall be able to persuade her. It's rather a hurry for her, though, isn't it? She does so dislike being hurried.'

'Tell her at once, then,' he suggested; 'she'll have all the more time to prepare in. Run up to her now.'

'Let—let us think,' murmured Cynthia; 'we'll consider. . . . Ann must be sent away, and we shall have to give her a month's wages instead of notice.'

'She's no loss,' he observed. 'I don't know what your mother ever saw in her. She can't even cook a steak, the wench!'

'She fries them, dear.'

'I know she does,' said Kent. 'A woman who'd fry a steak would do a murder! Well, we shall have to give her a month's wages instead of notice—it's an iniquitous law! But what about nurse?'

'Perhaps,' said Cynthia nervously, 'if **you** were to mention it to her, darling—if you don't mind—'

'Of course I don't mind,' he answered, but without alacrity. 'What an idea! Tell Ann to send her down.'

She entered presently, an important young person in a stiff white frock; and he played with the newspaper, trying to feel that he had grown quite accustomed to seeing an important young person in his service.

'You wished to speak to me, madam, but baby will be waking directly.'

'I shan't keep you a moment,' said Kent. 'Er—er—your mistress and I are going to Paris; we shall be there some time. I suppose it's all the same to you where you live? We want you to be ready by Thursday, nurse.'

'To Paris!' said nurse, with cold amazement, and a pause that said even more.

Cynthia became immediately engrossed by a bowl of flowers over which she had been bending, and Kent felt that, after all, Paris was a long way off.

'I suppose it's all the same to you where you are?' he said again, though he no longer supposed anything of the sort. 'And there are three days for you to pack in, you know—three nice full days.'

'Three days sir,' she echoed reproachfully, 'to go abroad! May I ask you if you would be staying in a place like that all the winter, sir?'

'Yes, certainly through the winter—or probably so. It might not be so long; it depends.'

'I could not hundertake to leave 'ome for good, sir,' said the nurse. 'I am engaged! Which my friend lives in 'Olloway, and—'

'Oh, it wouldn't be for good,' declared Cynthia ingratiatingly; 'we couldn't stay there for good ourselves—oh no! And, of course, if you found we stopped too long to suit you, nurse, why, you could leave us when you liked, couldn't you? Though Mr. Kent and I would both be very sorry to lose you, I'm sure.'

They looked at her pleadingly while she meditated.

'What baby will do, I dunno, madam,' she said, 'a-changing his cow, poor little dear!'

'Will it hurt him?' demanded the mother and father, in a breath.

'If you have the doctor's consent, madam, you may *chance* it. It isn't a thing that *Hi* would hever advise.'

'Well, well, look here,' said Kent; 'we'll see Dr. Roberts about it to-day, and if he says there's no risk, that'll settle it. You will get ready to start Thursday morning, nurse.'

'I will *hendeavor* to do so, sir,' she said with dignity.

They felt that on the whole she had been gracious, and Kent, having obtained Dr. Roberts' sanction to change the cow, commissioned a house-agent to try to let No. 64 furnished at four guineas a week.

CHAPTER XIV.

IN case he should feel unduly elated, 'The Eye of the Beholder' came back on Wednesday afternoon, but this time he did not post it to another firm instanter. He could not very well ask for it to be returned to Paris, and he left it with Turquand when he bade him good-bye. 'Send it where you like,' he begged; 'perhaps you might try Farqueharsen next. Yes, I've rather a fancy for Farqueharsen; but let it make the round, old chap, and drop me a line when there aren't any more publishers for it to go to.'

The nurse's 'Endeavor' had been crowned by success, and the Walfords, having congratulated him so warmly that he almost began to think they were nice people again, the departure was made on Thursday morning as arranged.

They traveled, of course, by the Newhaven route, and reached the Gare St. Lazare after dark on a rainy evening. The amount of luggage they possessed among them made Kent stare, as he watched half a dozen porters hoisting trunks, and a perambulator, and a bassinet on to the bus, and it seemed as if they would never get out of the station. At last they rattled away, however, through the wet streets, the baby whimpering, and the nurse flustered, and he and Cynthia very tired. They drove to a little hotel near the Madeleine, where they intended to stay until they found a suitable pension, and where dinner and the warmth of 'grave' was very grateful. Nurse also picked up after the waiter's appearance with her tray and a half-bottle of vin compris, and, as their fatigue passed, exhilaration was in the ascendant once more. Cynthia recovered so much that, finding the rain had ceased and the moon was shining, she wanted to go out and look at the boulevards. So Humphrey and she took a stroll for an hour, and said how strange it was to think they should have come to live in Paris, and how funnily things happened; and they had a cura-çoa each at a café, and went back to their fusty red room on the third-floor, with the inevitable gilt clock and the festooned bedstead, quite gaily.

The chambermaid brought in their chocolate at eight o'clock next morning, and her brisk 'Bon jour, m'sieur et madame!' sounded far more cheerful to them both than Ann's knock at the door, with 'The 'ot water, mum!' to which they were accustomed. The sun streamed in brilliantly as she parted the window-curtains, and, after the chocolate and rolls were finished, Kent proceeded to dress, and, leaving Cynthia in bed, betook himself to the office of the paper in the Rue du 4 Septembre.

Beaufort had not come yet, and, pending his chief's arrival, he occupied himself by examining a copy. The tone of the notes struck him as decidedly poor, and a lengthy 'interview' with one of the prominent French actresses abounded in all the well-wornclichés of the amateur. The 'luxurious' apartment into which the interviewer was ushered, the lady's 'mock' despair, which gave place to 'graceful' resignation and 'fragrant' cigarettes, made him sick. Beaufort was very cordial when he entered, though, and it was reassuring to the new sub to see how light he made of everything. The work was as easy as A, B, C. 'Turf Topics' was contributed by a fellow called Jordan, and, really, Mr. Kent would find a few hours daily more than enough to prepare an issue. They went into his private room, where a bottle of vermouth and a pile of French and English journals, marked and mutilated, were the most conspicuous features of the writing-table; and Kent came to the conclusion that his editor was an extremely pleasant man, as the vermouth was sipped and they chatted over two excellent cigars.

At first the duties did not prove quite so simple as they had promised to one who had never had anything to do with producing a paper before, and the printer worried him a good deal. But Beaufort, who had been aware he was engaging zeal rather than experience, was highly satisfied. The novice was swift to grasp details, and took such an infinity of pains in seasoning and amplifying the réchauffés, that really his stuff read almost like original matter. As he began to feel his feet, too, he put forth ideas, and, finding that the other was quite ready to listen respectfully to them, gained confidence, and was not without a mistaken belief that in so quickly mastering the mysteries of a weekly and painfully exiguous little print, of which four-fifths were eclectic, he had displayed ability of a brilliant order.

Primarily the labor he devoted to the task was ludicrously disproportionate to the result, but by degrees he got through it with more rapidity. When a month had passed since the morning he sat down in the subeditorial chair of *The World and his Wife,* he discovered that he was doing in an afternoon what it had formerly taken him two days to accomplish, and marveled how he could have been so stupid. The work had devolved upon him almost entirely by now, for Beaufort, having shown him the way in which he should go, dropped in late, and withdrew early, and did little but drink vermouth, and say, 'Yes, certainly, capital!' while he was there. Kent proposed the subject for the week's 'interview,' wrote—or re-wrote—the causerie, and secured the majority of the few advertisements that they obtained. Also, when the subject of the semi-biographical sketch was not a good-looking woman, it was he who interviewed her. When the lady was attractive, 'Billy' Beaufort attended to that department himself.

Cynthia had found a pension in the Madeleine quarter, which had been highly recommended for a permanency, and here they had removed. They had two fairly large bedrooms, communicating au quatriéme, and paid a hundred and fifty francs a week. It did not leave much surplus out of the salary for incidental expenses, after reckoning the nurse's wages; but it was supposed to be very cheap, and Madame Garin and her vivacious daughter, who skipped a good deal for thirty years of age, and was voluble in bad English, begged them on no account to let any of the other boarders know they were received at such terms, for that would certainly be the commencement of Madame Garin's and her daughter's ruin. The establishment was well patronized, and the meals, with which about twenty-five French people down the long table appeared contented, would have been pronounced execrable in a third-rate boarding-house in Bloomsbury. The twenty-five people were waited on by a leisurely and abstracted Italian, and the intervals between the meagre courses were of such duration that Kent swore he had generally forgotten what the soup had been called by the time the cold entrée reached him.

Yet they were not uncomfortable. Their room was cozy in the lamplight when the winter set in, and Étienne had made a fire, and the curtains of the windows were drawn to hide the view of snowy roofs; and though the dinner often left them hungry, they could go out before retiring, and have chocolate and cakes. As a pressman, too, Kent got tickets for the theatres and the concerts. It was livelier than Leamington Road, to say the least of it—more lively for him than for Cynthia, perhaps; but an improvement for her as well, since one or two of the women were companionable, and did to take walks with, while he was at the office, or to polish her French on in the chilly salon.

One afternoon when he was sitting at his desk, and Beaufort had gone, the clerk came in to him with a card that bore the name of Mrs. Deane-Pitt. She was staying in Paris, and the editor had accepted his suggestion that it might be a good idea to interview a novelist for a change. Kent had sent the proofs to her the day before, but he had never seen her. He told the clerk to show her in with some 'satisfaction, and wished he had had his other jacket on; for the authoress of 'Two and a Passion' was a woman to meet.

He felt shabbier still when she entered; she looked to him like an animated fashion-plate of human height. From the courage of her hat to the swirl of her skirt, it was evident that Deane-Pitt made money, and knew where to spend it. An osprey in the hat was the only touch of vulgarity. Everybody would not have termed her pretty; but her eyes and teeth were good, and both flashed when she talked. Her age might have been anything from thirty to thirty-five.

'I wanted to see Mr. Beaufort,' she said, in a clear, crisp voice; 'but I hear he's out.'

'Yes; he is out,' said Kent. 'Is it anything I Can do?'

'Well, I don't like the "interview." I dare say it was my own fault; but I object to suffering for my own faults—one has to suffer for so many other people's in this world. It's all about "Two and a Passion." I wrote "Two and a Passion" seven years ago; and I didn't get a royalty on it, either. Why not quote the books I've done since, and say more about the one that's just out? You say, "Mrs. Deane-Pitt confessed to having recently published another novel," and then you drop it as if it were a failure or a hot coal. And "confessed"—why "confessed"? That's the tone I don't like in the thing. You write about me as if I belonged to another profession, and dabbled in Literature.'

He felt that 'Billy' Beaufort would not be sorry to have missed her.

'May I see the proofs again?' he asked.

She gave them to him, and settled herself in her chair. He looked at them pen in hand, and she looked at him.

'It can easily be put right, can't it, Mr.—'

' "Mr. Kent." Easily—oh yes! Will you tell me something about your new book? I'm ashamed to say I haven't read it yet.'

'Don't apologize,' she said. 'It's called "Thy Neighbor's Husband."'

'Does she bolt with him, or do you end it virtuously?'

'Virtuously, monsieur,' she said, smiling. 'You travel fast!'

'And—please go on! Are there cakes and ale, or does she tend the sick and visit the poor?'

'You appal me,' said Mrs. Deane-Pitt. 'Whatever my faults, I am fin-de-siécle. Forgive me saying "fin-de-siécle"—a modern version's needed badly; I end with a question-point.'

'Not questioning the lady's—'

'Oh, her *happiness* of course!'

' "This brilliant and analytical study, which is already giving rise to considerable discussion," would be the kind of strain, then, would it not?'

'Entirely,' she said. 'I'm awfully sorry to give you so much trouble.'

The "trouble's" a pleasure. You don't want your "favorite dog" mentioned, do you? Favorite dogs are becoming banal. Er—'

'Three,' she said. 'Yes; a boy and two girls.'

'Does the boy—"in a picturesque suit"—come into the room, and lead up to "evident maternal pride"?'

He's a dear little fellow!' she answered. 'But do you think "evident maternal pride" would be quite in keeping? No; I'd stick to me and the work. Besides, domesticity is tedious to read about; the dullest topic in the world is other people's children.'

Kent laughed.

I'll explain to Mr. Beaufort,' he declared; 'you shall have a revise sent on tomorrow. I'm sure you'll find it all right when he understands the style of thing you want.'

'Thank you,' she said dryly. 'I assure you I have no misgivings, Mr. Kent. "Kent"! I've never had any correspondence with you, have I? The name's familiar to me, somehow.'

'An alias "The Garden of England," 'he said.

'No, you haven't written anything, have you?'

'Two novels. One is published, and the post is wearing out the other.'

'I remember,' she cried, uttering the title triumphantly; 'I read it. What grand reviews you had! Of course, I know now. I liked your book extremely, Mr. Kent. Humphrey Kent, isn't it?'

'Thank you,' he said. 'Yes, Humphrey Kent.'

And you go in for journalism, too, eh?'

Oh, this is a new departure. I was never in a paper office until lately.'

'Really!' she exclaimed. 'You aren't giving fiction up?'

'I'm pot-boiling, Mrs. Deane-Pitt. Do you think it very inartistic of me?'

'Don't!' she said. 'Inartistic! I hate that cant. There are papers that are always calling *me* inartistic. One's got to live. Oh, I admire the people who can starve in West Kensington, and take three years to write a novel, but their attitude is beyond me. I write to sell, moi—though you needn't put that in the "interview." But I shouldn't have thought you'd have any trouble in placing your books—you oughtn't to to-day. I expect you've been too "literary "; you'll grow out of it.'

'You don't believe in—'

'I'm a practical woman. The public read to be amused, and the publishers want what the public will read, good, bad, or indifferent; that's my view. You mustn't make me say these things, though,' she broke off, laughing, and getting up; 'it's most indiscreet—to a pressman. . . . I shall send you a copy of "Thy Neighbor's

Husband"—to a coleague. Good-afternoon, Mr. Kent. I'll leave you to go on with your work now. Pray don't look so relieved.'

'I should value the copy extremely', he said. 'It was anything but relief—I was struggling to conceal despair.'

She put out her hand, and a faint perfume clung to his own after the door had closed. Though her standpoint was not his own, her personality had impressed him, and, as he watched her from the window reëntering her cab, Kent was sorry she had not remained longer.

He trusted she would not forget her promise to send him her novel, and when it reached him, a few days later, he opened it with considerable eagerness. The perusal disappointed him somewhat, and the story seemed to him unworthy of the pen that had written 'Two and a Passion.' But he replied, as he was bound to do, with a letter of grateful appreciation, and endeavored, moreover, to persuade himself that he liked it better then he did. The lady, on her side, wrote a cordial little note, thanking him for the amended proof-sheets—'I had no idea I was so clever or so charming.' She said she should be pleased to see him if he could ever spare the time to look in; she could give him a cup of 'real English tea,' and she was very truly his—Eva Deane-Pitt.

CHAPTER XV.

She was living in the Avenue Wagram—she had taken a small furnished flat there for a few months—and when he encountered her on the boulevards, about a week afterwards, Kent was puzzled to discover a reason why he had not availed himself of her invitation. He called a day or two later, and found her cynical but stimulating. In recalling the visit, it appeared to him that she was more entertaining in conversation than in print, which suggested that her good things were not as good as they sounded, but while she talked he was amused. He left the flat with the consciousness of having spent a very agreeable half-hour, and was sorry that her 'Day,' which she had mentioned to him, was a fortnight ahead. She seemed to know many people in Paris whom he would be glad to meet, and the entrée to the little yellow drawing-room promised to be pleasurable, apart from the hostess, with whom he had drunk 'English tea' and smoked Egyptian cigarettes. That she was a widow he had taken for granted from the commencement, and his assumption proved to be correct. She was a woman who struck one as born to be a widow; it was difficult to conceive her either with a husband or living in her parents' home. As to her children, she spoke of them frequently, and saw them seldom. Kent decided that she was too fashionable and a trifle hard, but this did not detract from the pleasure the visits afforded him; perhaps his perception of her character was responsible for much of it, indeed, for it rendered it additionally complimentary that she was nice to him.

She was surprised to learn he was married, and declared that she looked forward to knowing his wife. She did not, however, take any steps to gratify the desire, and Kent was not regretful. He felt that few things more productive of boredom for two could be devised than Mrs. Deane-Pitt and Cynthia would find a tête-à-tête, and, though he was reluctant to acknowledge it to himself, he had a feeling also that the lady would be a little contemptuous of him afterward if it occurred. He knew her opinion of young men's marriages in the majority of cases, and was uncomfortably conscious that she would not pronounce his own to be one of the exceptions.

Mrs. Walford's letters to her daughter hitherto had been in her most enthusiastic vein. Mr. McCullough had given the disappointed bass a berth in Berlin, and in her epistle this was alluded to as a 'position,' upon which she showered her favorite adjectives of 'jolly' and 'extraordinary' and 'immense.' Cæsar was 'McCullough's right hand,' the 'best houses in Berlin' were open to him, and his prospects, social and pecuniary, were dazzling. Of late, however, he had been dwelt on less, and one morning a letter came which contained a confession of personal anxiety. The recent heavy drop in American stocks, and the failure of two or three brokers, had seriously affected the jobber. They thought of trying to let The Hawthorns, which was much too large for them now, and moving out of the neighborhood. Cæsar remained McCullough's right hand but quite briefly, and it was evident that the writer was in great distress.

Cynthia was terribly grieved and startled. She dashed off eight pages of love and inquiries by the evening mail, and when the news was confirmed, with more particulars, she felt she could do no less than run over to utter her sympathy in person.

Kent agreed that perhaps it was advisable, and raised the money that was necessary cheerfully enough by pawning his watch and chain. Only when she sent him a rather lengthy telegram from Streatham, detailing her mother's frame of mind, he felt that she was exaggerating his share in her solicitude.

The chilly salon, where the ladies played forfeits after dinner, or the vivacious daughter thumped the piano, was not attractive during Cynthia's absence. Neither was it lively to smoke alone in his room, or to go to a theatre or a music-hall by himself, and when, in calling on Mrs. Deane-Pitt, he mentioned his solitariness, and she proposed that he should take her to the Variétés, he accepted the suggestion with alacrity.

As he obtained the tickets for nothing, his only expense was the cabs and the liquors between the acts, and it was so enjoyable, laughing with her on the lounge of the café, that the recollection of their being paid for out of the balance of his loan from the mont-de-piété was banished. Mrs. Deane-Pitt made some more of her happy remarks while they sipped the chartreuse, and her teeth and eyes flashed superbly. The piece was a great success, but Kent thought the entr'actes were even gayer; and when the curtain had fallen, and they reached the Avenue Wagram, she would not hear of his leaving her before going in and having some supper.

The liquors looked rather mean to him contrasted with the little table that he saw laid with its mayonnaise and a bottle of champagne, and his exhilaration was momentarily damped by envy. Fiction meant a good deal when one was lucky; how jolly to be able to live as this woman did! Her maid took away her cape and hat, and he opened the bottle. She drew off her long gloves, and patted her hair before the mirror with fingers on which some rings shone.

'Let's sit down,' she said. 'Am I all right?

He thought he had never seen her look so charming or so young.

'You have a color,' he admitted.

'A proof it's natural; when we went out I was as pale as a ghost. I work too hard. I do—what are you smiling at?—I work horribly hard. Life's so dear—yes, "expensive"—don't say it, it would be unworthy of you. And I can't do a fifth part of what's offered me, with all my fag.'

'Am I supposed to sympathize with you for that?' he asked.

'Certainly you should sympathize; what do you suppose I tell you for—to be felicitated? Do you think it's agreeable to have to refuse work when one needs the money it would bring in? The trials of Tantalus were a joke to it. I had to let a twenty-thousand-word story for **The Metropolis** slide only the other day, and I could place half a dozen shorter tales every week if I'd the time to write them.'

'You do write a great number,' said Kent, 'and you seem fairly comfortable.'

' "Wise judges are we of each other!" Where from? You don't know "The Lady of Lyons." You ought to see my bills; that music-stand over there is full of them. That's the place I always keep them in; I'm naturally tidy, it's one of my virtues. I had to turn out Chopin's Mazurkas yesterday to make room for some more. I only came to Paris because people don't write you so many abusive letters when they have to pay twopence-halfpenny postage. Oh, I'm comfortable enough in a fashion, but I've my worries like my neighbors. I suppose I'm extravagant, but I can't help it. Besides, I'm not. Do you think I'm extravagant?'

He looked at her, and nodded, smiling.

'No,' she said, 'not really? Why?'

'Heavens! you haven't the illusion that you're parsimonious? I believe you spend a small fortune on cabs alone.'

'I don't spend a solitary franc on one when I'm **not** alone.'

'You **never** walk, so far as I can ascertain.'

'No; not so far as that,' she said; 'but—'

'But shorter distances, yes,' he laughed. 'Your champagne is beyond criticism, and you dress like—like an angel. The simile is bad—'

'And improper. Go on; what other faults have I? I like to know my friends' opinion of me.'

' "If to her share some human errors fall," ' he murmured.

'**Don't** look, then. Shall I hide it behind my serviette? That is sheer cowardice. Fill your glass, and mine, please. Go on; tell me how I strike you frankly. I know. You think I don't approach literature reverently enough, and that I ought to devote twelve months to a book, and let my poor little children go barefoot in the meanwhile. Well, I did give twelve months to a book once; but I had a husband when I wrote "Two and a Passion," and **he** provided the boots. Now, if I didn't work as I do, I should have to live in Battersea, and buy my frocks in Brixton, and take my holidays in Southend. You wouldn't calmly condemn me to Southend? My income, apart from what I make, barely pays my rent.'

'Your rent is somewhat heavy,' suggested Kent, 'with two flats going at once.'

'Wretch! do you lecture me because I couldn't find a tenant for the Victoria Street place? He blames me for my misfortunes!'

She caught the long gloves up, and swirled them round on his cheek. Like the others, they were perfumed; but now their scent was in his face. They looked in each other's eyes an instant, smiling across the corner of the table. Then, as the smile died away, they remained looking in each other's eyes attentively. He drew the gloves from her hold, and played with them. Her hand lay upturned on the cloth to receive them back, and in restoring them his own rested on it. She averted her gaze, but her palm did not slip away as quickly as it might have done.

'You know you may smoke,' she said, rising, and going over to the fire. 'I'll have one, too.'

Isn't it too late?' he asked, joining her.

His voice was not quite steady, and now he did not look at her as he spoke.

'You can have one cigarette,' she declared, sinking into an armchair, and crossing her feet on the fender. 'How is the paper going, Mr. Kent? Eclipsing *Le Petit Journal?*'

'Of course,' he said. 'Did you ever know anybody's paper that wasn't?'

'You count Paris your home, I suppose? You mean to stop here permanently? I go back in March; the people are returning here then. I loathe London after Paris; but I shall have escaped most of the winter there, that's one thing. Where did you live in town?'

'*My* neighborhood *was* Battersea,' answered Kent; 'that is to say, it was suburban wilds. We had a villa in Streatham—have it now, in fact,' he added, remembering with dismay that there was a quarter's rent due. 'No; I'm afraid I can't condole with you, Mrs. Deane-Pitt.'

' "Pride sleeps in a gilded crown, contentment in a cotton nightcap," ' she said. 'An address is only skin-deep, after all; besides, Streatham is pretty.'

'Pretty *well;* and it looks prettier out of a big house.'

'Make money, my friend,' she said languidly; 'you are young enough, and I think you're clever enough. When all things were made, nothing was made better. And it's really very easy; as soon as you are popular, the editors will take anything.'

'First catch your hare,' he observed. 'I'm not popular.'

The clock on the mantelshelf struck one, and he threw away his cigarette-end and got up.

'Good-night, Mrs. Deane-Pitt.'

'Good-night,' she said.

Her touch lingered again, and her personality dominated him as he walked back to the pension through the silent streets. He was angry with himself to perceive that it was so. What the devil had he been about in that business with the gloves over the table? She had let him do it, too! Did she like him? He would not go to see her any more. Well, that was absurd, but he would not go as frequently as he had. And he must keep a rein on himself. Nothing could come of it, he was convinced, even if he wished; and he did not. It would be too beastly to deceive a girl like Cynthia . . . and their baby only a year old. He decided as he mounted the stairs he would tell Cynthia when she came back that he had been to the Variétés with Mrs. Deane-Pitt. It would not disturb her to hear that, and, though it was juggling with his conscience, he should feel cleaner afterwards. There was a letter from her waiting for him on the bedroom table, and he washed his hands before he opened it.

Cynthia wrote to say she should be home the next evening but one, and that her parents had been rejoiced to see her. On the whole, things did not seem to be so desperate as she had feared; but it was quite determined that The Hawthorns should be let, for, fortunately, there was a Peruvian family who were prepared to take it just as it stood, and mamma had already been to view a house in Strawberry Hill which was quite nice, and far cheaper. Whether Miss Wix would remove with them was doubtful.

'Mamma's temper is naturally not of the best just now, and I gather that the dissensions have been rather bad. Papa talks of allowing Aunt Emily a pound a week to live by herself, and really she seems to prefer it.'

She added, underlined, that Cæsar was still 'the right hand of McCullough.' She had learned to smile a little at Cæsar, and Kent winced as he came to that allusion to a mutual joke. And then there followed a dozen affectionate injunctions: he was not to be dull, 'poor boy who had no watch and chain!' but to go somewhere every night; he was to hug baby for her, and to give and keep a score of kisses. She was 'always his loving wife.' He read it under the paraffin lamp with his overcoat on, and wished it had not arrived till the morning.

Mrs. Deane-Pitt's inquiry how **The World and his Wife** was going had had more significance than Kent's perfunctory reply. The band of 'Paris Correspondents' in the vicinity of the Boulevard Magenta and elsewhere were already beginning to talk about 'Billy' Beaufort, for, not only was he neglecting the first chance of a competence that had fallen in his way for years, but he was squandering the whole of a very handsome salary, and getting into difficulties besides. The amount of energy which this man, when in his deepest waters, devoted to seeking opportunities was only equalled by the abundant folly by which he had ruined, and always would ruin, all that he obtained. He was one of the fools who devote their lives to disproving the adage that experience teaches them. The circulation of the paper was purely nominal, and the Baronet had constantly to be applied to for increased remittances; indeed, the only work in connection with the journal which 'Billy' now did was to write euphemistic reports to the proprietor. Nor did the drafts supply the journal's deficiencies alone. Card debts had to be settled somehow. And an ephemeral attachment to a girl who tied herself in knots at the Nouveau Cirque was responsible for some embarrassment.

Hitherto, however, Beaufort had always spared the hundred and seventy-five francs at the end of the week to his subeditor, but on the Saturday after Cynthia's return he asked him casually if he would mind waiting for it a few days.

'Sorry if it puts you out at all,' he remarked. 'I can't help myself. You shall have the money for certain Wednesday or Thursday. Devil of a nuisance! But I suppose you can finance matters in the meanwhile, Kent, eh?'

Kent could do no less than answer that he would try, but on Monday morning Madame Garin's bill would come up with the first breakfast, and he saw himself confronted by the rather unpleasant necessity of making an excuse to her, or pretending to forget it till he could pay.

CHAPTER XVI.

Their liabilities had been discharged with such exceeding regularity up to the present that he decided to take the bolder course, albeit it remained distasteful to him. He had been obliged to ask landladies to wait longer in his time, but it was one thing to be ' disappointed' as a bachelor, and quite another when one had a wife, and baby, and nurse in the house. Madame Garin's countenance, moreover, was of a rather forbidding type, and did not suggest a yielding disposition in money matters; and he was agreeably surprised when she rejoined, 'Cela ne fait rien, monsieur,' after a scarcely perceptible pause, as he spoke to her in passing her little office in the hall on Monday morning. Cynthia's relief was immense; it had been quite a serious crisis to her, her earliest experience of having to ask for credit; and, to be on the safe side, he had not promised to settle the bill before Thursday. Both trusted, though, that the salary would be forthcoming on the earlier of the dates mentioned by Beaufort, for if the nurse wanted anything bought in the meanwhile they would be compelled to temporize with her, and that would have its awkwardness.

Beaufort did not refer to the subject on Wednesday, and Kent went home with sixty-five centimes in his pocket. He got in late, and Cynthia was already at dinner. She glanced at him inquiringly as he took his seat, and he shook his head.

'Not yet,' he murmured.

She disguised her feelings, and continued to talk chiffons with the woman opposite; but when they mounted to their room, and the proprietress looked out of the bureau at them with a greeting, she felt a shade uncomfortable, and hastened her steps.

'I hate that bureau,' she said as soon as they had reached the haven of the first landing. 'The Garins seem to live in it, and you can't get by without them seeing you. Well, he didn't give it to you, eh?'

'No; it will be all right to-morrow, though. It's lucky I said Thursday instead of to-day. Has nurse been to you for anything?'

'Thank goodness, she hasn't! But baby is bound to be out of something directly. You do think we are sure of it to-morrow, Humphrey, ***don't*** you?'

He said there was no doubt about it, and they drew their chairs to the hearth. The night was cold, and he went out presently to a grocer's close by and spent sixty centimes on a bottle of the kind of claret which was included by the humblest restaurants in the cheapest meal à prix fixe, smuggling it upstairs under his overcoat. In Madame's wine-list it figured as médoc at two francs, and she would not have been pleased with him for obtaining it at a shop. They made it hot over their fire in one of the infant's saucepans, and, sweetened with the sugar that they kept secreted for that purpose in the wardrobe, they found it comforting. Though their capital was now a sou, they were not unhappy, with the prospect of a hundred and seventy-five francs in the course of twenty-four hours, and once Cynthia laughed so gaily that the nurse came in and intimated that ' the rooms hopening into one another' made the noise very disturbing to her charge.

Kent went to the office next day without a cigarette, for he had smoked his last, and he awaited his chiefs arrival with considerable impatience. The editor had not been in when he returned to the pension for luncheon, but in reply to Cynthia's eager question he assured her he was certain to have the money in his pocket when he saw her again in the evening. He wanted a cigarette by this time very badly indeed, and when three o'clock struck he left his desk, and stood pulling his moustache at the window moodily. He began to fear it was going to be one of the days when ' Billy' Beaufort did not look in at the office at all.

His misgiving proved to be well founded, and dinner that night was agreeable neither to him nor the girl. She had been reluctant to go down to it, on hearing that Madam Garin could not be satisfied, and, though he had persuaded her to do so, sped past the bureau with averted eyes. It was useless going in search of Beaufort; the only thing of which one could be positive with regard to his movements at this hour was that he would not be at his hotel; but Humphrey promised her to see him before commencing work in the morning, and declared that he would send the necessary amount round to her at once.

The editor was staying at the Grand, and when he called there Kent learnt that he was still in his room. He found him lying in bed and reading his letters. A suit of dress-clothes trailed disconsolately across a chair, and by the window a fur-coat and a hat-box had rolled on to the floor. He had not drunk his chocolate, but a tumbler of soda water and-some-thing, and a syphon, stood on the table beside him, surrounded by his watch and chain, some scattered cigarettes, and the bulk of his correspondence. He looked but half awake and cross.

'What's the matter?' he murmured. 'Sit down. There's a seat there, if you move those things. Will you have anything to drink?'

I won't have a drink, but I'll take one of those cigarettes, if I may,' said Kent, sticking it in his mouth and inhaling gratefully. 'I'm sorry to dun you, but you told me I could have the money "Wednesday or Thursday," and I'm pressed for it. I wish you would let me have it now; I want to send it up to my pension before going on to the shop.'

Beaufort put out his tongue and drank some more of the contents of the tumbler thirstily.

'That will be all right,' he said, yawning; 'don't you bother about that.'

'But the point is, that I want it now,' repeated Kent. I dare say it would be "all right," but I'm in need of it this morning. My bill came up on Monday, and I put the woman off till yesterday—I can't put her off any more.'

'What! is this the first week you owe her? My boy, a week! I haven't paid my bill here for eleven weeks. Let her wait.'

You haven't a wife,' said Kent. '*I* have. It's damned unpleasant for a girl, I can tell you!'

How much does the old hag want?' inquired the editor, with resentment.

A hundred and sixty, more or less, with extras. I have the interesting document with me, if you'd like to see it.'

Billy gasped again.

'Oh, well,' he said, 'we'll engineer it. You—you tell your wife not to worry herself; and don't trouble any more—don't break your head. I'll see you through.'

He settled his head on the pillow, and appeared to be under the impression that the difficulty was disposed of.

It's very good of you,' answered Kent, as his tone seemed to call for gratitude. 'I'm glad to hear you say so; but how soon can I have it?'

'Eh? Oh, I shall be able to draw to-morrow. You shall have a hundred and sixty to-morrow. I give you my word of honor on it. I'll work it for you somehow. I won't see you in a hole.'

Kent stared at him. On the morrow a second week's salary would be due, and on the next day but one a second account from Madame Garin. He pointed the fact out to Beaufort quietly, but with emphasis. He said that, if matters were financially complicated, it would be well for him to understand their position, in order that he might realize his outlook, and, if essential, make a temporary removal to a pension where he could live more cheaply. He did not want to badger him, he explained, but Beaufort's own programme was not capable of imitation in his own case, and, as a family man, he must cut his coat according to his cloth.

'If you want me to let part of my salary stand over for the next few weeks, and it's unavoidable, I suppose it *is* unavoidable,' he said finally; I only, I can't be left in the dark about it. Am I to gather that what you propose is to pay me a hundred and sixty francs to-morrow, instead of three hundred and fifty? Or shall I have the lot?'

What he received was a peaceful snore, and he perceived that 'Billy' Beaufort had fallen asleep. He contemplated him for a minute desperately, and lit another cigarette. The thought of Cynthia sitting at home in the bedroom, and waiting in suspense for a messenger's knock at the door, nerved him to upset a chair, and Beaufort opened his eyes with a grunt.

'What can you do?' demanded Kent, briefly this time, lest slumber should overtake him again. 'Can you give me any money before I go?'

'I've told you I'll do my utmost. You shall have a hundred and sixty francs to-morrow; I can't give it you now—I haven't got it. If I had, you may be sure you wouldn't have to ask twice for it. I'm not a chap of that sort, Kent. By George! I never desert a pal. I've my faults, but I never desert a pal! . . . If a louis on account is any good, I can let you have that.'

'Well,' said Humphrey, seeing that there was no more to be done, 'I rely on you, and—thanks—I'll take the louis to go on with.'

He went down and out on to the boulevard, and sent Cynthia a petit bleu, saying: 'Got something. Balance to-morrow,' and wondered gloomily whether Madame Garin would continue complacent when she discovered that, after all, he only suggested paying one week's bill instead of two. Perhaps it would be easier to arrange with the vivacious daughter.

He resolved to try, and 'Mademoiselle' was all smiles and 'Mais parfaitment, monsieur,' when he spoke to her. He congratulated himself on having had the idea; but, though Beaufort provided him with the sum agreed upon next day, and repeated that he 'never deserted a pal' with an air of having achieved a triumph, he did not make up the deficit, and, instead of being able to square accounts with the Garins, the subeditor gradually found himself getting deeper into their debt. From its being a doubtful point whether he would receive his salary in full, it became a question whether he would get any of it at all; and when he obtained half, he learned by degrees to esteem it a fortunate week. Beaufort overflowed with promises and protestations. Everything was always 'on the eve of being righted,' but the day of righteousness never dawned. 'Mademoiselle' began to stop 'Monsieur Kent' in the hall, and convey to him with firmness that her mother had very heavy obligations to meet, and Cynthia sat at the dining-table in constant terror of the old woman , coming in and publicly insulting them.

One morning, when the laundress brought back their linen, Humphrey had to feign to be asleep, while Cynthia explained that 'monsieur had all the money, and was so unwell that she did not like to wake him.' The poor creature was sympathetic, and went away bidding madame not disquiet herself—it was doubtless only a passing indisposition; but after she had gone, the girl begged Kent to take a loan on her engagement-ring, and after some discussion he complied. Everything is more valuable in Paris than in London until one has occasion to pawn it, and then it is less so, especially jewelry. From the mont-de-piété Kent procured about forty per cent. of what a London pawnbroker would have advanced. However, the loan was useful. Though it did not clear them, it went some way toward doing it, besides paying the nurse's wages, which were due the same day, and afforded temporary relief. Cynthia said she had become so 'demoralized'—she used a happy term now with a frequency he would have found astonishing if he had recalled how she talked when they first met—that a substantial payment on account 'made her feel quite meritorious,' and there was a week in which they went to the theatres again, and walked past the bureau erectly.

March had opened mildly, and people were once more beginning to sit outside the cafés, and Mrs. Deane-Pitt was returning to England. Kent had kept his resolution not to enter the yellow drawing room in the Avenue Wagram when it could be avoided—partly, no doubt, because of the anxieties he had had to occupy his mind, but partly also by force of will. When he heard that she was leaving, though, he could do no less—nor did he feel it necessary to do less—than call to bid her au revoir, and he was conscious, as the servant replied she was at home, that he would have been disappointed otherwise.

Her gown betokened that visitors were expected; teacups demonstrated that visitors had been. She welcomed him languidly, and motioned him to a seat.

'I thought you must have gone to London, or to Paradise, 'she said. 'What have you been doing with yourself?'

'I've been so fearfully busy,' he answered lamely.

'On the paper?'

'Of course.'

'I don't hear good reports of the paper,' she said. 'I hope they aren't true.'

'The paper is as good as it always was,' responded Kent—'neither better nor worse. May I ask what you hear?'

'I heard that Sir Charles Eames is getting tired of it: says he is running a journal that nobody reads but himself, and *he* "don't read it much." He told a man in confidence in his club, who told it privately to another man, who told it, between him and her, to a woman who told me—I wouldn't breathe a word of it to anyone myself—that "if the price didn't improve soon he should scratch it." What will the robin do then, Mr. Kent?'

Humphrey look grave. This was the first plain intimation he had had that *The World and his Wife* was likely to collapse, and badly as the post was paying him now, it was more lucrative than any that awaited him should it terminate. He thought that Mrs. Deane-Pitt might have communicated her views more considerately.

'The robin will manage to find crumbs, I suppose,' he replied; 'I wasn't born on *The World and his Wife.'*

'May I offer you some tea and cake in the meantime?'

'No, thanks.'

Her tone annoyed him this afternoon; it was hard and careless. He fancied at the moment that his only feeling for her was dislike, and sneered at the mental absurdities into which he had strayed. There was a lengthy pause—a thing that had seldom occurred between them—followed by a brief inters change of platitudes.

'Well,' he murmured at length, getting up, 'I'm afraid I must go.'

She did not press him to remain.

'Must you?' she said. 'I dare say we shall meet again. It's a little world in every sense.'

'I hope we shall. Au revoir, and bon voyage, Mrs. Deane-Pitt.'

'If you should go back yourself, you'll come to see me? You know where I live.'

'Thank you; I shall be very glad.'

But as he went down the stairs Kent was surprised to perceive that he felt suddenly mournful. The noise of the door closing behind him was charged with ridiculous melancholy, and there appeared to him something sad in this conventional ending which had the semblance of estrangement. The sentiment and impression of the hour that he had spent in the room after the Variétés recurred to him, and contrasted with it their adieu became full of pathos. He questioned reproachfully if, in his determination not to be more than a friend, he might not have repaid her own friendship by ingratitude, and so have wounded her. He decided that he would send her a letter, and that he would not send her a letter. He made his way through the Champs Élysées reflectively, and once half obeyed a violent temptation to turn back. He would have obeyed it wholly but that he felt its indulgence would be laughable, or that Mrs. Deane-Pitt would be likely to look upon it in that light. So he restrained the impulse. But he could not laugh himself.

CHAPTER XVII.

THE respite afforded by the mont-de-pété was brief, and all that Kent received from Beaufort in the next three weeks was twenty francs. The Garins' faces in the hall were very glum now, and the sum against 'Notes remises' at the top of the bills that came up to the bedroom on Monday mornings, and were perforce ignored, had swelled to such disheartening dimensions that the debtor no longer gave himself the trouble to decipher the various items. In addition to this, the affairs of **The World and his Wife** had reached a crisis, and he learned from the editor that it was doomed. An interval of restored hope succeeded the intelligence, during which the life of the paper hung in the balance, and it looked likely that the Baronet would continue it, after all, and then they went to press no more.

Beaufort declared that Kent's claim would be discharged without delay, and, knowing the ex-proprietor's position, Humphrey could not believe that he would be allowed to suffer. That the Baronet was ignorant his claim existed, and it was 'Billy' Beaufort who had to find the money for him, he had no idea; any more than he had suspected, when he took Cynthia to the Nouveau Cirque, and applauded the contortions of 'Mdlle. Véronique,' that the artiste who stood on her head, and kissed her toes to them, was in part responsible for their plight. 'Billy,' realizing that the matter must be squared somehow, if things were not to become more unpleasant, spoke reassuringly of Sir Charles being momentarily in tight quarters, and Humphrey, in daily expectation of a check, made daily promises of a settlement to the Garins, while he discussed with Cynthia what should be their next move.

To remain in Paris was useless, and they decided that they would go back to England as soon as the check was cashed. Perhaps it was fortunate, after all, that No. 64 had not been let. In London he must advertise again, and a post might be easier to find now that he could call himself a subeditor in the advertisement. The days went by, however, and Beaufort, whom he awoke, like an avenging angel, at early morning, and tracked in desperation from bar to bar until he ran him to earth at night, still remained 'in hourly expectation of the money.' Both Cynthia and Kent had the fear that their inability to pay was known to everybody in the house, even to the servants; and they imagined disdain in the face of the Italian who waited on them at meals, and indifference in the bearing of Étienne when he laid the fire. The chambermaid's 'Bon jour, m'sieur et madame,' had a ring of irony to their ears, and on Mondays, in particular, they were convinced that she sneered when she put down their tray.

The thought made the girl so miserable that Kent took an opportunity of asking Miss Garin if it were so, and she informed him that he was mistaken.

'Nobody 'as been told, monsieur,' she said; 'oh, not at all! But, monsieur, it is impossible that you can remain longer, you know, if your affairs do not permit of a settlement. Your intentions are quite honorable—well understood; but my mother cannot be able to wait for the payment. Her expense is terrible 'eavy 'ere; vraiment, c'est épouvantable je vous assure; et—and—and my mother 'as an offer for your rooms, and she require that you and ma- dame locate yourselves elsewhere, monsieur, on Saturday.'

After an instant of dismay, Humphrey was, on the whole, relieved by the idea of being allowed to depart in peace, and to await his check where the situation would not be strained. It was rather a nuisance, having to make a removal for so short a time; but when it was effected, he felt that they would be a great deal more comfortable. He replied that they would, of course, do as they were asked, and that Madame Garin could depend upon his sending her the amount he owed the very second that his arrears were forthcoming. He said he thoroughly appreciated the consideration she had shown them, and could not express how deeply he regretted to have inconvenienced her.

'Yes, monsieur,' murmured Miss Garin. She hesitated, and then added, in a slightly embarrassed tone: 'You know, monsieur, my mother must keep your luggage 'ere. Her lawyer 'as advised that.'

'What?' said Kent. 'Oh, my dear Miss Garin! I will give your mother an acknowledgment—a promissory note—whatever she likes! She will only have to trust me a few more days; I am perfectly certain to have the money in the course of a week. She won't keep the luggage, surely? My—my dear girl, think what it means with a wife and child!'

Miss Garin spread out her hands with a shrug.

'It is always "a few days," monsieur,' she said. 'My mother will permit that you take your necessaries for the few days, and the things belonging to the little one. No more.'

'Can I see her?' inquired Kent, rather pale.

'Oh yes; she is in the. bureau.'

'The servants can hear everything that goes on in the bureau,' he demurred. 'Can't I talk to her in her room?'

Miss Garin preceded him there, and he tried his best to wring consent from the old woman, but she was as hard as nails, and would not listen for long. An 'acknowledgment of the debt,' certainly—the lawyer had advised that, too, and he would prepare it—but their luggage, jamais de la vie! The baby's box, and the bassinet; and for madame and himself such articles as were indispensable for a week. She would agree to nothing else.

Cynthia was upstairs, with the baby on her lap, and Kent went in and shut the door that communicated with the nursery.

'What is it?' she asked, after a glance at his face. 'Is anything wrong?'

He wondered if he could soften the news, but it did not lend itself to euphemisms. He told her what had occurred in as light a tone as he could acquire.

'It won't be for any length of time, and we can easily make shift for a bit,' he said. 'It isn't as if the kid's things had to be left behind, you see. A hand-bag will hold all we really need for ourselves. What do we want, after all, for a week. It isn't a serious matter, if one comes to look at it. It sounds worse than it is, I think.'

She sat startled and still. Then she cuddled the baby close, and forced a smile.

My brown frock will do,' she assented; 'I shall go in that. Oh, it isn't so dreadful, no. Of course just for a moment it does give one a shock, doesn't it? But—but, as you say, it sounds worse than it is. Were they nasty to you?'

'The old lady wasn't very affectionate," said Kent; 'the girl wasn't so bad. It's cussed awkward, darling, I know. Poor little woman! I was funking telling you like anything. It took me ten minutes coming up those stairs, and I nearly went out for a walk first.'

She laughed; she was already quite brave again.

'We shall get through it all right,' she declared. 'Where shall we go? We might go back to the hotel where we stayed first, mightn't we? We paid there.'

I thought of that,' he replied; 'but it was rather dear, wasn't it? We had better spend as little as possible; there are our passages, and we can't arrive in London with nothing. I'm afraid we shan't be able to get your ring out in any case.'

'That can't be helped,' she said; 'I'm sorrier about your watch and chain. A man is so lost without a watch. Saturday? Saturday will be micarême, won't it? We shall celebrate it nicely. . . . Oh! She sat upright, and stared at him with frightened eyes. 'Humphrey—nurse!'

His jaw dropped, and he looked back at her blankly.

'I'd forgotten her,' he said.

'To see our luggage detained—it could only mean the one thing. Humphrey, what would she think? Whatever can we do? She mustn't, mustn't know; I should die of shame.'

'No,' he said; 'she mustn't know, that's certain. Good Lord! what an infernal complication at the last minute! *I* don't know what's to be done, I'm sure. Take the child in to her, and let us consider.'

He filled a pipe, and puffed furiously, until Cynthia came back.

'Couldn't we,' he suggested—'couldn't we say, as we're on the point of going home, that we don't think it's worth while carting the heavy trunks to another place for a week? Madame Garin has "kindly allowed us to leave them here in the meantime." Eh?'

Cynthia mused.

'Then, what are we going to another place ourselves for?' she said.

'Yes,' said Kent; 'that won't do. Hang the young woman! she's a perfect bug-bear to us; we're all the time struggling to live up to the teapot. I wish to heaven we could get rid of her altogether!'

'That,' answered the girl, after a pause—'that is the only thing we *can* do. We must send her away, and *I'll* take baby.'

'You? A nice job for you! You could never go down to a meal; and traveling too—imagine it!'

'I can do it; I'd like it. Anything, anything rather than she should see us turned out, and our luggage seized. That would be too awful! Yes, we must get her away, Humphrey. We must get her away before we leave here. Whatever happens afterwards is our own affair. She'll be gone, and know nothing about it.'

'That's very good,' he said thoughtfully. 'But there'll be her wages, and her passage back. Great Scot! and another month's wages because we don't give her proper notice ! How much would it come to? I've got two francs fifty, and I've pawned my match-box. I'm afraid we must think of something else.'

'We could send her second-class on the boat as well. Yes, certainly second-class. What does that cost? Have you got the paper you had? Look for it, do; it used to be in your bag.'

Kent searched and found it. He felt also that their lot would be comparatively a bed of roses if they were spared the astonished inquiries of the nurse.

'Second-class tickets are twenty-five and seven-pence,' he announced, and two months' wages are four pounds. Say five pounds ten. Well, my dear, I might as well try to raise a million.'

He blew clouds, and waited for an inspiration, while she walked about the room with her hands behind her.

'If we could get it,' she remarked, breaking a heavy silence, 'I don't know what reason we could give for packing her off so suddenly. It would look rather a curious proceeding, wouldn't it?'

'We could say,' said Kent, 'that we have decided to live in Paris permanently. She'd want to go then. The charms of 'Olloway.'

'Yes,' answered Cynthia, 'we could say that. But why in such a gasping hurry?"

'Yes; it would be rather a rush, it's a fact. Well, I'll tell you. We are going on a visit to some friends in the country, and they haven't room for another nurse. Mrs. Harris's nurse will do all that's needed while we're there. . . . But five pounds ten! I can see Beaufort, and make the attempt; but the man hasn't got it till the draft comes. You can't get blood out of a stone.'

'Let *him* go and pawn his match-box, then, and his watch and chain, and his engagement-ring. He must find it for you. Humphrey, tell him you must have it. Say it's—it's a matter of life or death. Think of what we've gone through already, trembling in case she suspected what a state we were in. The blessed relief it will be to be alone, and have no pretences to make! I shall feel newborn.'

'I'll see him to-day,' said Kent, catching her enthusiasm. 'He's often in a place in the Rue Saint-Honoré about four o'clock. What time is it now? Go in and ask her; she's the only one among us with a watch. Tell her mine has stopped—unless it has stopped too often.'

'Yours is u being cleaned." ' She disappeared for a second, and returned to say it was half-past three. 'Hurry, and you may catch him now,' she continued; 'and—and, Humphrey, be very firm about it, won't you? If he hasn't got it, make him give you a definite promise when you shall have it. To-day's Tuesday—say you *must* have it by Thursday, at the latest. And come back and tell me the result as quickly as you can. Wait; here's a kiss for luck.'

Kent kissed her warmly—she had never before seemed to him so companionable, such 'a good fellow,' as she did in this dilemma—and, picking up his hat and cane, he ran down the stairs, and made his way to the buffet in the Rue Saint-Honoré at his best pace.

Beaufort was not to be seen in the bar when he pushed back the door, nor was he in the inner room, but upon inquiring at the counter, Humphrey learnt that a gentleman there was now waiting for ' Billy,' who had made an appointment with him for a quarter to four. This was very lucky, and Kent took a seat on the divan and ordered a bock. Rolling a cigarette, he debated how he could put the matter strongly enough. He had expended so much eloquence of late without deriving any benefit from the interviews that he did not feel very hopeful of the upshot.

However, he was resolved that he would not fail for any lack of endeavor, and after Beaufort came in, a little before five, he sat watching him warily until the other man took his leave.

Beaufort expressed pleasure at seeing him, and asked him to have a drink. Kent did not refuse the invitation, for it would be easier to talk there in the corner than if he had to dodge by his side among the crowd in the streets, and he opened fire at once. He felt that his best card was absolute frankness, and explained the situation without reserve. Billy was entirely sympathetic. He romanced about Sir Charles, but was subsequently truthful. A draft from the Baronet might be delivered any morning or evening; but supposing it did not come in time, he would straighten matters out himself. 'He was damnably short, but he had arranged with a pal to jump for him. If he touched a bit to-morrow—of which there was, humanly speaking, no doubt—Kent should have a hundred and forty francs at night, and the balance of what was owing to him early in the week.' Damon would repay himself when the draft arrived.

Such devotion demanded another drink, and though this left him with less than a franc in his pocket, Kent went back to the pension in much better spirits, and feeling that he had good news to impart. Cynthia looked upon the tidings in the same light, and, as the nurse might learn from the servants that their rooms were to be vacated Saturday, they decided to speak to her without delay. Kent informed her that they were going to friends in the country, preparatory to settling in Paris for two years, and that she must make her preparations to return to England on Saturday morning. This gave a margin for delay on Beaufort's part. The young woman was greatly taken aback, and though she did not wish to stay, there was real feeling in her voice as she said how sorry she would be to leave the baby. She hung over the bassinet, and tears came into her eyes. Then Cynthia choked, and began to cry too, and Humphrey found her five minutes later with her face buried in her pillow, sobbing that she felt ashamed to have told lies to such a conscientious, nice-minded girl.

CHAPTER XVIII.

Kent's appointment with Beaufort next evening was for half-past eight, outside the Café de la Paix. The sous remaining after the conversation in the Rue Saint-Honoré had gone for a nursery requirement, so he was unable to sit down while he waited. His man was very late, and he walked to and fro before the stretch of tables on the Boulevard wearily for nearly an hour, tacitly confessing himself penniless to every idler in the crowd of chairs. When 'Billy' arrived at length, he began by saying that his news was 'not altogether unsatisfactory,' whereat Humphrey's heart sank within him, and when details were forthcoming, it appeared to him about as unsatisfactory as it could be. Stripped of the circumlocution by which the speaker sought to palliate its asperities, the news was that the completion of his business had been deferred till Saturday, and while he was confident of 'touching' then, he feared he could do nothing in the meantime. Kent took no pains to conceal his despondency. Seeing that he and Cynthia must leave the pension by noon, and get the nurse out of the way and into the train by ten o'clock in the morning, Saturday sounded as hopeless as Doomsday. He explained the urgency of the situation afresh, over a petit verre, and, after reflection, 'Billy' thought that, assisted by somebody else's signature, he could raise a hundred and fifty francs in another quarter. When he had had a second petit verre he was sure of it, and bade Humphrey meet him there again on the morrow at a quarter to two.

The morrow was Thursday, and when Kent descended about eleven, Madame Garin requested that the document her lawyer had drawn up should now be signed. After that had been done, and duly witnessed—one may do anything one likes in France excepting not pay—Kent told her that his wife wished her to view the contents of the baby's trunk before it was closed. As a matter of fact, it was rather a large one, and they were anxious to avoid the possibility of its giving rise to any remark in front of the servants in the hall at the moment of departure. She replied that such an examination was not necessary; it would be sufficient if they instructed their nurse to pack nothing that did not belong to the little one. This led to his informing her that the girl was quitting their service, and, to Kent's horror, Madame

Garin said frigidly:

'You know to what I have consented, monsieur? The things of the child, and for madame and yourself what is essential for one week. Besides that—nothing.'

'My God!' exclaimed Kent with a gasp; 'you don't mean to say you won't let the girl take her box?'

'But certainly I mean it,' she returned. 'What I have said. It is perfectly understood. I have already been too liberal.'

'But—but—heavens above!' he stammered,' the girl doesn't owe you anything! My wife is dismissing her, so as to keep our humiliation from her knowledge, madame. If you refuse to let her box go, the exposure is complete.'

The proprietress shrugged her shoulders:

'That is nothing to me,' she answered. 'Once more, for the little one and your own necessaries—that is all. There!'

This time Kent literally had not the courage to tell Cynthia what had occurred. He went out, and dropped on to the first bench he came to, sick in his very soul. What was the use now if Beaufort did bring him the money when they met? The girl could not be sent home without her luggage, and they would have to make a clean breast of the whole affair to her, and beg her to be tolerant with them. Cynthia had been very plucky; she had taken the disappointment of last night like a brick, and was at the moment full of hope for the result of the appointment at a quarter to two, but he felt that this unexpected blow would surely crush her. It was the death-stroke to their scheme, and entailed even more mortification than they had originally feared. He was at the foot of the Champs Élysées, and he sat staring at the passers-by with wide eyes—at the bonnes, big of bosom, with the broad, bright ribbons depending from their caps; at the children with their hoops, and the women in knickerbockers, flashing through the sunshine on their bicycles. Paris looked so light-hearted that woe was incongruous in it, but its air of gaiety seemed to turn his empty pockets inside out.

Now, it happened, about half an hour subsequent to his leaving the pension, that Cynthia decided to go with her baby and the nurse for a walk. Halfway down the stairs it was perceived that something had been forgotten, and she continued the descent alone. To her dismay, she saw the gaunt figure of Madame Garin standing at the office door, and as she came timorously down the last flight, the proprietress stood at the bottom with folded arms watching her. Perhaps her nervousness was very evident, perhaps the other had been sorrier for her than she had shown, but as the girl reached the hall the grim old woman moved toward her, and, with a gesture that said as plainly as words, 'Oh, you poor little soul!' took her face between her hands, and kissed her on the forehead.

'Listen,' she said; 'that's all right about your servant's box. Rest easy.'

Cynthia murmured a response to her kindness without realizing what was meant, but presently Kent became aware that among the stream of nurses and infants flowing up from the Place de la Concord were his own nurse and infant, and that Cynthia accompanied them. She recognized him before they reached the bench, and came over to him with surprise, and sat down, and then each spoke of what the other did not know.

'What a half-hour you have had!' she cried, when she understood. And he exclaimed:

'But the relief! Heaven be praised you came this , way!'

Their fate now hung once more on what 'Billy' Beaufort would have to say, and Humphrey sped to the rendezvous with restored energy. By the clock in the middle of the road it was twenty minutes to two when he reached the Café de la Paix, and, as before, it was impossible for him to sit down. He rolled a thin cigarette with a morse of tobacco that remained in his pouch, and paced his beat smoking. At two Billy' had not come. He had not come at half-past two. Kent doubted if this augured well for the tidings that were to be communicated, but fortified himself by remembering that he awaited a man who was rarely punctual for an appointment under any circumstances. Nevertheless, the later it became, the worse the chance looked, and when the clock showed that the hour was three, he began to lose both hope and patience. At a quarter to four there was still no sign of Beaufort. The watcher's feet ached, and the asphalt seemed to grow harder, and his boots to get tighter, with every turn. A little tobacco-dust yet lurked in the corners of his pouch—he thanked God to see it—and carefully, as if it had been the dust of gold, he shook it on to a paper, and assuaged his weariness and rage with another cigarette. Beaufort meant the success or the failure of their plan, and while he had but scant expectation of his turning up now, he dared not go away. He promised himself to go at four, but at four dreaded lest he might just miss him by five minutes, and determined to stop until a quarter past. Despair had mastered him wholly when a cab rattled to a standstill, and, forgetting the pain of his feet, he saw 'Billy' spring out. A glance at his face, however, assured him that he had waited to no purpose, and after 'Billy' had made many apologies, and recounted a series of misadventures, the point was that he was unable to obtain any money until Saturday afternoon.

Kent dragged himself home, and Cynthia and he sat and looked at each other with bowed heads.

'We're done,' said Humphrey, and that's all about it. I must tell the girl we can't pay our bills, and are turned out. But *she's* always been paid up to the present. What the devil is it to do with her, after all!'

'We *won't* be done!' declared Cynthia; 'we won't! Humphrey, if—if I wrote——' 'No, by Jove!' he said; 'I do bar that. We've kept our affairs from your people all along, and we won't give ourselves away now. . . . Do you mind very much?'

She did, but lied valiantly.

'You're perfectly right,' she answered; 'I was a coward to think of it.'

Kent squeezed her hand.

'You are a trump,' he said. Little woman, I've another idea—Turquand!'

She was breathless.

'Beautiful!'

'If Turquand has got it, Turquand will part; but—but has he? Anyhow it's worth trying. Let's see: I can catch the post; he'll get the letter in the morning; if he answered on the instant, we could have the money to-morrow night. Good Lord! how tired I am! Where's the stationery?'

He dashed off a note begging his friend to send him five pounds ten—or six pounds, if he could manage to spare so much—immediately, and then recollected that he could not buy a stamp. There was a ghastly pause; defeat confronted them again.

'There's nothing for it,' he said; 'I must go and ask the Garins. I'd post it without one if we were in England, but here—'

He went down, and left her walking about the room in excitement; but the bureau was shut, and he learnt that the ladies were out.

'Do you think nurse has got one herself?' he suggested, coming back, 'or—or twenty-five centimes?'

'She is out too. She took baby ten minutes ago. . . . Humphrey!'

'Another inspiration?'

'The bottles!' she cried triumphantly, pointing to the wardrobe; 'there are three.'

On an empty bottle of the wine which they sometimes boiled in the evening, two sous were refunded if a customer chose to give himself the trouble to take it back. They had had occasion to acquire the knowledge. Kent pulled the bottles out, and, after an abortive effort to make a parcel of them, caught up his letter and ran to the shop. He obtained thirty centimes, bolted to the post office, and saved the mail. Nothing could be done now but pray that Turquand might be in a position to oblige him.

In the meantime the young woman, all unconscious of the jeopardy in which it had been, packed her box calmly in the room behind their door, and prepared for her departure on Saturday morning with the composure of one whose ticket and wages were as good as in her purse. By Friday evening the box was corded and labelled, and when Kent and Cynthia entered, and beheld it so, suspense tightened its grip about their hearts.

The mail would not be delivered until about nine o'clock, and they sat with tense nerves, straining to hear Étienne's heavy footsteps on the landing when they judged the hour was near. They had not made arrangements yet where they would remove to on the morrow, and they spoke disjointedly of the necessity. Kent said it would be desirable to have two rooms in the new place also, for then they would be able to talk when the baby was asleep; in one room it would be awful. This assumption that the nurse would not be with them was followed by intensified misgivings, and in imagination both saw her sitting, on her tin box, with her bonnet on, while they faltered to her that, after all, she could not go.

'If it comes in the morning, you know,' he said, at the end of a long silence, 'it will be in time. Her train doesn't start till ten.'

'Y-e-s,' said Cynthia; 'she *expects* it to-night. . . . Is that someone coming up-stairs?'

'Nobody,' answered Kent, listening intently. . . . 'No; her train doesn't start till ten. I don't think, in point of fact, that we can look for it to-night. You see—'

'We needn't *give up* if it hasn't come when we go to bed.'

'No; that's what I mean. One must allow for—hark! . . . no; it's nothing—one must allow for him having to—'

Cynthia uttered a cry.

'It *is!* Come in—entrez—yes!'

Étienne appeared.

'A letter for monsieur!'

Kent snatched it from his hand; it was from Turquand. He tore it open. Postal orders for six pounds—brilliant and blue, the color of hope—dazzled their eyes. In pencil was scribbled:

'Here you are, sonny!—Yours ever, TRUK.'

Cynthia gave a hysterical laugh. They were saved.

Ten minutes later, after she had blessed Turquand and her eyes were dried, she opened the door of the adjoining room with great dignity, and said:

'By the way, nurse, I had better give you your money now. You can change enough postal orders for your ticket, you know, opposite the station.'

Then she came back radiant, and Kent said salvation must be celebrated, and, as their cab next day wouldn't cost ten shillings, they would go out on the Boulevards, and drink Turquand's health, and he could buy some tobacco on the way.

They were, compared with what their state of mind had been, supremely contented now that the danger of their servant witnessing their disgrace was over; and in the morning, when they had bidden her good-bye, and watched her drive away, and their misfortunes were nobody's business but their own, they drew such a breath of thanksgiving that they might just have inherited a fortune.

Cynthia's trunks, and Humphrey's, and his hat-box, and the dressing-case which somebody had given to the girl as a wedding-present, were drawn together in a corner of the room to be left behind; and, with intermittent attentions to the baby, they stored their toilet articles, and all the linen it would hold, in the handbag which was to be taken with them. The bassinet was already shut up, and sewn in its canvas wrapper; and the blankets, and such of the child's clothing as would not go in its box, had been packed downstairs in the perambulator. There was nothing further to do but to put the oatmeal, and the saucepan, and a few other infantile necessities, in a basket before they went; and, leaving Cynthia to collect these, Kent hastened out to obtain accommodation at an hotel. He went first to the one where they had stayed on their arrival, which was close at hand; but all the communicating rooms were occupied, and he was forced to try somewhere else. Jordan, who had done Turf Topics' for *The World and his Wife,* had once mentioned a place to him in the Rue de Constantinople as being cheap and comfortable, and he bent his steps there impatiently, regretting that they had not made their arrangements earlier. The mother had intended to see to the matter, so as to make sure that everything was healthy, and that there was not a draught from the window, and the rest of it, but, being so worried, she had put it off.

When he reached the address in the Rue de Constantinople, he was not favorably impressed. The terms were low, but the proprietress seemed so, too; and, though her manner was jovial enough, and the place looked clean, he hesitated to settle with her. After he had essayed an hotel in the Rue des Sœurs Filandières, at which he was obliged to own the rate was higher than he was prepared to pay, he decided that he had been hypercritical, and went back; but, as ill-luck would have it, the woman had let the apartments she had shown him five minutes after he had gone away. It was Mi-Carême, and the streets were beginning to be blocked by sightseers. He remembered that Cynthia would be sitting anxiously in the chaotic bedroom, wondering why he was gone so long; and, hurrying through the crowd, he returned to the Rue des Sœurs Filandières, and said he had changed his mind.

He was glad when he had done so. It was only for a week, perhaps for less; and there was a chambermaid who declared she would be willing to assist madame with the little one when she could, since madame found herself temporarily without a bonne. She had a cock eye, but seemed to have a good heart, and Kent assured her that any extra services she might render should not go unrewarded.

He regained the pension as quickly as possible, and instructed the waiter to send at once for a cab constructed to carry luggage on the roof. Cynthia was in a chair, with the baby on her lap, and looked up eagerly. On the table was a tray with luncheon, for which she would have been unable to go down, even if she had had the audacity; and she explained that Madame Garin, finding that she did not appear, had sent it up to her unasked. Cynthia had not been hungry, but that was very nice of her. They were not entitled to the déjeuner to-day.

The little basket was now ready, and Kent cast a gloomy glance at the impedimenta to be detained, questioning if he could manage to disburse more than three francs among the servants. Almost at the same moment there was a knock, and Étienne entered.

'I have called a cab,' he announced surlily. 'The mistress says there is no need for a voiture-en-galerie, because monsieur cannot take his trunks.'

The color fell from their faces, and for a second they remained mute and stock-still.

'Oh yes,' stammered Kent at last, 'we are leaving our heaviest trunks; we are going to send for them. But it is necessary, all the same. I will speak to Madame Garin.'

He found her erect in the hall in her favorite position, her arms folded across her flat breast. Her face was as pale as his own, and her eyes were angry. He looked at her amazed.

'I don't understand your message, madame,' he murmured. 'I "cannot have a voiture-en-galerie"? But it is for the things you have allowed!'

Not at all,' she exclaimed. 'What, then, do you suppose you will remove from my house, monsieur? You will take "what I have allowed"? But for that you need no voiture-en-galerie. My God!'

Pray speak quietly,' he implored. 'See, there's the baby-carriage over there; and there's the box; and bassinet! Of course they must go on the roof; we can't put them inside.'

Never in life,' she answered; 'I have not permitted you to take such things. All is said; I will not talk with you. I will carefully watch what you take, be certain! Fetch your things down.'

'Do you mean to say,' muttered Kent with dry lips,' that you refuse at the last moment to let us take the child's bassinet?'

'I have never consented to it. You lie!

'Good Lord!' he said. Isn't Mademoiselle Garin at home? I want to see mademoiselle—where is she?'

'My daughter is out. No; you will not take the bassinet, and you will not take the perambulator. You will take what you can carry in the hand, and nothing else.'

'The perambulator we must have,' he insisted. 'If you keep the bassinet, you must let us have the perambulator. The child's bedding and half its clothes are in it.'

'Never!' she repeated, and hugged herself determinedly.

'You have had my acknowledgment of the debt, and then you repudiate the agreement,' said Kent, trembling with passion. 'It is very honest, such behavior!'

' "Honest"?' she echoed. 'Ha! ha! ha! it was perhaps "honest" that you came here with your wife, and your little one, and your nurse, to live in my house, and eat at my table, and do not pay me for it. You are a thief, monsieur—you are a rogue and a thief!'

His fingers twitched to smash some man in the face.

'And the box?' he gasped, fighting for the ground inch by inch. 'Do you allow *that?*'

'Never, never, never!' Unlike her daughter, she did not speak English, and her yellow teeth were clenched upon her furious 'nevers.' 'Go and fetch your things, I say!'

He went up slowly with weak knees. Cynthia was standing in the middle of the room, pale and frightened. She had her hat on, and the baby, dressed for the streets, was clasped in her arms.

'She won't let the luggage go,' said Kent hoarsely. 'God knows what's come to her—*I* don't! Perhaps she thinks we were trying to get more out than was arranged; but she swears now she promised nothing. Come on; it's no good waiting. There's a cab at the door; let's go. I'll bring the small things down.'

'But—but what shall we do?' said the girl, with agitation. 'Humphrey, baby *must* have his things; it's impossible to do without them. Oh, this is awful!'

'Awful or not, we must put up with it. For Heaven's sake, let's get out of the damned place as quickly as we can! Where were the most important things put?'

'I don't know; they are everywhere,' she declared tremulously. 'I want the basket when we get in; but afterwards I want the box, and the bedding—I want everything of baby's. She must be a perfect wretch!'

He seized the basket and the hand-bag, and they descended the stairs, the baby crying loudly, and the tears dripping down the girl's cheeks as she strove ineffectually to hush it. Fortunately, the boarders had all gone to see the procession; but Madame Garin was still where Kent had left her, and Étienne, and the chambermaid, and the Italian waiter, suppressing a smile, stood watching about the hall. In an agony of shame that seemed as if it would suffocate her, Cynthia slunk past them to the cab, her head bent low over the child, and, the driver opening the door, fell, rather than sank, on to the seat. Kent made to follow her immediately, but this was not to be. Madame Garin, stopping him, demanded that he should display the contents of the bag; and then ensued a scene in which she was not a woman any longer, but a mouthing, shrieking harridan. Remonstrance was futile. Collars, stockings, handkerchiefs, slippers, were wrested from him piece by piece, and flung upon the office floor, while she loaded him with invective, and the servants nudged one another and grinned. Kent clung to the basket like grim death, but the hand-bag, when she threw it back at his feet at length, had been emptied of so much that he dreaded to guess what was left in it. He picked it up without a word, and, more dead than alive, strode through the hall, and leaped into the cab. Even then the ordeal was not quite over. As the man mounted to the box, a woman approached with whom they had become rather friendly in the house, and, seeing Humphrey getting in with the bag in his hand, came to the cab-window, and put amiable and maddening questions as to where they were going and when they were coming back. Kent was voiceless, but Cynthia leaned forward and replied, and, in the midst of his misery and abasement, he admired his wife for the composure she could contrive to simulate in such a moment.

On reaching the hotel it was necessary to invent some story to account for the absence of luggage, and Kent remarked as carelessly as he could manage that it would arrive on the morrow. He had ordered luncheon to be ready for them, not knowing that Cynthia would get any at the pension, and in the room intended for her and the boy a fire had been lighted. She flew to the basket, and boiled some oatmeal while Humphrey endeavored to soothe the mite, whose meal the disturbance had delayed, and who cried as if he would never be pacified any more. When the food was cooked at last, and something like order was restored, the lunch was allowed to be brought up, the filet overdone, and the potato-chips hard and stiff. However, after what they had gone through, it tasted to them delicious; and emboldened by the knowledge that there would be no bill to discharge for a week, Kent told the waiter to take away the claret which was included in the cost, and to bring them a bottle of burgundy. The wine put heart into them both, and as their fatigue passed, they drew their chairs to one of the windows, the doors of which had been laid back, and found courage to discuss the situation, while they gazed upon the little ornamental garden at the corner of the street below.

The baby slept, tucked in the quilt of the high big bed, and Cynthia said that by-and-by he must be put inside for the night in the frock he wore. Every minute revealed some further deficiency. They opened the bag, and they had neither brushes, nor sponges, and but a single comb. Tet she laughed again, for instinctively she realized that she was at the apex of her opportunity, that in such a crisis a wife must be either a solace or an affliction, and whatever happened to them during the rest of their lives, there would always be moments when he looked back at their experiences in Paris and remembered how she had behaved. As they sat there beside the open window, with the remainder of the bottle of burgundy between them, and a smile forced to her lips, the philistine might have been a Bohemian born and bred, and, as he had done in the cab, Kent silently marveled at her pluck.

By the time the dinner was laid their nerves were almost as equable as their speech. But this renewed calmness received a sudden shock. It was the rule of the proprietress, they were told politely, to ask for a deposit from strangers, and she would be obliged if Monsieur Kent would let her have twenty or thirty francs, purely as a matter of form.

Cynthia started painfully, and Kent refastened the paper of his cigarette before he answered.

'Certainly,' he said. 'Is thirty francs enough? I've only a check in my pocket, but tell madame I'll give it to her to-night.'

When the waiter had withdrawn, he and Cynthia looked at each other aghast. Their breathing-space had been brief. They knew that their having no luggage had made the woman suspicious of them, and that, unless they were to be turned out here as well, almost before they were in, the thirty francs must be found for her. Dinner had to be eaten, lest they should appear discomfited by the message; but the coffee was no sooner swallowed than Kent prepared to go out. Swearing to the girl he would obtain two or three louis before they slept, and reminding her that if Beaufort's expectations had been fulfilled he would now be in a position to let them have much more, he left her, and went to search for 'Billy' among his various haunts. The streets were thronged, and in his impatience the slowness of progression permitted by the mob infuriated him. All Paris seemed to have surged on to the Boulevards, filling the pavements and the road, and playing the fool. He pushed forward as best he could, and tried the Grand, in the faint hope either that the other might be dining there, or that something could be learned of his movements, but he was able to ascertain nothing. After all, he thought, it would have been wiser to have inquired at the bar in the Rue Saint-Honoré, and he now retraced his steps, pressing through the crowd in the direction of the Madeleine, impeded and pelted with confetti at every yard. At the corner of the Rue Canmartin a clown in scarlet satin thrust a pasteboard nose into his face. Kent cursed him and shoved him aside, and the buffoon span into the arms of a couple of shop-girls, who received him with shrill screams. The concourse appeared to grow noisier and more impenetrable each moment. It was the first Mi-Carême celebration the young man had witnessed, and with fever in his veins, and wretchedness in every fibre of him, this carnival confusion, with its horseplay and hindrance, was maddening. The gaslight sparkled with the rain of colored discs—they were pitched into his eyes and his ears as he struggled on—the asphalt was soft and heavy with them. When he reached the Madeleine things were better, but at the buffet Beaufort had not been seen since five o'clock. Somebody there believed he had an appointment at nine at the Café de la Paix. Kent plunged into the throng again, and fought his way steadily until the café was gained. The figure he sought was in none of the rooms. He proceeded in turn to all the principal cafés on the Boulevards, and in one he descried Jordan, whom he buttonhole eagerly. Yes, Jordan had met Beaufort this evening. Beaufort had said that later on he might go to the Moulin Rouge. This was a clue, at least, and Kent tramped on wearily until the glittering sails of the windmill revolved in view. The price of admission had been raised to-night, but he could not hesitate. The dancing had already commenced when he entered, and here two-thirds of the assembly ran about in carnival attire. A quadrille was going on, and in different parts of the ballroom three sets of dancers were enclosed by vociferous spectators, while the band brayed a tuneless measure. His gaze roved among the company vainly, and he fancied he could make his examination better when the sets broke up. The ill-dressed women, with their skirts and petticoats lifted to their shoulders, looked like factory hands as they lumped perfunctorily to and fro over the floor. Momentarily a mechanical smile would lighten the gloom of their excessive plainness; at long intervals, spurred to energy by the cries of the audience, one of them would give a kick higher than ordinary, or jerk a bit of argot to her vis-à-vis; but for the most part the performers appeared as spiritless as marionettes, and the air of gaiety and of interest was entirely confined to those who looked on.

It was midnight when Beaufort was encountered, and he was partially drunk. Humphrey caught him by the arm, and heard that his business had not been completed to-day, but was—once more—certain for 'next week.' Completed or not, however, Kent had to have money, and he made the circumstances of the case clear, a task which, in his companion's condition, was somewhat difficult. He said they were in new quarters, penniless, and the woman demanded a deposit; their luggage was detained at the pension, and could not be recovered unless he paid the Garins' bill, or, at all events, a substantial portion of it. In the meanwhile, they possessed literally nothing, and a good round sum on account of his claim was absolutely essential. 'Billy' was very grieved by the recital. He answered that he could lend him twenty francs, and repeated with emotion that 'he never deserted a pal.' In the end Kent extracted fifty, and, secretly relieved even by this, but dog-tired, dragged himself down the Rue Blanche toward the hotel.

Cynthia was waiting up for him, and reading a sheet of an old newspaper, that had lined one of the drawers, to keep herself awake. She learnt the result of his expedition with gratitude. They could now give the proprietress what she wanted, and out of the remaining louis would be able to buy a hairbrush and one or two other immediate necessities in the morning. She kissed him, and retired to the next bedroom, where she prayed that the child would allow her a good night, and Kent, whose fatigue was so great that it was a labor to undress, bade her call him if there should be any need for his assistance. It seemed but a few minutes afterwards when he was startled back to consciousness by the baby's crying, and, listening in the darkness, heard Cynthia moving about. Blundering to the door with half-opened eyes, he found her attempting to quiet the boy and to heat some food at the same time, and the weariness of her aspect made his heart bleed. The fire, which had been built up to last until the chambermaid's entrance, had gone out, and rocking the child on her lap with one hand, with the other the girl, semi-nude, held a saucepan over the flames of a candle. She rebuked him for coming in, for, 'poor fellow! he must be so tired.' He took the saucepan from her, and, fetching the candle from his own apartment, held the food to warm over the two, while maternity paced the floor. A clock in the distance told them the hour was three. At last a bubble rose upon the placid surface of the milk. The baby was fed, and coaxed to repose again, and, oblivious now of everything but the desire to sleep, they dropped upon their beds and slept.

CHAPTER XIX.

'Good-morning, monsieur. Here is your chocolate.'

Ah, thank you! Put it down. And madame, has hers been taken in?'

'Oh, madame had hers three hours ago. . . . Look, it is a beautiful day, monsieur!'

Then, when the waiter had let sunshine between the window-curtains and withdrawn, Kent would rise, and find Cynthia busy and hot, and either stirring more food over the fire or preparing the boy's bath. Afterwards she would carry him into the little enclosure opposite, and, what with her unfamiliarity with a nurse's duties and the makeshifts she was put to, it often seemed to her that this was the only time that she was able to sit down until evening came.

Their meals, as on the day of their arrival, were all served in Kent's bedroom; but just as he was taking his seat at the luncheon-table, the baby, who was feverish and fretful, would surely cry, and she would be obliged to call out that Humphrey was not to wait for her. For dinner, she made desperate efforts. Before this the child was bathed once more, and supposed to be already asleep; and then further oatmeal had to be stirred and carefully watched for five-and-twenty minutes, an operation that entailed burning cheeks and occasionally despair, for the saucepan had a habit of boiling over without the slightest warning, and requiring to be filled and stirred for twenty-five minutes again. When the task was accomplished, there followed a hurried attempt to make herself look cool and nice before the soup appeared, for Kent was apt to be irritable if she was not ready, and if she had succeeded, and the baby did not wake at the very last moment and prevent her going in after all, the dinner-hour was very agreeable.

Thanks to the chambermaid, they had been able to dispense with the tallow candles at sixpence each, and had obtained a lamp, which was much more cheerful.

The vin compris had turned out to be rather good, too, and after the appalling meals at the pension the cuisine struck them as quite first-rate. Not infrequently, when the coffee was brought in, they sent down for liquors, and their evenings, despite the worry of the day, and their ignorance where the money was coming from to pay the bill, were very jolly.

Beaufort's expectations were still unrealized. On Thursday he was certain 'things would be right on Saturday,' and on Saturday, with undiminished confidence, he repeated, 'Early in the week.' The proprietress of the hotel was a huge red woman, who had been a low-class domestic servant. The 'gracious service unexpressed' by which she had attained her present prosperity, the squinting chambermaid did not know, and she added, with a grin and a grimace, that it was really very difficult to conjecture it. The flaming countenance and belligerent eye of the 'missis' would assuredly have scared Kent from the door, under the circumstances, if she had been visible when he came there to arrange, and on Sunday night he slept uneasily. She delivered the bill next morning at nine o'clock, and at twelve sent him a message that she desired it settled at once. His interview with her was eminently unpleasant, and on Wednesday, when the fire for the child was not laid, and Cynthia inquired the reason, she learned that the woman had forbidden the servant to take up any fuel.

But for Nanette, their position would now have been untenable. She smuggled wood to the room, pacified her mistress by the recital of purely imginary telegrams she had picked up on Monsieur Kent's floor, and wound up by squeezing Cynthia's hand one afternoon, and offering to bring down some money she had saved out of her wages. This was the last straw. Cynthia put her arms round her neck and kissed her, and when Humphrey came home, and she told him what had happened, they both felt that to have to decline such a loan, and wish it could be accepted, was about the deepest humiliation to which it was possible people could sink. They were mistaken, but it was the lowest point which they themselves were called upon to touch. The day following, Beaufort wired, asking Humphrey to meet him at the Cabaret Lyonnais, and gave him a little dinner at a moderate price than which no one in the world need wish to eat a better. 'Billy' had not had his loan made yet— that, he said cheerfully, was certain for next week—but he had had a lucky night at baccarat, and after the bénédictine he pulled a bundle of notes out on to the table of the shabby restaurant, and, disclaiming any thanks, paid what he owed in full.

With a cigar in his mouth and delight bubbling in his veins, Kent jumped into a cab, and, rattling to the Rue des Sœurs Filandières, threw their receipt and the rest of his arrears into Cynthia's lap. She nearly dropped the baby with astonishment, and though they were unable to go out anywhere, it was perhaps the liveliest night they had spent in Paris. After adding together the Garins' account, and the cost of their return, and a present to Nanette, it was momentarily disconcerting to perceive how few of the notes would be left; but the relief was so enormous that their spirits speedily rose again, and, extravagant as it was, they ordered champagne, and invited the chambermaid in to drink some of it.

Kent recovered their luggage the next morning, and the morning after that they departed for London, having heard in the meanwhile that the Walfords could easily put them up until No. 64 was in readiness for them. The journey without a nurse was awkward, and though it had been essential to go to the Walfords' on arrival, Kent was secretly chagrined to reflect that explanations would have to be forthcoming of her absence. Compared with the crossing from Newhaven, this passage, to Cynthia, who had to remain, below all, the time, was a long voyage, and when at last they reached Victoria, she felt that she would have given a good deal to be going into the Grosvenor Hotel. Strawberry Hill was gained about nine o'clock, and Kent found the house a pathetic descent from The Hawthorns. Mr. and Mrs. Walford, however, were not unamiable, and as they did not refer to the nurse's absence otherwise than by inquiring presently how soon he expected to obtain another, he concluded that his wife had anticipated their surprise, and discounted it more or less dexterously in her letters.

'So the paper was a failure?' said Walford, when the excitement of the entrance had subsided. 'Oh, well, you will be able to get something to do here, I dare say, before long. What do you think of the place? Not so bad, eh?'

'Not bad at all,' said Kent—'very pretty! That was awful news, sir. I was infernally sorry to hear about it. Might have been worse, though—a good deal.'

'Ups and downs,' said the jobber; 'we'll get square at the finish. Grin and bear it, Louisa, old girl. You'll always have enough to eat.'

Mrs. Walford laughed constrainedly. She did not relish allusion to their reverses; it appeared to her insult added to injury.

'I don't think we've either of us much cause to grieve,' she answered. 'We're very comfortable here, don't you think so, Humphrey? There are such nice people in the neighborhood, Cynthia—people who move in the best society, and—hee! hee! hee!—we are making quite a fashionable circle; we are out almost every night. Well, I don't hear much about Paris. Did you have a jolly time?'

'We went everywhere and saw everything,' said Cynthia. 'Humphrey got no end of tickets, and—well, yes, Paris is lovely.'

'Why "well, yes"?'

'Well, of course, the paper's stopping was an anxiety to us, mamma. Naturally. How's Aunt Emily?'

'Emily writes us once a week, acknowledging the receipt of her allowance. How she is I really can't tell you; she says very little more than that she has received the money. She is living in apartments in Brunswick Square, and I believe she is very glad she is alone. *I* am, I can tell you. She has become very sour, Emily has.'

'Apartments in Brunswick Square aren't so remarkably cheap,' observed Kent. 'Aunt Emily must be expensive, mater?'

'Well, she has—er—one room. It's a nice large room, I understand, and quite enough for one person, I'm sure. There was no occasion for her to take a suite; she isn't going to give any parties.'

'No occasion whatever,' he rejoined. 'A bedroom can be very cosy when the lamp is lighted and there's a bottle of wine on' the table, can't it, Cynthia?'

'She won't have any bottles of wine. What are you thinking of?' said Mrs. Walford. 'Not but what she could afford wine,' she added hastily; 'but it doesn't agree with her; it never did. I suppose you know that Cæsar is still in Germany? He has settled there. If there **are** moments when I feel "out of it" in spite of the company we see in Strawberry Hill, it's when I read of the life that boy leads in Berlin. He is in a brilliant circle—most brilliant!'

'Cynthia told me he had a first-rate thing.'

'Capital thing!' affirmed Sam briskly. 'I tell you, he's going to the top of the tree. When he's my age Cæsar will be a big figure in Europe.'

Kent thought he was a fair size already, but replied briefly that he had been very fortunate.

Ability, my lad! He's got the brains! Do you know, Louisa, it was damn foolishness of us ever to persuade that boy to go on the stage? He was meant for what he is; we'd no right to divert his natural bent! He's in the proper groove, because his tendency was too strong for us. But we were wrong—I say we did very wrong! By George! he might never have made more than a couple of hundred a week among greasy opera singers all his life. What a thing!'

By dint of many midnight conferences with Louisa, he had almost succeeded in believing that he meant part of what he said.

'Are his prospects now so very wonderful, then, papa?' asked Cynthia, with wonder in her eyes. 'What is it he *is* doing? He has only a sort of clerkship, has he?'

'A clerkship!' shrieked her mother. 'How can you talk such ridic'lous nonsense? A clerkship!

Absurd! He is McCullough's right hand—quite his right hand. McCullough says he would be worth double the amount he is to-day if he had met Cæsar five years ago. He told your papa so last week—didn't he, Sam?'

'Certainly,' said the jobber, but there was less conviction in his tone. This was new, and he had not taught himself to try to credit it yet.

'He told your papa that Cæsar's power of—er—of gripping a subject was immense; he had never met anything like it. He consults him in everything; he doesn't take a step without asking Cæsar's opinion first; I don't suppose a young man ever had such an extraordinary position before. Ho, you don't know what you're talking about!'

Kent gave the conversation a twist by inquiring Miss Wix's number, as he and Cynthia would have to pay her a visit, and, on searching for her address, Mrs. Walford discovered, with much surprise, that she was not in Brunswick Square, after all, but that her one room was in a street leading out of it.

The mistake was unimportant, and Kent, moreover, had too much to occupy his mind to really think of making social calls on anyone but Turquand. To the office of *The Outpost* he betook himself next morning, and learnt that his friend was at Brighton until Monday. This did not look as if he had been pressed for his six pounds, but was otherwise disappointing. Humphrey proceeded from *The Outpost* to *the Daily News* and Athenæum offices, where he left his advertisements, and after that he had only to stroll through the streets, which looked very ugly and depressing to him after Paris, back to Ludgate Hill. Lunch was over when he reëntered the villa, but it had not been cleared away, and he found Cynthia in the dining-room alone, reading a novel. He noted, with as agreeable surprise as she could have afforded him, that it was the copy of his own which he had given to Mrs. Walford on their return from Dieppe. He looked at his wife kindly.

'Turk's not in town,' he said, helping himself to cold sirloin and salad; 'gone to Brighton for a day or two. I've paid for my advertisements; did you send off yours yet, to try to induce a general servant to accept a situation?'

Cynthia shook her head meaningly, and came across and took a chair beside him.

'Kemp is awfully nice with baby,' she said; 'she is upstairs with him now, and on the whole I've been thinking that we had better not hurry to get home again; we had better be a long time arranging matters, Humphrey. While we are here we haven't any expenses.'

Kent stared, and then smiled.

'This is abominable morality,' he said. 'Paris has certainly corrupted you, young woman. And, besides, your people would worry my life out with questions. Nothing puts me in a worse temper than being asked what my news is when I haven't any.'

'That's all very well, my dear boy, but we haven't any money. There's a quarter's rent overdue now, isn't there? and we should only have a month's peace before the tradespeople began to bother. I really think we ought to take two or three weeks, at all events, finding a girl; I do indeed. Mamma and papa would beg us to stop if they knew what a state we were in; it seems to me we ought to do it without giving them the—ahem—needless pain of listening to our confession.'

'You're very specious,' laughed Kent. The semi-serious conclusion might have been uttered by himself, and he approved the tone without recognizing the model. 'Has your mother noticed that you haven't got your ring on?'

'No. I couldn't tell her a story about it, and I'm praying that she won't. I've been envying you your trouser-pockets ever since we arrived. Don't take ale, Humphrey; have some claret, it will do you more good. If we sold our furniture—'

'What would it fetch at a sale?' he replied; 'and apartments would cost us more than the house. No; at any rate, we'll make ourselves welcome here for a week or so. And—well, let's hope the advertisements will turn up trumps. Then we shall be independent.'

The ***Daily News*** advertisement would appear on Monday.

CHAPTER XX.

IT was slightly disheartening to perceive how many other subeditors were open to offers, and he had the uncomfortable consciousness that his competitors' experience was probably a great deal wider than his own. He knew that for him to consider subediting a 'daily' was out of the question, and his chance of securing a post on a periodical seemed scarcely better on Monday morning, as he perused the 'Wanted' columns. Cynthia declared that his own advertisement 'read nicer than any in the list,' and that if she were an editor it would certainly be the one which attracted her attention; but Cynthia was his wife, and not an editor, and this encouraged him no more than Sam Walford's supposition at the breakfast-table, that he might obtain the management of 'a sound magazine.'

He went in the evening to Soho, and Cornelia's successor, in opening the door, informed him that Turquand had returned. The journalist was at the table, writing furiously, and Kent declined to interrupt him more than he had already done by entering. Turquand indicated the cupboard where the whisky was kept; and, picking up a special edition, Humphrey took a seat by the window, and read silently until the other laid down his pen.

'*That's* off my chest!' said Turquand, looking up after twenty minutes. 'Well, my Parisian, how do you carry yourself? Do you still speak English?'

'I can still say "thanks" in English,' answered Kent. 'I was devilish obliged to you, old chap. Here's your oof.'

'Rot!' said Turquand. 'Have you been "poping" anything to get it?'

'The "popping" took place before I wrote you. Don't be an ass; I couldn't take the things out if I didn't pay you back. Well, I've had some bad quarters of an hour in the pleasant land of France, I can tell you.'

'That's what I want you to do,' said Turquand. 'Let's hear all about it. What do you think of that whisky? Half a crown, my boy; my latest discovery. I think it's damned good myself.'

He listened to the recital with an occasional smile, and somehow, now the trouble was past, many of the circumstances displayed a comic side to the narrator. What was quite destitute of humor was the present, and when they fell to discussing this, both men were glum.

'I suppose you haven't been able to do anything with the novel?' Kent asked. 'Has it made the round yet, or does a publisher remain who hasn't seen it?'

'It came back last week from Shedlock and Archer. Oh yes; publishers remain. It's at Thurgate and Tatham's now; I packed it off to them on Friday. Farqueharsen was no use. I tried him, as you asked; he rejected it in a few days. I wrote you that, didn't I?'

'You did communicate the gratifying intelligence. Where has it been?'

Turquand produced a pocket-book.

'Farqueharsen, Rowland Ellis, Shedlock and Archer,' he announced. 'I must enter Thurgate and Tatham. I dare say you'll place it somewhere in the long-run; we haven't exhausted the good firms yet. By-the-bye, the front page has got a bit dilapidated; you'd better copy that out, and restore the air of virgin freshness, when Thurgate sends it home.'

'You expect he will, then?'

'I don't know what to expect, you seem so infernally unlucky with it. For the life of me, I don't know why it wasn't taken by Cousins, in the first instance. I looked it through again the other night, and I consider it's—I don't want to butter you, but I consider it's a great work; by Jove, I do!'

Kent glowed; he felt, as he had done all along, that it was the best of which he was capable, and praise of it was very dear to him, even though the praise was a friend's.

'I say, you know about your wife's aunt, I suppose?' said Turquand. 'What do you think of her?'

'She has left the Walfords, you mean? Who told *you?*'

'Miss Wix told me. But I didn't mean that departure; I meant her new one.'

'Not heard of any other departure of the lady's. What? Where's she gone to?'

'She has gone to journalism,' said Turquand, with a grin; 'the fair Miss Wix is a full-blown journalist! Don't your wife's people know? She's keeping it dark. She came to see me, and said her income was slightly inadequate, and she thought she could do some writing. Wanted to know if I could put her in the way of anything.'

Get out!' scoffed Kent. 'Did she really come to see you, though? Very improper of her!'

'Oh, Miss Wix and I always took to each other. I think she dislikes me less than anybody she knows. I'm not kidding you; it's true, honor bright.'

'What, that's she's writing?'

Turquand nodded. His face was preternaturally solemn, but his eyes twinkled.

'I got her the work,' he said; 'it just happened I knew of a vacancy.'

'Well, upon my soul!' exclaimed Humphrey. 'I wish you'd get some for *me.* Doesn't it just happen that you know of another?'

'Ah! you aren't so easy to accommodate. Miss Wix is a maiden, and her exes aren't large. She gets a guinea a week, and is affluent with it. It's a beautiful publication, sonny—a journal for young gals—and it sells like hot cakes. I tell you, *The Outpost* would give its ears for such a circulation.'

Kent stared at him incredulously.

'A journal for young girls!' he echoed. 'The acidulated Wix! Is this a fact, or delirium tremens?'

'Fact, I swear. She does the "Correspondence" page; she's been on it a fortnight now. She's "Aunt" something—I forget what, at the moment; they're always "Aunt" something on that kind of paper. The young gals write and ask her questions on their personal affairs. One says she is desperately in love with a gentleman of her own age—seventeen—and isn't it time he told her his intentions, as his "manner is rather like that of a lover"? and another inquires if "marriage between first cousins once removed is punishable by law." She calls them her nieces, and says, "No, my dear *Plaintive Girlie;* I do not think you need despair because the gentleman of your own age has not avowed his feelings yet. A true lover is shy in the presence of his queen; but, with gentle encouragement on your part, all will be well. I was so glad to have your sweet letter."'

'Miss Wix?'

'Miss Wix, yes. Her comforting reply to "Changed Pansy" the first week was quite a masterpiece, I assure you. And occasionally she has to invent a letter from a mercenary mother, and admonish her. The admonishments to mercenary mothers are estimated to sell fifteen thousand alone. You should buy a copy; it's on all the bookstalls.'

'Buy it!' said Humphrey; 'I'd buy it if it cost a shilling. What's it called? Well, I'm not easily astonished, but Miss Wix comforting "Changed Pansy" would stagger the Colossus of Rhodes. Does she like the work?'

' "Like" it? My boy, she execrates it—sniffs violently, and gets stiff in the back, whenever the stuff is mentioned. That's the cream of the whole affair. The disgust of that envenomed spinster as she sits ladling out gush to romantic schoolgirls makes me shriek with laughter in the night. I've got her name now—she's "Auntie Bluebell." "Auntie Bluebell's Advice to our Readers" in ***Winsome Words.*** One penny weekly.'

Kent began to yell himself, and but that the bookstalls were shut when he took his leave, he would have carried a copy home with him. He told the news to Cynthia, and she went into such hysterics that Sam Walford, underneath, turned on his pillow, and remarked gruffly to Louisa that he didn't know what Cynthia and Humphrey had got to be so lively about, he was sure, considering their circumstances, and he was afraid that Humphrey was 'a damn improvident Bohemian.'

Their mirth was short-lived, unfortunately. The ***Daily News*** advertisement was productive of no result, and the solitary communication received after the issue of the Athenæum ***was a circular from an employment agency. The outlook now was as desperate as before the post on*** The World and his Wife turned up, and their pecuniary position was even worse than then. When they had been at Strawberry Hill a week, moreover, the warmth of the Walfords' manner toward their son-in-law had perceptibly decreased; and though Kent did not comment on the difference in his conferences with Cynthia, he knew that she was conscious of it by her acquiescing when he declared that they had been here long enough.

At this stage he would have taken a clerkship gladly if one had been obtainable with a salary sufficing for their needs; and after they had returned to Leamington Road, and had temporized with the landlord, and sold a wedding present for some taxes, and were living on credit from the tradespeople, he began to debate if the wisest thing he could do would not be to drown himself, and relieve Cynthia's necessities with the money accruing from his life policy.

The idea, which primarily presented itself as an extravagance, came, by reason of the frequency with which it recurred to him, to be revolved quite soberly, and he wondered if Cynthia would grieve much, and if, when his boy could understand, she would talk to him of his ' papa,' or provide him with a stepfather. He did not, in these conjectures as to the post-mortem proceedings, lose sight of 'The Eye of the Beholder,' and he devoutly trusted it would see the light after he was dead, and make so prodigious a stir that the papers disinterred its history, and the names of the publishers who had refused it were held up to obloquy and scorn.

He was walking through Victoria Street toward the station one afternoon, and mentally lying in his grave while the world wept for him, when he was brought to an abrupt standstill by a greeting. He roused himself to realities with a start, and found that the gray-gloved hand which waited to be taken by him belonged to Mrs. Deane-Pitt.

'How d'ye do, Mr. Kent? I thought at first you meant to cut me,' she said.

'I beg your pardon, I didn't see. It's awfully stupid of me; I'm always passing people like that.'

'You've returned, then,' she said. 'For good?'

'Oh yes; we live in town, you know—in the suburbs, at least'

'You told me,' she smiled. ' "Battersea."'

'So I did. "Battersea" is Streatham, but that's a detail.'

The mechanicalness of his utterance passed, and animation leapt back in him as he recovered from his surprise. The sun was shining, and the sequins of her cape were iridescent. There was a bunch of violets in it. His impression embraced the trifles with a confused sense that they formed a delightful whole—the smart, smiling woman in the sunshine, the deep purple of the flowers, which seemed to gain a touch of sensuousness in her costume, and the warmth of her familiar tones.

'So you come to Victoria every day, and you haven't been to see me,' she said. When did you leave Paris?'

'I've done nothing,' he replied. 'Of course you know *The World and his Wife* is dead, Mrs. Deane-Pitt? When did I leave? Oh, soon after the funeral.'

' I trust you've recovered from the bereavement,' she laughed. 'Are you on anything here?'

'Not yet. Editors are so blind to their own interests.'

'Well.' She put out her hand again, and repeated her number. 'When will you come in? I'm nearly always at home about five. Good-bye; I'm going to the Army and Navy, and I shall be late.'

Kent continued his way cheerfully. The brief interchange of conventionalities had diverted his thoughts, and his glimpse of this woman who took her debts with a shrug, and had candidly adapted her ideals to her requirements till the former were all gone, acted as a fillip to him. She typified success, of a kind, and in a minute he had seemed to acquire something of her own vigor. It made him happy, also, to observe that the manner of their parting had had no sequal; and, in recalling the mood in which he had walked through the Champs Élysées afterwards, he decided that he had been extremely stupid to attach so much importance either to that or to their acquaintance. She was an agreeable woman toward whom his feeling was a friendship he had once been in danger of exaggerating; he should certainly call upon her at the first opportunity. It was quite possible she might be able to tell him something useful too.

Before he fulfilled his intention, an unlooked-for development occurred, however. The office of the agent who had endeavored to find him a tenant was on the road to the station, and a day or two later, as he passed the door, the man ran out after him, and asked if he was willing to let No. 64 still. Kent replied shortly that the opportunity had presented itself too late; but after he passed on, the gentle flow of detail the other had let fall caused him to reflect. The house was wanted at once by some people who had considered it previously. They now made an offer of three and half guineas a week for a period of six or twelve months. It appeared to Kent he had been very idiotic in dismissing the suggestion off-hand. With three and a half guineas a week, less the rent and taxes, he could send Cynthia for a few months to the country, which was exactly what she stood in need of; and though he could not leave London himself, he could retain a pound, and shift alone somewhere till he found a berth and they rejoined him.

Cynthia and he discussed the idea lengthily, and while she was opposed to the separation, she agreed that it would be very unwise of them to refuse to let the house. She said that they might all live together in apartments on the money, and that, although the fresh air and peace would be delicious if Kent were with her, she thought she would rather stay with him in London than go away by herself. This point was debated a good deal, but there was much against it. It was absurd to deny that their anxieties, and the restraint imposed by her charge of the baby, had told upon her health, and in a little village where living was cheap she would not only recover her roses, but as soon as he earned a trifle might be able to afford a nurse-maid. If they took lodgings together, on the other hand, town would be impossibly dear, and they must be reconciled to going to a suburb—twice as expensive as the country, however—where there would be, again, the item of railway-fares. By himself Humphrey could get a top bedroom in Bloomsbury for the same sum that he now spent on his third-class tickets.

The logic was inexorable, and the only further question to decide was where she should go. She recollected that a few years back Miss Wix had been sent to a cottage in Monmouth to recoup after an attack of influenza. The spinster had spoken very highly of it all—of the picturesque surroundings, the attention she had received, and the cosy accommodation. If Miss Wix praised it, there could be little to complain of, surely. As to the terms, Cynthia knew what her aunt had been given to spend; they were so moderate that they were ridiculous. She determined to write immediately, and ask her if she remembered the address.

On second thoughts, though, she declared she must ask her in person. She had not paid her a visit yet, nor had Kent, and an inquiry by post would render their remissness ruder. They went the following morning, having looked in on the agent, and informed him they were prepared to accept the offer, and to give up possession at the end of the week. The payments were of course to be made monthly in advance.

Miss Wix resided in Hunter Street, W. C., and they found that in her improved circumstances she now boasted two rooms. The parlor she had acquired was chiefly furnished by a large round table, a number of Berlin-wool antimacassars, and a wax work bouquet under a flyblown shade, and at the table, which was strewn with manuscripts, the spinster sat, sourly engaged upon her 'Advice' for **Winsome Words.** She welcomed them politely, and offered to have some tea made if they would like it, but, as it was one o'clock, they said that they were not thirsty. The request for a five-years-old address evidently perturbed her very much, but after a rummage behind the folding doors, she emerged with a note book in which it was entered, and, to mollify her, Cynthia referred again to her new pursuit, and reiterated congratulations.

'Mr. Turquand told Humphrey, or we should never have known, Aunt Emily. Why have you kept it so quiet? We were delighted by the news; I think it is very clever of you indeed.'

'There is nothing to be delighted about,' said Miss Wix. 'I kept it quiet because I did not wish it known—a very sufficient reason. Mr. Turquand is much too talkative.' 'I think you ought to be very proud,' observed Kent—'a lady journalist! May I—am I allowed to look at some of the copy?'

'As I can't prevent you seeing it whenever you like to spend a penny,' said Miss Wix bitterly, 'it would be mere mockery to prevent you now.'

'You underrate your public,' he murmured. **'Winsome Words** has an enormous circulation, I hear.'

'Among chits,' exclaimed the spinster, with sudden wrath—'among chits and fools. Smack 'em and put 'em in an asylum. Since you wish it, read it aloud. Cynthia shall hear what I have to do in order to live. If Louisa weren't your mamma, my dear, I'd say that it's a greater shame to her than to me, I would. If she weren't your mamma, I'd be bound to say that.'

'Well, let's hear,' said Humphrey quickly. 'Where is it? Now, then—what's this? Oh, *Miserable Maidie!* "Yours is indeed a sad story, *Miserable Maidie,* because you seem to have no one to turn to for help and counsel. I am so glad you resolved to come to your Auntie Bluebell, and tell her all about it. So you and your lover have parted in anger, and now you are heartbroken, and would give worlds to have him back? Ah, my dear! it's the old, old story—" '

'That'll do,' snapped Miss Wix. ' "The old, old story"! I'd "old story" the sickly little imbecile if I had her here!' She sat bolt upright, her eyes darting daggers, and her pink-tipped nose elevated and disdainful. 'Is it necessary to go on, do you think?'

'I think so,' said Kent. 'I see there's one to *Anxious Parent.* May I—er—glance at your advice to *Anxious Parent?* "My dear friend, were you never young yourself? And didn't you love your little Ermyntrude's papa? If so, you can certainly feel for two young things who rightly believe that love is more valuable than even a good settlement. Let them wed as they wish, and be thankful that Ermyntrude is going to have a husband against whom you can bring no other objection than that he is unable to support her." '

'I'm a sensible woman, Cynthia,' said Miss Wix, quivering; 'and for me to have to write that incomes don't matter, and sign myself "Auntie Bluebell," is heavy at your mother's door.'

Her mortification was so evidently genuine that Kent gave her back her copy, with replies to *A Lover of 'Winsome Words'* and *Constant Daffodil* unread, and as soon as was practicable he and Cynthia rose and made their adieux. The apartments in the cottage proved to be vacant, and as the references of the incoming tenants were satisfactory, and the inventory was taken without delay, there was nothing in the way of the migration being effected by the suggested date. Cynthia had proposed that her husband should try to obtain his old bedroom at Turquand's, where he could have the run of a sitting-room for nothing, and this idea was adopted with the approval of all concerned. Humphrey saw her off at Paddington, and told her to get strong, and the close of the week that had opened without a hint of such an occurrence saw Cynthia living with her baby in Monmouth, and Kent reinstalled in his bachelor quarters in Soho.

CHAPTER XXI.

IT was very jolly to be back with Turquand. The earliest evening, while they smoked with the enjoyable consciousness of there being no last train to catch, was quick with the sentiment of their old association, and after a letter arrived from Cynthia, in which she clapped her hands with pleasure, the respite was complete. Kent had been impatient to hear how the place struck her, and she wrote that she had been agreeably astonished. The cottage was roomier than she had expected, and beautifully located. It was furnished very simply, of course; but there was a charm in its simplicity and freshness. The landlady was a rosy-cheeked young woman who had already 'fallen in love with baby,' and overwhelmed her with attentions. 'If you do not see what you want, please step inside and ask for it.' Kent smiled at that; it was a quotation from one of the Streatham shop-windows. Also there was quite a respectable garden, which her bedroom overlooked. 'There are fruit-trees in it— not my bedroom, the garden—and a little, not too spidery, bench, where I know I shall sit and read your answer when it comes.' She wrote a very happy, spontaneous sort of letter, and Kent's spirits rose as he read it. There was the rustle of dimity and the odor of lavender in the pages, and momentarily he pictured her sitting on the bench under the fruit-trees, and thought that it would be delightful if he could run down one day and surprise her there.

It was very jolly to be back with Turquand, albeit his satisfaction, perhaps, was a shade calmer than he had fancied it would be during the first year of his married life, when he recalled his lost paradise. It was convenient, moreover, to be in town, and a relief to feel that the unsettled accounts with the tradespeople round Leamington Road were, at least, not waxing mightier. Nevertheless, he missed Cynthia a good deal; not only in the daytime when he was alone, but even in minutes during the evening when he was in Turquand's company. It was curious how much he did miss her—and the baby: the baby, whose newest accomplishment was to stroke his father's cheek, and murmur 'poor' until the attention was reciprocated, when he bounded violently, and grew red in the face with ridiculous laughter. Soho, too, though it saved him train-fares, soon began to appear as distant from a salary as Streathain. Turquand remained powerless to put any work in his way, and, despite his economies and the cheapness of Monmouth, Humphrey was dismayed to perceive that his expenses were heavier than they were entitled to be. He was encroaching on the money laid aside for the landlord and the rates, and, if nothing turned up, there would speedily be trouble again. The butcher who had supplied No. 64 had been to the agent for Mr. Kent's address, and presented himself and his bill with no redundancy of euphemism. When another advertisement had been inserted ineffectually, the respite was over and anxiety returned.

Kent had not called on Mrs. Deane-Pitt yet, and on the afternoon following his interview with the butcher he paid his visit to the lady. He was very frank in his replies to her questions. He did not disguise that it was imperative for him to secure an appointment immediately, and when she agreed with him that it was immensely difficult, instead of answering that it was likely some opening might be mentioned to her, his face fell. He at once felt that it behoved him to deprecate his confidences.

'You must forgive my boring you about my affairs,' he said. 'And what are you doing, Mrs. Deane-Pitt? Are you at work on another book now?'

'I've a serial running in *Fashion,*' she said; 'and they print such ghastly long installments that it takes me all my time to keep pace with them. You haven't bored me at all; I'm very interested. A post on a paper is a thing you may have to wait a long time for, I'm afraid. You see, you aren't a journalist really, are you? You're a novelist.'

'I'm nothing,' said Kent, with rather a dreary laugh. 'For that matter, I wouldn't care if it weren't on a paper. I'd jump at anything—a secretaryship for preference.'

'Secretaryships want personal introductions; they aren't got through advertisements.' She hesitated. '*I* can tell you how you might make some money, if you'd like to do it,' she added tentatively. 'It's between ourselves, Mr. Kent. If it doesn't suit you, you'll be discreet?'

'Oh, of course,' said Kent with surprise. 'But I can promise you in advance that *any* means of making some momey will suit me just now. What are you going to say?'

She looked at him steadily with a slow smile.

'How would you like to write a novel for me?' she asked.

He did not instantaneously grasp her meaning.

'How?' he exclaimed. 'Do you mean you are offering to collaborate with me?'

'I can't do that,' she said quickly. 'I'm sure you know I should be delighted, but I shouldn't get the same terms if I did, and I haven't the time. That's just it. I'm obliged to refuse work because I haven't time to undertake it. No; but it might be a partnership as far as the payment goes. If you care to write a novel, I can place it under my own name, and you can have—well, a couple of hundred pounds almost as soon as you give it to me. I can guarantee that. You can have a couple of hundred pounds a week or two after it is finished, whether I sell serial rights or not.'

She took a cigarette out of a box on a table near her and lit it, a shade nervously. Kent sat pale and disturbed. That such things were done, at all events in France, he knew, but her proposal startled him more than he could say, or than he wished to say. His primary emotion was astonishment that Mrs. Deane-Pitt had had the courage to place her reputation in his hands, and then, as he reflected, an awful horror seized him at the thought of a year of his toil, of effort and accomplishment, going out for review with another person's name on it. The pause lasted some time.

'I don't much fancy the idea,' he said at last slowly, 'thanks. And it wouldn't assist me, either. I want money now, not a year hence.'

'A year hence!' she murmured. 'A year hence would be no use to *me,* but you could do it in a month. Pray don't mistake me. I'm not anxious to get any kudos at your expense; I don't want you to do the kind of thing I suppose you have done in this novel of yours that's making the round now; I don't want introspection and construction, and all that. All I want is to buy shoes for my poor little children, and what I suggested was that you should knock off a story at your top speed—good, bad, or indifferent. I don't care a pin what it's like; only turn me out a hundred thousand words.'

'A hundred thousand words,' cried Kent, 'in a month! You might as well suggest my carrying off one of the lions out of Trafalgar Square! "The Eye of the Beholder" isn't a hundred thousand words, and I worked at it day and night, and then it took me a year! Besides, that's another thing; it *is* going the round. The story mightn't be any use to you if I did it.'

'I can place it,' said Mrs. Deane-Pitt with emphasis. 'Don't concern yourself about its fate, my friend; your responsibility will be limited to writing it. Your book took a year? I've no doubt you considered, and corrected, and spent an afternoon polishing a paragraph. Supposing you take six or seven weeks, then. Do you mean to say you couldn't write two thousands words a day?'

'No, I don't believe I could—not if you offered me the Mint!' said Kent.

'But you can put down the first that come into your head,' she declared, 'and leave them. *Anything* will do. Naturally, it would be no use to me if you wrote "Mother Hubbard went to the cupboard" over all the pages, but any trivial thing in the shape of a story, I assure you, I can arrange for at once. Indeed, it *is* practically arranged for; it only remains for you to give it to me.'

She puffed her cigarette silently, and the young man mused. The plan was repugnant to him, but if, as she said, anything would serve—well, perhaps he *could* do it in the time; he did not know. Two hundred pounds would certainly be salvation, and, for seven weeks' work, a magnificent reward.

'I'll tell you,' she continued, after a few moments: 'if you liked to do me a short tale or two now and again, we should have money from those in the meanwhile. I don't want to persuade you against your convictions, if you have any, but our business together would pay you better than an appointment, even if you found one; and—though that's nothing to do with it—it would be a tremendous benefit to me as well. See, with our two pens we can produce double the work, and we share the advantage of the popularity I've gained.'

'Oh, I quite appreciate the pecuniary pull,' he answered. 'I could hardly write short stories while I was fagging at a novel, though.'

'I think myself one goes back to the novel all the fresher for the break,' she said; 'but, of course, everybody has his own system of working. Would you care to write me a couple of three-thousand-word stories first? We can discuss the book later. If you let me have two tales to-morrow night, I could give you five guineas each for them on Saturday.'

'To-morrow is out of the question. You don't realize how slowly I write, and I haven't the motives.'

'Say the next day—say by Thursday. But it must be by then. The man goes out of town on Saturday, and I want him to read them before he goes. If *I* can have the manuscripts on Thursday, **you** can have ten guineas Saturday night.'

'It's a very good offer,' said Kent. 'You must get a royal rate.'

'Well, I couldn't always offer you so much, but, then, I don't often want them quite so long. Two or three thousand words, and to end happily, for choice. Not too strong. If they will illustrate well, all the better, but you needn't give yourself any trouble on that score—it's the artist's affair.'

'I'll do them,' said Humphrey; 'I suppose I must 'make an attempt to imitate your style?'

'It isn't necessary. I generally begin with a very short sentence, like "It was midday," or "It rained"; you might do that, but I really don't know that it matters. Mr. Kent!'

'Yes,' he said.

'This is a confidential matter; I rely on your honor not to mention it to a living soul, of course! I don't know how much married you are, but I depend on you not to tell your wife. It would ruin me if it came out.'

He assured her she might trust him, and, having pledged himself to the lighter task, he resolved on his way home that he would undertake the heavier, too. She did not want a year of his best work—he doubted if he could contemplate that, if refusal meant Strawberry Hill for Cynthia and the baby, and the workhouse for himself—she asked only a few weeks of his worst. Money was indispensable; he must make it in whatever way he could. A ghost, eh? He was rising finely in the career of literature. His first novel had received what was almost the highest possible cachet; his second was 'declined with thanks'; and now no mode of livelihood was left him but to be a ghost. His throat was tight with shame; there were tears in it.

That passed. He reflected that with two hundred pounds in his pocket he would be able to sit down to another novel on his own account, with which he might be luckier than with 'The Eye of the Beholder.' What were a few weeks compared with two hundred pounds? Mrs. Deane-Pitt must have thought him rather a fool to hesitate. Practical herself, indeed! But—well, for all that, it was rather fascinating to feel that so intimate a confidence was going to subsist between them. She had been a trifle nervous, too, as she took that cigarette; he hoped he had not been a prig. She was very nice; it distressed him to think that she had been afraid of him even for a second. Two hundred pounds? He wondered what share it was—half, or more than half, or less. With a woman, however, he could not go into that. His admission that five guineas sounded a lot to him for a three-thousand-word story had probably been injudicious, and must have seemed rather ignorant besides. Well, that couldn't be helped. And he would be glad if the partnership paid her well. Whatever terms she obtained, she must be perfectly aware that her offer was a liberal one to a man in his position, and he was grateful to her. He felt it again; she had been 'nice.' He began to revolve a plot for the first of the feuilletons, and by the time he reached home he had vaguely thought of one. When Turquand came in, it had shaped. Saying that he had work to do, Kent left him, and went upstairs. He drew a chair to the table, and sat down and wrote—slowly, painfully. The man was an artist, and he could not help the care he took. He sneered at himself for it. Mrs. Deane-Pitt had impressed on him that anything would do, and here he was meditating and revising as if it were a story to submit to the most exclusive of the magazines in his own name. He dashed his pen in the ink, and threw a paragraph on the paper, but he could not go on. The consciousness of that slip-shod paragraph higher up clogged his invention, so that he had to go back to it and put it right. Presently a touch of cheerfulness crept into his mood. That was well said. Yes, she would praise that! The pride of authorship possessed him, and he wrote with pleasure, and at two o'clock, when a third of the tale was achieved, he went to bed feeling exhilarated.

It was no easy duty to him to complete both stories by Thursday morning, and, confronted by the necessity for making Turquand a further excuse for retirement, he almost wished he were living alone now. He was vastly relieved that the other accepted his allusions to something that would keep him busy for a month or so with no apparent perception of a mystery. After the first inevitable question was shirked, the journalist put no more, and behaved as if the explanation had been entirely explicit. Neither Kent's friendship, nor his admiration for him, had ever been so warm, as while he decided that Turquand's experience must lead him to suspect something like the truth, but enabled him to conceal the suspicion under his normal demeanor.

With Cynthia the ghost was less fortunate, though he barely divined it by her answer. He told her as much as he was free to tell: he wrote that he had work on hand at last, and they would have ten guineas on Saturday, and a large sum in a couple of months. Where the stuff would appear, he could not say without ft false-hood, and he trusted she would not be curious on the point. The reservation, he regretted, gave to his tone an aloofness he did not design, and Cynthia refrained from inquiring; but she was hurt. She felt that he might have imparted such intelligence a little more enthusiastically, at a little greater length. Did he suppose her interest was limited to the payment? Was she only held sympathetic enough to mind the baby when they were obliged to discharge the nurse? Nowhere-turned to work, her husband was going to treat her as a child again, just as he had done when he was engaged on his book. She did not perceive that, while he had been writing the book, she had occupied the position most natural to her; she did not detect that the attitude in which she recalled it was a new one. It was, however, the attitude of a woman; the hidden chagrin and urbanity of her reply was a woman's. These things were part of a development of which, while they had remained together, neither she nor the man who had missed her had been acutely aware.

CHAPTER XXII.

MRS.DEANE-PITT paid Kent the ten guineas a few days after the Saturday on which she had expected to receive the editor's check, and she made no secret of being delighted with the two tales. They were written upon rather original ideas, and after she had had them typed, and read them, she talked to him about them with the frankest appreciation possible. Kent almost lost sight of his regret that they were not going to appear under his own name, as the lady expressed her approval, and declared enthusiastically that to call them 'excellent' was to say too little. He found it very stimulating to her hear his work praised by Mrs. Deane-Pitt, especially as it was work done for her. Although she had professed to be careless of the quality, it was not to be supposed that she would not rather sign good stuff than bad, and the warmth and gaiety of her comments took the sting from the association, and lent it a charm.

When he commenced her novel, it was with the discomfiting consciousness that the breakneck speed imposed on him would prevent the laborer being worthy of his hire. He was too hurried to be able to frame a scenario, and neither he nor the lady who was to figure as the authoress had more than a hazy idea of what the book was going to be about. He had mentally sworn to keep his critical faculty in check, and to produce a chapter of two thousand words every day—if he did not bind himself to the accomplishment of a fixed instalment daily, the book would not be finished in double the time at his disposal—and he rose at seven, and worked till about midnight, on the day on which Chapter I. was done. He had corrected in a fashion as he composed, and he did not read it through when he put down his pen—that would be too disheartening. He remembered the opening chapter of 'The Eye of the Beholder,' and, contrasted with the remembrance, these pages he had perpetrated appeared to him puerile and painful. He folded them up, and posted them to Mrs. Deane-Pitt with a note before he slept.

'Whether you will want the novel after you have seen this, I don't know,' he wrote; 'I am sending it to you to ascertain. It is a specimen of the rubbish the thing will be if I have to turn it out at such a rate. I will call, on the chance of your being in, tomorrow afternoon.'

He found her at home, and she welcomed him with a humorous smile.

'You have read it?' asked Kent, with misgiving.

'Yes; I've read it,' she said. 'Violet! Pray don't look so frightened of me!'

'Why "violet"? Well?'

'The type of modesty. Well, what's the matter with it? It will do all right.'

Kent drew a breath.

'I'm glad to hear you say so. I am bound to confess I thought it very slovenly myself.'

'Oh, nonsense!' she said. 'Have you gone on with it?'

'No; I waited for your verdict. I thought you might call me names, and cry off. I'll go on with it now, though, like steam.'

'Do. I suppose you couldn't manage a five-thousand-word story for me this week, could you? It would be good business.'

He stared ruefully.

'No, indeed, Mrs. Deane-Pitt; not if I'm to write a chapter a day.'

'Oh! the chapter a day, please, if you can't do the story too. Get the novel done at the earliest moment possible; that's the chief thing. You will, won't you, Mr. Kent? I should be so grateful to you if you finished it in six weeks.'

'I promise to finish it as quickly as I can,' said Kent. Even if I didn't care to serve you, I should do that, for my own sake. When I get two hundred pounds, I shall be at the end of my troubles.'

'Happy man!' said Mrs. Deane-Pitt. 'Would that two hundred pounds would see the end of mine! And as you do want to serve me, you'll do it even more quickly than you can?'

'Or try.'

'That's very nice of you. I wonder how true it is. One of the answers one has to make, isn't it? Then when you're behind with the work, and your wife wants to be taken out somewhere, you'll nobly remember there's a miserable woman in Victoria Street depending on you, and persuade madame to go with a sister, or a cousin, or an aunt? You'll say to yourself "Excelsior!" and other improving mottoes, meaning "Loyalty forbids"?'

'I'll say "Loyalty forbids" when I want to go out by myself,' said Kent; 'my wife's in the country.'

'Tant mieux! if it isn't shocking,' she laughed. 'I'm afraid a woman on the spot would prove too strong for me. Am I grossly selfish? Poor boy who has got no wife!'

She looked at him as she had looked across the supper-table in the Avenue Wagram. He could not think of anything to say in reply of a nature which he desired to say, and exclaimed abruptly:

'Oh, you may rely on me, Mrs. Deane-Pitt; I'll never go anywhere; I'll be a hermit. By the way, you don't know I'm in Soho now. Perhaps I'd better give you the address?'

'Certainly,' she said; 'I may want to write to you. The hermit of Soho! Well, when you've been good, and done penance thoroughly, hermit, you may come and see me sometimes; I'll allow you that distraction. Come in whenever you like, and you can tell me how the thing is going; any afternoon you please at this time. And don't come in trembling at me any more. I don't expect you to write me a master-piece in six weeks, I assure you.'

Kent kept his word to her doggedly, and, although he continued to rise early, he was seldom free to join Turquand until about nine o'clock in the evening. When the chapter was done, he would go downstairs, and light another pipe, and Turquand would put away his book or his paper without any indication of curiosity whatever. With a woman such a state of things would have been impossible; but Turquand's manner was so unforced that by degrees Kent came to own that he was tired, or to make some other allusion to his labors quite freely. Nor did the other once say to him, 'Well, but what is it you're doing?' On the days upon which he called on Mrs. Deane-Pitt, it was later still before Humphrey could ensconce himself in the parlor; the temptation to go to her, however, was more than he could resist. He realized very soon that she had an attraction for him which was not in the least like friend-ship, and which he could never term 'friendship' any more. In moments, as he sat writing in his shabby bedroom under the tiles, the thought of her would suddenly creep in to him, and beat in his pulses till he was assailed by a furious longing to be in her presence; and while he often denied the longing, he frequently obeyed it. He would throw down his pen, and change his coat, and leave the house impetuously, seeing her, in fancy, all the way until he reached the flat. During a fortnight or so, he sought some reason for the visit. Would she like the heroine to go on the stage when her husband lost his money? Did she think it would be a good idea to kill the husband off, and introduce a new character, who could reinstate the girl in luxury? But presently such excuses were abandoned. For one thing, Mrs. Deane-Pitt was too much occupied with her serial to accord any serious consideration to his work; and for another, she welcomed him as a matter of course. It was agreeable to her to see this man who was in love with her, and whom she liked, looking at her with eyes that betrayed what he would not allow his tongue to acknowledge. 'Oh, I'm glad,' she would say, 'I was hoping it was you. Sit down and make yourself comfortable—no, bring me that pillow first—and talk to me, and be amusing.' Sometimes she received him radiantly, sometimes wearily. On one afternoon she declared herself in the best of spirits, and had just been wishing for someone to bear her company; on the next, she sighed that she was worried to death, and he had only arrived in time to save her from extinction. 'Bills,' she would yawn, when he questioned her, 'bills! A dressmaker, a schoolmistress—I forget which. Some wretch threatens something, I know. Don't look so concerned; I shall survive. Cheer me up.' Then the servant would enter with the tea-equipage, and afterwards, in the cool shadows of the drawing-room, through which the perfume of the heliotrope that grew in a huge bowl under the crimson lamp floated deliciously, there would be cigarettes, and a half-hour he found exquisite in its air of intimate familiarity. Though no verbal admission was ever made, there were seconds in which Kent's voice, as plainly as his face, told her what he felt for her, and seconds in which the tones of the woman said, 'I'm quite conscious of the effect I have on you; we both understand, of course.' Occasionally he had a glimpse of her children, and ogee when he was there, Mrs. Deane-Pitt took the boy on her lap—among the folds of her elaborate tea-gown—and fondled him. 'Do you think I make a nice mother, Mr. Kent?' she said, flashing a glance. 'This monkey doesn't properly appreciate his privileges.' She kissed the child three times, and in the gaze she lifted over his curly head there was, for an instant, provocation that shook the man.

But such incidents as this were exceptional, and, as a rule, Kent would have been puzzled to cite a single instance of coquetry on her part when he took his leave and returned to the attic. Nor did the passion she had aroused in him militate against the success of his undertaking, taking 'success' to mean its completion by the given date. Perhaps he was more industrious, even, in the perception that she was always warmest when he had done the most. 'I finished the thirtieth chapter last night.' Then she would be delightful, and if she had appeared harassed at all, her languor would speedily give place to gaiety. The tremulous afternoons were never so quick with the sense of alliance, so entirely fascinating to him, as when he was able to surprise her by some such report. The desire to please the woman became fully as strong a stimulus to the ghost as his eagerness to receive the money which would permit him to commence a third novel for himself. The two short stories had been published now, in a periodical in which Kent would have been very proud to see his own name above them, and, though he did not grudge them to Mrs. Deane-Pitt, he could not help feeling, as he read them, that they were better than he had known, and that it would be eminently satisfactory to resume legitimate work.

After the fortieth chapter was accomplished, conclusion was in sight, and albeit he could not quite sustain his earlier pace, he never turned out less than one thousand words a day. Had anybody told him a couple of months before that he could do even this, he would have ridiculed the statement, but the consciousness that acceptance was certain had been very fortifying. He scarcely allowed himself leisure to eat after passing the fortieth chapter. The stuff was undeniably poor, though it was not so jejune as it seemed to Kent. The worst part was the construction, for, ignorant what the next development was to be, he was often forced to write sheets of intermediate and motiveless dialogue until an idea presented itself; but for the style, hasty as it was, there was still something to be said. Instinctively Kent gave to a commonplace redundancy a literary twist, and the writing had almost invariably a veneer, though the matter written might be of no account.

During the final week Kent did not go to Victoria Street at all. He could, not suppress the artist in him wholly, and for the climax he meant to do his utmost. It was a sop to his conscience—he could remember the last chapter, and forget the rest. He had sent or taken the, manuscript to Mrs. Deane-Pitt piece by piece, and he took her the last of it on the evening that he wrote 'The End,' having sent her a telegram to say she might expect him. He had written the book in seven weeks, but he felt as exhausted as if he had built a house in the time, brick by brick, with his own hands. She read the pages he had brought while he watched her from an armchair, and, with the candor which was so striking a feature in such an association, she cried that the scene was admirable—that she could not have done it so well. Kent's weariness faded from him as they talked, and momentarily he regretted that he had not been able to write her a book as good as 'The Eye of the Beholder.'

With regard to her negotiations, however, Mrs. Deane-Pitt was not so outspoken—it was only by chance that Kent had seen the two short tales, nor had she even told him for what paper they were intended—and some delay occurred in paying the two hundred pounds, of which her explanations were vague and various. The partner with whom she always dealt was on the Continent; she would not sign an agreement before American copyright was arranged; she generally ran her stories as serials before they were issued in book-form, and it was not decided what she was going to do—half a dozen reasons for the postponement of the settlement were forthcoming. She gave Kent his share at last, though, and very cordially, and he felt some embarrassment in taking her check when the moment arrived, it being his earliest experience of business with a woman. If he had had others, he would have appreciated her action in paying him in full, and only a little late, more keenly, though he was far from ungrateful to her as it was. He put the cheek in his pocket as carelessly as he could manage, and said:

'Well, you've done me a tremendous service, Mrs. Deane-Pitt, and, by Jove! I thank you for it—heartily.'

'Oh, nonsense!' she replied; 'the work's been as useful to me as to you; you've nothing to thank me for.'

'It makes more difference to me, 'said Kent; 'it means—you hardly know what it means. I needn't look out for a berth now; I can sit down to another novel. I owe you that.'

'If you like to think so——' She smiled, but her tone was constrained. 'I should be glad if somebody owed me something; I'm more used to the reverse.'

'I feel a Crœsus,' he said. 'We ought to celebrate this accession to wealth, Mrs. Deane-Pitt; it demands a festivity. If I get seats for a theatre, will you go to dinner with me somewhere to-morrow night? Do. What shall we go to see? have you been to Daly's yet?'

'I'm engaged to-morrow night, and the next.'

'To-night, then?'

'This evening I am dining out; there's the card on my desk.'

'What a fashionable person you are!' exclaimed Kent, rather enviously. 'Would Friday evening suit you?'

'Yes, I'm free on Friday; but a theatre is awfully stifling this weather, isn't it?'

'We needn't go to a theatre,' he suggested; 'we might dine at Richmond. Will you drive down to Richmond, and have dinner at the Star and Garter on Friday?'

Mrs. Deane-Pitt promised that she would, but the animation with which she had given him the check had deserted her and after a minute, she said:

'I suppose your starting another novel for yourself needn't stand in the way of our business together? There are several things I can offer you, if you care to do them.'

'Oh, thanks,' said Kent; 'but I'm afraid I'd better stick to the novel. I want to do all I can with it, you see.'

'L'un n'empêche pas l'autre—a short tale now and again won't interfere with it, surely? I can place a ten-thousand-word story at once if you like to write it for me.'

The refusal was difficult, and he hesitated how to express himself. He had never contemplated the association as a permanent one, and now that an alternative was open to him, its indignity looked doubly repellant. He was surprised that Mrs. Deane-Pitt had thought it possible it could continue. Could she not understand that he felt it a humiliation; that he had adopted the course merely as a desperate measure in a desperate case. He had taken her comprehension for granted.

'I'd rather not, if you don't mind,' he said awkwardly. 'It would take me off my own work more than you can imagine. My motive for doing this book for you was to be free to devote myself heart and soul to a novel, and that is what I want to do.'

She looked downcast.

'When do you mean to begin it? You could knock off a ten-thousand-word story first, couldn't you? And I believe an occasional short tale would come as a relief to you, too. I wouldn't persuade you against your will—pray don't think that—but, as a matter of fact, there is no reason why you shouldn't make a few pounds a week all the time you're writing your book, you know, if you like. I don't want another novel yet, but I can take almost any number of feuilletons, or, if you preferred it, you might write me a short thing that could be issued in paper covers at a shilling. Will you think it over? I don't want to hurry your decision.' She hummed a snatch of tune, and picked up a new song that was lying on the piano. 'Have you seen this?' she said carelessly. 'It's pretty.'

Kent took it from her, and played with the leaves in a pause. He was conscious that he must decline now, and definitely, and the insistence of her request made the duty harder every second. Mrs. Deane-Pitt sauntered about the room; she felt blank and annoyed with herself. Was this her reward for liking the man enough to give him two hundred pounds in a lump, instead of paying him by instalments, which would have been infinitely more convenient to her?

'If you won't think me boorish,' he said at last abruptly, 'I'd rather keep to my intention. I'm not a boy. I need all the time at my disposal to succeed in.'

She gave a forced laugh.

'How much younger do you want to be? If the money doesn't attract you, at all events it won't be in your way, I suppose; and—you can do it to oblige me. It will be all the more chivalrous of you. Come, I'm quite frank: I own that you're very useful to me. You don't mean you're going to "strike," and leave me in the lurch, Mr. Kent?'

The face upturned to him was more earnest than her words. Her brown eyes widened, and fastened on him, and for an instant his resolution broke down. But it was his work, and his ambition, his fidelity to his art, that she was asking him to waive—he would not!

Nobody so sorry as the "striker," ' he said, in a tone to match her own. 'Let me be your banker when I'm going into a dozen editions, Mrs. Deane-Pitt, and I'll serve you all you want. The service you ask me to-day is just the one I can't do.'

'Bien,' she murmured; 'I suppose you know your own business best.'

But she was plainly disappointed, and, though she speedily spoke of another subject, her voice lacked spontaneity. Kent's courage knew no approving glow, and if, during the minutes he remained, she had begged him to assist her by returning the check, he would most certainly have done it. He considered that she must hate him, though in truth he had never appealed to her so strongly, and it was the only occasion on which he had ever bidden her adieu without regret.

To Cynthia he wrote immediately, telling her he had been paid two hundred pounds, and enclosing twenty-five, that she might have a surplus to draw upon when she required it, without applying to him. He also remitted to Paris the amount necessary to redeem her ring and his watch and chain, and the rest. He had now an opportunity of going down to see her, and he told her she might expect him on Monday or Tuesday in the following week. The picture he had once seen of surprising her in the garden had long since ceased to present itself to him, nor was he impatient to find himself in his wife's company under the circumstances. He questioned if Mrs. Deane-Pitt would be disposed to go with him to Richmond after what had passed. To refuse a woman's petition to augment her income, but to invite her to dinner at Richmond, was rather suggestive of the bread and the stone. Yet, now that propinquity was not her ally, he was fervently glad he had had strength to refuse. It was an alliance that would have become more difficult to sever every month, and she had, apparently, looked for it to extend over years. As to Richmond, he could only trust the engagement would be fulfilled; it would pain him intensely otherwise. He owed her too much to be reconciled to their illicit partnership ending in coldness, and he determined to send her a note, reminding her of her promise.

The lady's reply allayed his misgivings, but not more than her demeanor when they met. Indeed, the delicacy which he perceived prompted her to the display of even more good fellowship than usual caused Kent primarily to feel some guilty restraint.

She seemed to divine his reflections, and to assure him indirectly that such self-reproach was needless and far-fetched. She had never been brighter or more informal with him than in the hansom as they drove down. Her air implied that their previous interview had been a trivial folly which, as sensible people, they must banish from their recollection, and she talked of everything and nothing with the gaiety of a schoolgirl on an unforeseen excursion, and the piquancy of a woman who had observed and lived.

Her vivacity was infectious, and Kent's embarrassment gradually melted in a rush of the warmest gratitude for her forbearance. He was so entirely at her mercy here, and he thought that few women similarly placed would have refrained from planting at least one little sting among their verbal honey. His admiration began to comprise details. He remarked the style of the bonnet she wore, and the gleam of her pink ear against the hair's duskiness. He noted with pleasure the quick, petulant twitch of a corner of her mouth as her veil got in the way, and the appreciative gaze of the young men, whose stiff white shirt-fronts made stains on the twilight from the cabs that rolled toward them—a gaze which invariably terminated by a swift scrutiny of the charming woman's companion.

When the hotel was reached, he had never been livelier, and, while he had often read an opposite opinion, he found it very delightful to see the woman he was in love with eat, and drink her champagne. The humanity of the gourmandize appealed to him—lessened the 'noli me tangere' mien of feminine fashion, and brought her closer. The attire of an attractive woman who has never belonged to him has always a mystery for a man, though he may have had three wives and kept a milliner-shop. But, in turn, liveliness was succeeded by a vaguer emotion, as they lounged on the terrace over their coffee and liquors. Under the moon the river shone divinely, limitless and unspeakable in its glint and shadow—Desire touched with the awesomeness of the Beyond. Her features took a tenderness from the tremulous light, and sometimes a silence fell between them, which, as he yielded himself to the subtle endearment of the moment, soft as the breath of love on his face, Kent felt to be the supplement of speech. A woman who could have uttered epigrams in the mood that possessed him now would have disgusted him, and insensibly their tones sank. She spoke gently, seriously. Presently some allusion that she made begot a confidence about her earlier life—her marriage. It disturbed him to hear that she had been fond of Deane-Pitt when she married him, and he was grieved when she owned how quickly her illusions had died. Her belief that she might have been 'a better woman 'if she had married a different man was pathetic in its revelation of unsuspected heart-aches, and sympathy made him execrate the feebleness of words. Her voice acquired an earnestness that he had never heard in it before, and while he was stirred with the sincerest pity for her, a throb of rapture was in his veins that she could be talking so to him. These minutes were ineffable, in which the woman, lowering the social mark, surrendered more and more of her identity to his view; spiritually she appeared to be lying in his arms, and when she checked herself, and rallied with a laugh which was overtaken by a sigh, he felt that he could have listened to her for ever.

'How solemn we have become!' she exclaimed; 'and we came out to be "festive" to-night.'

'I shall always remember the "you" of to-night,' he said.

They were silent again. She passed her hand across her eyes impatiently, as if to wave away the pictures of the past. By transitions their tones regained their former cheerfulness. She mentioned the hour, and drew her cape about her. It was time to return.

'It has been delicious,' she murmured, looking up at the stars. 'Only you let me bore you.'

'By talking of yourself?'

'So stupid of me!'

'You know,' said Kent—'you know.'

'I **wanted** to tell you; you won't think so badly of me, perhaps.'

'I?'

'I am sure you have. Now, sometimes?'

'If I confessed my thoughts, you would never say so any more.'

'Really?' Her eyes flashed mockery. 'You musn't tell me, then—I might be vain.'

The cab bowled over the white roads rapidly. The flutter of her cape upon his shoulder stole through his blood, and the clip-clop sound of the horse's hoofs seemed to him to waken echoes in his inside.

'Do you know, it was very indiscreet of me to come down here with you,' she laughed; 'supposing somebody had met us!'

'And then?'

'What would be thought?'

'**What** could be thought?' he asked unsteadily.

'Scandal, perhaps. Now I reflect, I'm very indignant with you; you have made me do wrong. Why did you make me do wrong when I had such faith in you?'

'You've given me the happiest evening of my life,' said Kent; 'is that the wrong?'

'Do you think happiness must be always right? it's a convenient creed. Happiness at any price—and let the woman pay it. Eh? That's a man's philosophy, isn't it? You're quite right, though; but, then, you're at the happiest time of life—no, nobody is ever that. What is the happiest time of life—twenty—thirty? Nonsense! the happiest time of life's the past. Believe me or not, the past is always beautiful; to-morrow I shall regret to-day.'

'So shall I,' said Kent; 'but I can assure you I appreciate it now. . . . What are you cynical for? You only put it on. It's not "you" really.'

'Wise judges are we of each other. How do you know?'

'You said that to me once before—in Paris.'

'Said what? Oh, the quotation. When?'

'At your place, after the Variétés.'

'What a memory! Yes, you're certainly resolved to try to make me vain. But

I'm adamant. Did you know that? I'm made of steel. Do you treasure up what every woman says to you? The answer is a wounded gaze; it's dark to see expressions, but I'll take it for granted.'

'I remember what *you* said to me half an hour ago, and I know your bitterness is a sham. You were meant to be—"

'Oh, "meant"!' she cried recklessly; 'a woman's what she's made. I'm afraid *I've* been made untidy. Do you mind driving in a hansom with such a figure?'

She plucked at her veil and hair in the strip of looking-glass, and bent her face to him for criticism. The brilliance of the eyes she widened glowed into him as she leaned so, and his arms trembled to enfold her. His mouth was dry as he muttered a response.

The sweetness of June was in the air that caressed them as they sped through the moonlight. With every sentence she let fall, and every glance she shot at him, she dizzied Kent more, and he sat strained with the intensity of his struggle to retain his self-command. Through his febrile emotions, the horror of proving false to Cynthia loomed like an angel betokening the revulsion of his remorse. He could imagine the afterwards—he knew how he would feel—and there were instants in which he prayed for the drive to finish and permit escape. But there were instants also in which he ceased to fight against his weakness, and, steeped in the present, only yearned to forget his wife, though the tardy remembrance should be a double scourge.

Her fingers were busy at a knot of violets under the cape, and she held the flowers to him, looking round, smiling.

'Shall I give you a buttonhole?' she inquired gaily. 'It would be quite an appropriate conclusion—my ideals, my withered hopes, and my dead violets. Oh, I shiver to think of what I said to you! Did I gush toward the last? I've a fearful, a ghastly misgiving that I gushed. If you acknowledge that I did, I'll never forgive you; but you shouldn't have encouraged me. Stoop for the souvenir of the occasion. They cost a penny—emblematical of the sentiment. . . . Though lost to sight, to memory dear! It will be a very dear memory, won't it? Use me one day; I shall come in as material—the hard woman of the world, who bares her soul on impulse, and the Star and Garter terrace, to the man she likes, and stands revealed as—as what? I wonder what you'd make of me. Mr. Kent, I shall never get this buttonhole in if you don't turn. I've admitted I'm a spectacle, but you might suffer for a second.'

Her hair swept his cheek as she wrestled with refractory stalks, and the dark eyes grew, and fastened on him again.

The hansom sped on. The quietude was left behind, and the lights of the West End twinkled around them. There was the rattle of traffic. Kent was laughing at something she had said, and he heard himself with surprise—or was it himself? He seemed to be two entities—antithetical and antagonistic. The cab rolled to a standstill, and Mrs. Deane-Pitt descended, and they were borne to her landing in the lift.

'Good-night,' he said, as the servant opened the door. 'I won't come in.'

'Oh, come in; it's not ten o'clock. You'll have a brandy and-soda before you go?'

She entered without waiting for his reply, and Kent followed her reluctantly. Only the lamp had been lighted, and the room was filled with crimson shadows. He stood watching her unpin her bonnet before the mirror, and pull at her gloves.

'I don't think I'll stop,' he said again, 'really. I've something to do.'

'If I can't persuade you——' she answered listlessly.

Her gaiety had deserted her, and there was a weariness in her attitude as she drooped by the mantelshelf; her air, her movements, had a languor now. She put out her bare hand slowly, and Kent's clung to it.

He stood holding her hand in a pause.

'I can't leave you,' said Kent.

CHAPTER XXIII.

IT was a little less than a fortnight after the dinner at Richmond that Kent brought Mrs. Deane-Pitt the ten-thousand-word story she had wanted, and, like the two earliest tales he had written for her, it was work to which he would have been glad to see his own name attached. He had promised to let her have half a dozen short stories as soon after its completion as possible, and it was his delight to surprise her by the versatility, as well as the originality, of the invention he displayed in these. In one he wrote an idyll; in another a grusome little sketch, whose conception would not have been disdained by Poe; in a third he seemed to be running through the stalest of devices toward the most commonplace of conclusions, until, lo! in the last half-column there came a literary thunderclap, and this story was even more original than the preceding ones. But all the links fitted, if a reader liked to take the trouble to look back, and the tragedy had been foreshadowed from the beginning. The tales tickled the editor for whom they were intended mightily—so much so that he asked Mrs. Deane-Pitt to contribute regularly for a few months; and the lady accepting the compliment and the invitation, Kent continued to supply *The Society Mirror* with an idyll, or a tragedy, or a comedy every week after the initial half-dozen were done, astonished at his own fecundity.

It was amazing how his hand was emboldened, his imagination stimulated, by the knowledge that his stuff was accepted before it was penned. There were weeks during which he turned out a story for Mrs. Deane-Pitt nearly every day, each built upon a more or less brilliant idea, each noteworthy and distinctive when it appeared in *The Society Mirror* or elsewhere; and if his share of the swindle had been punctiliously paid to him now, he would have been making a good deal of money. Even as it was, he was making it in a sense, for his partner always credited him with the sums that were not forthcoming—entering them in an oxidized silver note book that she kept in one of the drawers of her desk—and when he said that it did not matter, would laughingly command him not to be a fool.

His conscience was not dull, however, and there were hours when Kent suffered scarcely less acutely than one realizes that a wife may suffer sometimes under similar circumstances. His remorse then was just what he had known it would be while he struggled. From making his projected visit to Monmouth he had excused himself—it was repugnant enough to play the hypocrite in his letters—and by degrees Cynthia ceased her allusions to his coming; but while her silence on the point relieved him from the necessity for telling her further falsehoods, it intensified his shame as well.

His abasement was completed by the seventh rejection of 'The Eye of the Beholder.' He sent it off again at once, to Messrs. Kynaston, to get it out of his sight; but the return of the ill-starred package had revived all the passion of his disappointment concerning it, and he could not get rid of the burning at his heart so easily as he did of the parcel. The weight of the slighted manuscript lay on his spirit for days after Thurgate and Tatham's refusal, and the irony, the cruelty, of Fate lashed him, by which Mrs. Deane-Pitt could place his hasty work in the best papers, was enabled to pay him two hundred pounds for writing a novel he was ashamed of, while his own book, to which he had devoted a year, was scorned on all sides. True, he had had in his own name very much better reviews than those which had been accorded so far to the novel he had written for her; but one could not fill one's belly with, reviews when one was hungry, or warm one's hands at them when too poverty-ridden to procure a fire.

Once he owned to her something of the mortification that was galling him. He could not restrain himself; he wanted her to comfort him.

' "The Eye of the Beholder" has come back again,' he groaned.

'Really?' she said. 'How many is that?'

'God knows! It's awfully hard that *you* can place whatever I do, Eva, and *I* get my best stuff kicked back to me from every publisher's office in London. I'm miserable!'

She smiled. She did not mean to be unfeeling, but Kent hated her for it furiously as she turned her face.

'There's much in a name,' she said with a shrug. 'What's the difference, though? Your terms aren't bad, "miserable one," whether the name is mine or yours. By the way, I can work another tale for *The Metropolis,* if you'll knock it off for me; I was going to write to you.'

Kent never appealed to her for sympathy again, but a little later there came a letter from Cynthia, replying to his brief announcement of Thurgate and Tatham's rejection; her consolation and prophecies of 'success yet' overflowed four sheets, and the man's throat was tight as he read them.

Well, he must do the tale for *The Metropolis* but he would write some short stories for himself as well as for Eva, Kent determined. It had not been a lucrative occupation when he essayed it before, but those early stories had been designed from a bad model—he perceived it now: he would write some short stories of the pattern which were so successful when they were signed 'Eva Deane-Pitt.'

He begun to see his work over her signature soon in almost every paper he looked at. If he turned the leaves of a magazine on a bookstall, a tale of his own met his eyes, signed 'Eva Deane-Pitt'; if he picked up a periodical in a restaurant, on two out of every four occasions a familiar sentence would flash out of the pages at him, and he would encounter a story written by him, and published by 'Eva Deane-Pitt.' Yes, he would submit to the editors on his own account. He would not receive the same terms as were obtainable by her; that he knew—he doubted strongly whether he would even get as much as she spared to him after retaining the larger share— but he could, and he would, get what was dearer to him than the extra pounds, the recognition and the kudos to which he was entitled.

He found be did not phrase so quickly when he put pen to paper for himself as he did in his capacity of ghost, but he was not discouraged, for he felt that he was phrasing better. For a week he did nothing for the woman at all; he wrote all day and half the night as Humphrey Kent, and when a manuscript was declined by *The Society Mirror* he sent it to *The Metropolis,* and forwarded the story rejected by *The Metropolis* to *The Society Mirror.* He could not abandon his work for her entirely, but, under the pressure she put upon him and his new interests, he wrote for her more and more hastily, wrote frank and unmitigated rubbish at last, and on one occasion candidly told her so.

She had telegraphed him at six o'clock, begging him to call, and he had risen from his table feeling his head a void. She clamored for a two-thousand-word story by the first post the following morning, and insisted, as usual, that 'anything would do.' Kent assured her that he was too exhausted to even invent a motive, still less could he produce two thousand words before he slept; but she overruled his objections, hanging about him with caresses, and made him promise that the sketch should reach her in time.

'Write twaddle, dearest boy,' was her parting injunction; 'but write it. A motive? A mercenary girls jilts her lover because he is poor, and then her new fiancé loses his fortune, and the jilted lover succeeds to a dukedom, and says, "Get out," like Mrs. Guppy. Write a story that Noah told to his family in the Ark, only cover enough pages. Put " 'Yes,' she said" on one line, and " 'No?' he exclaimed" on the next—simply fill it out. I depend on you, Humphrey, mind.'

He went home and did it, on the lines she had laid down. She wanted bosh— she should have it. He did not stop to think at all. He sat down, and wrote, without a pause or a correction, as rapidly as his pen would travel, and posted the tale to her before half-past ten. He slipped a note in with it:

'I have done as you ordered,' he scribbled. 'Don't blame me because no editor will take it now you are obeyed.'

She had no complaint to make, however, when he saw her next, and it was after this occurrence that Kent's stuff for her became fatuous, while he lavished on his own a wealth of fastidious care for which she would have mocked him had she known it. He visited her also at much longer intervals, for a disgust of her caresses, a horror of the febrile afternoons, which always ended with a petition for additional tales, was forming in his mind; but that cowardice prevented him, he would have stayed away altogether. Something like horror formed of the woman herself, insatiable, no matter with how much work he might supply her, coaxing him for 'two little stories more; anything will do,' while a batch of manuscripts that he had brought her lay in her lap. He could remember now, with her arms about him, the many original ideas she had had from him at the commencement, and he felt with a shudder that her embrace was as destructive as the clutch of an octopus. First she had had his brains, and now she was stealing his conscience. He foresaw that, sooner or later, a day must come, if the strain she put upon him continued, when the imagination that she was squeezing like an orange would be sterile, or fruitful, at least, of nothing better than the literary abortions with which his mistress was content.

His dismay at his position increased rather than diminished, and it became so plainly evidenced that by degrees a coldness crept into the woman's manner toward him, which Kent, on his side, was at no pains to dispel. That their relations had drifted on to a business footing alone, inspired him with no other fear than presently she might make him a scene, and entail upon him the disagreeable necessity for declaring as delicately as he could that his infidelity to his wife had been a madness he violently regretted, and would never repeat. The obvious retort would be so superficially true that he fervently trusted the necessity would not arise.

Meanwhile the short stories submitted in his own name, with silent prayers, had all been refused; but, undeterred by the failure, he wrote more and more. The present tenants of No. 64 were anxious to renew their agreement for another six months, and Kent was pleased to hear it; the prospect of meeting Cynthia again frightened him, and, closing readily with the offer which would afford him a respite, he remained at his literary forge in Soho, writing for Mrs. Deane-Pitt and for himself, seeing sometimes three of the tales done for her published in different papers in the same week, and finding those submitted in the humbler name of 'Humphrey Kent' returned without exception.

He would have pronounced such a thing an exaggeration formerly if it had been related to him, but now he discovered that it could be. There was not at this stage a periodical or magazine in London that Humphrey Kent did not essay in vain, and there were not more than three or four (of the kind that one sees in a club or an educated woman's drawing-room) in which his stuff did not appear during the same period, at a handsome rate of payment, when it was supposed to be by Mrs. Deane-Pitt. There were not five papers making a feature of fiction in London which did not consistently reject the man's best work, signed by himself, and accept his worst, signed by somebody else. Not five of the penny or sixpenny publications—not five among the first or second-class ones—not five editors appraising fiction in editorial chairs who did not either find or assume a story bearing the unfamiliar name of Humphrey Kent to be below their standard, while they paid five or ten guineas for a tale scribbled by the same author in a couple of hours when it was falsely represented to be by Mrs. Deane-Pitt. During nine months he was never offered a single guinea for a tale by an editor. Every story he submitted during nine months was declined, and every story he gave to Mrs. Deane Pitt was printed. Raging, he swore that one day he would describe the monstrous situation in a novel; but he knew, even as he swore it, that the circumstances would never be believed, that the 'extravagance' would be called the blot upon the book.

Once an editor did know his name. He was the editor of a very fashionable magazine indeed, and Kent called at the office with an inquiry about a manuscript, concerning which he had been hoping to hear for a long while. The gentleman was extremely courteous to him. He did not remember the title, and, unfortunately, he could not put his hand on the tale at the moment, but he would read it immediately it was found, and he promised to communicate his decision without delay.

A letter from him (and the manuscript) reached Kent the same week. It was as considerate a letter of rejection as anyone could indite. The editor commenced by saying that the story 'was clever, as all Mr. Kent touched was clever, but—' And then he proceeded to analyze the plot, to demonstrate that the motive was too slight for the purpose. The criticism was so kindly worded that, though Kent could not perceive its justice, he was sensible enough to try, and decided it was far-fetched. He felt a glow of gratitude toward the writer, and his appreciation was deepened when the following post brought him a copy of the newly-issued number of the magazine, 'With compliments.'

He opened it at once, and the first thing he saw was a story done for Mrs. Deane-Pitt—the story he had written, tired and insolently careless, about the mercenary girl, and the jilted lover, and the succession to the dukedom. After that he did not try to discern the acuteness of the criticism any more.

And now, when he was least expecting it, there came to him the first gleam of encouragement he had had since he received his last review. Messrs. Eynaston wrote, offering to undertake the publication of 'The Eye of the Beholder,' if he were willing to accept forty pounds for the copyright.

He did not hesitate even for an instant; he said 'Thank God!' as devoutly as if he had never expected more for it, and passed the missive to Turquand, who had just come in. The journalist gave it back to him with a grunt.

'It's a wicked price,' said Turquand; 'but I suppose you'll take it to-day if you can't get them to spring?'

'Take it!' echoed Kent; 'I could take them to my heart for it. Oh, thank God! I mean it. Yes, it's beggarly; it's awful; but, at any rate, the book will see the light. Price? It isn't a price at all, but the thing will be published. There's quite enough money for us to live while I'm writing my next, and this will send me to it with double energy. I shall go to Kynaston's to-morrow morning.'

He did go, and, though less enthusiastic in the publisher's presence, his attempt to induce him to increase the terms was but weak. Seven rejections had made a high hand unattainable.

'I got a hundred for my first,' he said, 'and you offer me forty for my second. It isn't scaling the ladder with rapidity.'

'The other was longer, perhaps,' suggested Mr. Kynaston, tapping his fingers together pensively—'three volumes?'

'Don't you reckon that this will make three volumes, then?' said Kent.

'Two. It's unfortunately short; that's the only fault I have to find with it. I like it—it's out of the common; but there isn't enough of it.' He sighed. 'I am sorry that forty is the most I can say. I considered the subject very deeply before I wrote you—

very deeply indeed.'

His expression implied that he had lain awake all night considering, and that regret that he couldn't quote a larger sum might even keep him awake again to-night.

He did not disguise his opinion of the novel, however, especially after the matter was settled.

'Send me something else, Mr. Kent,' he said warmly, as he saw the author downstairs and pressed his hand—'something a trifle longer—and I shall be able to make you a more substantial offer. Yours is a very rare style; you have remarkable power, if I may say so. If fine work always meant a fine sale, "The Eye of the Beholder" should see six editions. I shall get it out at once. Good-day to you: and don't forget—make your next book a little longer.'

Turquand would not be back for some hours, and Kent did not hurry home after leaving the office. He sauntered through the streets reflecting. He was resolved that now he would do ghost-work no more, and he wondered how Eva would receive the announcement of his decision. Disappointing as she would doubtless find it, she would not have had much to complain of, he thought, and he congratulated himself anew on their liaison having ended, since it left him but the one association to sever instead of two. Again an access of remorse in its most poignant form assailed him, and he wished he could carry his good news to Cynthia in lieu of writing it—wished he could confess to Cynthia—wondered if the desire to do so was mad.

This desire had fastened on Kent more than once. He thought he should feel less guilty toward her—would *be* less guilty toward her—if she knew. There had been moments when, if they had not been separated, he would have told her the truth in a burst, and, whether she pardoned him or not, have lifted his head, feeling happier from the mere fact that the avowal had been made. Nor did he deceive himself into imagining that his craving to confess to her was any shining virtue. He was conscious, just as he had been conscious in Paris, when he had informed her casually of the supper in the Avenue Wagram, that it was as much the weakness of his character as its nobility which urged him to voice the load that lay on his mind; but, weak or noble, the longing was always there, and at times it mastered him completely.

A little sleet began to fall, and he entered a restaurant, and ordered some coffee. A copy of **Fashion** lay on the table, and, mechanically turning the pages, he noticed that the feature of the issue was an instalment of a story in three parts by Lady Cornwallis. The name arrested his attention, for she was the widow of a baronet who had been a connection of the late Deane-Pitt's, and Kent was aware that Eva and she were on friendly terms. He glanced at the heading with an ironical smile; the lady was not known to him as an authoress, though she had figured prominently of late in the witness-box, where a shrewd solicitor and a smart modiste had posed her in quite a romantic light, and he surmised bitterly that her maiden effort in fiction had been remunerated more handsomely than his second novel. What was his astonishment, on glancing at the opening paragraph, to discover that the story 'By Lady Cornwallis' was another of those that had been written by himself for Mrs. Deane-Pitt!

As a matter of fact, the editor, believing that her name would be a draw just now, had offered Lady Cornwallis a hundred pounds for a tale that would run through three numbers. Lady Cornwallis, who bad never tried to write anything more elaborate than a love-letter in her life, and who was being dunned to desperation for an account at a livery-stable, had gone to Mrs. Deane-Pitt to do it for her. Mrs. Deane-Pitt, who wrote much less quickly than she pretended, had relegated the duty to Kent. It was a literary house-that-Jack-built. Lady Cornwallis, assuming that her friend might ascertain the sum the editor paid, had ingenuously halved it with her; Mrs. Deane-Pitt, confident that the young man would be unable to ascertain, had given to him ten pounds. The details of the transaction Kent could only guess at, as he sat in a restaurant staring at his work while his coffee got cold; but the evolution of the story which had been perpetrated in a Soho attic for ten pounds, and was published as Lady Cornwallis's at the cost of a hundred, was interesting.

He was fiercely and inconsistently resentful. In one way it mattered nothing to him. Since his stuff was not printed over his own name, it was really unimportant over whose it appeared; but the perception did not lessen his angry sense of having been duped. He remembered the circumstances under which he had written this tale, and the lies that Eva had told him concerning it. Was he to become the ghost of every imposter in London?

Though he did not refer to the discovery he had made, it lent a firmness to his tone when he informed her that 'The Eye of The Beholder' was accepted, and that he was going down into the country to devote a year to another, and she heard him without remonstrance. Whatever her faults, she had the inestimable virtue of being a woman of the world, and she did not endow the parting, for which she was partially prepared, with any tactless tragedy. For an instant only she considered the feasibility of tenderness begetting a reconciliation; then she dismissed the idea. The man was remorseful—not of having become estranged from her, but of having ever succumbed—and tenderness would be thrown away, besides making the interview extremely painful for him, which she had never been in love with him ardently enough to desire to do. She shrugged her shoulders.

'Everything has an end,' she said languidly—'even "Daniel Deronda." I owe you a lot of money, by-the-by. I'm afraid I can't square accounts with you at the moment, but I suppose you don't mind trusting me?'

'You owe me nothing,' answered Kent. 'If my boorishness has left any liking for me possible, let me have the pleasure of feeling that I did you one or two trifling services.'

But he did not go down to the country. More than ever he felt that to rejoin his wife with his guilt unacknowledged would be a greater trial than he could endure. She was so innocent. If she had been a different kind of woman, his reluctance would have been duller, and easier to overcome; but to have been false to Cynthia inspired him with the same sense of shame as if he had robbed a blind girl.

That he could not delay rejoining her much longer he was distressfully aware. It was ten months since she had gone away, and even if the people in Streatham wished to retain the house for a third half-year, as he understood was likely—their return to New York, or wherever they had come from, being postponed—it would be no reason why he and Cynthia should not live together either in Monmouth or somewhere else.

He had written her that Messrs. Kynaston had taken 'The Eye of the Beholder,' and during the next day or two he was in hourly expectation of her reply. On the third afternoon after he had posted his letter, the door opened, and she came into the room.

Kent had not heard the bell ring, but at the sound of her footstep he turned quickly, and then, almost before he realized it, his wife was in his arms, laughing and half crying, saying how glad she was to see him, how delighted she was at the book's acceptance, all in a breath.

'I had to come,' she exclaimed—'I had to I Oh, darling! you don't mind because the money isn't much? Think what Kynaston said of it! And for your next you'll get proper terms. . . . Well, are you surprised to see me? Let me look at you. You're different. What have you been doing to yourself? And baby—you wouldn't know baby. He talks!. . . I've been praying you'd be at home. I wouldn't let them show me in; I've been picturing walking in on you all the way in the train . . . Sweetheart!' She squeezed him to her again, and then held him at arm's length, scrutinizing him gaily. 'You've changed,' she repeated; 'you look more serious. And I? Am I all right—am I a disappointment?'

'You are beautiful,' said Kent slowly. 'You, too, have changed.'

He gazed at her with a curious sense of unfamiliarity, striving to define to himself the alteration that puzzled him. Her face had gained something besides the hues of health. It seemed to him that her eyes were wider and deeper in color; her smile was more complex. Vaguely he felt that he had thought of her as a girl, and was beholding a woman—that he had insulted a woman who was lovelier than any he had known.

'Aren't you going to invite me to take off my things?' she inquired. 'May I?'

'Do,' he answered, with the same sense of remoteness from her. 'Can I help you?' He took them from her awkwardly, and put her into a comfortable chair, and replenished the fire. 'It's a new hat,' he remarked; 'it suits you. I always liked you in a little hat. Did you get it down there?'

'I trimmed it myself,' she said. 'Mind the pin!'

'You shall have some tea—or would you rather have dinner? You must be hungry!'

'Tea, please, and cake. Can you produce cake?'

'There's a confectioner's just round the corner,' said Kent, ringing the bell.

'Then, Madeira. I didn't tell the servant who I was Better say "my wife" casually when she comes in. I suppose you don't have ladies to tea and Madeira cakes, as a rule?'

'Not as a rule,' he said—'no.'

She laughed again, and stretched her shoes to the blaze luxuriously.

'So this is the room,' she murmured; 'this is where you lived before we knew each other? How funny that it should be the first time I've been in it! I've often imagined you here, and it isn't the least bit like what I fancied, of course; I always saw the window over there. Well, talk to me—tell me all; what are you thinking about? I believe you find me plain now my hat's off.'

Tea was brought to them in about a quarter of an hour, and they sat before the fire sipping it, and stealing glances at each other—the woman's, amused, delicious; Kent's, guilty and tortured. He was tempted to kiss her, but could not bring himself to do it deliberately; and with every phrase that fell from her lips his heart grew heavier.

'You've scarcely been to Strawberry Hill all the time, I hear,' she said. 'This is very good tea, Humphrey.'

'Not very often, I'm ashamed to say; I've been so busy. Yes, it isn't bad, is it? the landlady provides it. Are they offended with me?'

'H'mph! they'll look it over. You'll have to be very nice and repentant, bad boy.'

'I must; I'll go this week if I can.'

'This week! You must take me to-night,' she cried, 'What do you suppose is going to become of me; I can't stop here. . . . Shall I give you another cup?'

Kent felt the blood sinking from his face. His hands shook as he bent over the stove, and for a moment he could not find voice to reply.

'You don't return to Monmouth to-night?' he asked harshly, without looking at her.

'N—no,' she said; 'I can't go back till to-morrow.'

'I was thinking of the child,' he muttered.

'He is as safe with the nurse as with me,' she answered; 'I wouldn't have left him even for a day otherwise.'

'I see,' said Kent.

His pause appeared to him to become significant and terrible.

'I can't go there with you this evening,' he said abruptly; 'it can't be done. I have to be here; there is some one I must meet. I mean I can take you there, but I can't possibly stay. You—you must forgive me, Cynthia.'

He still did not look at her; but when she spoke, the change in her tone cut him like steel.

'You will do as you like,' she said quietly.

He lifted himself, and faced her.

'Cynthia!'

'Well?'

'Cynthia, don't think I don't care for you.'

She did not reply, but she was very pale, and her lips were set proudly.

'You are angry with me?' he stammered.

'What prevents you—your business? If you are too late for a train, there are hansoms. It would be expensive, I know.'

' "Expensive!" '

'Perhaps it might cost half a sovereign.'

Cynthia! But it's impossible.'

'Oh, please don't let us talk about it!' she said. 'I made a mistake, that's all. I've made a good many since I married you; this was one more.'

'I *can't* go,' gasped Kent, fighting for his words. 'I—If I cared for you less, I should. I can't go because there's something I must tell you first. If . . . but you won't. I want you to know . . . I've a confession to make to you. It's over, but . . . I've acted badly to you; I haven't the right to go to you. For God's sake don't hate me more than you can help; I've been unfaithful.'

Her first sensation was as if, without any warning, he had turned and dealt her a brutal blow in the face. There was the same staggered sense of fright, succeeded by the same sick wave of horror. Another woman had known him! Her brain did not leap for details instantaneously, as a man's would have demanded them in the reverse of the situation; the name the woman bore, her position, the color of her hair—what had these things to do with it? A hot curiosity to compare her with herself in looks would follow; but now, while she stared at him with bloodless features, she was conscious of nothing but the pollution: another woman had known him. Kent stared back at her, appalled by her expression; but he divined what she felt no more than he could have understood her emotions had she analyzed them for him. 'Another woman had known him' was the tumult in her soul; he believed her pride outraged that he had known another woman. The difference was enormous. The curiosity and thirst for vengeance apart, the wife's sensation was what the husband's would have been, had he heard of her own defilement. But that he himself appeared to her defiled he could not grasp; unworthy, contemptible, corrupt, he realized, but' defiled,' no.

'Cynthia, forgive me.'

She swayed a little as his voice struck her agony.

'I will try.'

'You see why I couldn't go.'

'Yes,' she said hoarsely, 'I see.'

'I should have told you anyhow soon. . . . You aren't sorry I've told you?'

'I don't know. I think . . . I think I am sorry just now. I shall be able to thank you for that later.'

'I did it for the best,' said Kent.

'You were right.'

He leaned against the mantelpiece; his chin drooped on his chest. The only sound in the room issued from the kettle, upon which the woman's eyes were fixed intently. The clock of St. Giles-in-the-Fields tolled four.

'What am I to do?' he inquired.

'Oh,' she moaned, 'don't ask me; I can't think yet. . . . You have killed me, Humphrey—you have killed me!'

He dropped before her chair, and stroked her hand. Her pain writhed like a live thing at his touch, but, in pity for him, she let the hand lie still, and suffered.

'Did you . . . love her so much?' she asked.

'I swear I did not.'

'And yet—Humphrey, she wasn't——'

'I was mad. She was a lady. It wasn't love; I didn't love her at all. . . . If you were a man, you would understand. I sinned with my body, but my mind—she never had that . . . it was with you—with you. It was the animal in me. How can I explain myself to an angel!'

Presently she said:

'Does a woman ever learn to understand a man? She gives him her life, yet to the end——They begin differently. . . . He has known everything before he comes to her, and she has known nothing. She is told that it doesn't matter, that it's Nature, that it's right. She doesn't believe it in her heart—the more she loves him, the less she really believes it—but she tries to persuade herself she believes it. It's wrong—wrong. She is a new girl to him, and to her *he* is a new world. How can marriage be the same thing to both! You didn't love her, but you gave yourself to her. Could a husband think less of his wife's sin for such a reason?'

Kent rose, and stood beside her dumbly. Some glimmer of her point of view reached him, and confused him by its strangeness.

'I will do whatever you order,' he said, in a low voice. 'What can I say?'

'Help me to forget,' she said. 'Will you help me to forget?'

'You will let me come to you?'

'Give me a few days—wait a few days first. Only I can't be your wife again, Humphrey, all at once—I can't. . . . Ah, don't think me unforgiving; it isn't that. Come to me, if you will, and work, and we will be good friends together. Don't be afraid; I won't make it bad for you, I promise. I will never remind you even by a look. Are the terms too hard?'

'You are merciful to me.'

The seconds crept away.

'I must go,' she said; 'I will write to you.'

'Shall you go to your mother's?'

'I must; there is no train to Monmouth after three. Will you send for a cab to take me to Waterloo? I'll tell them you were coming with me, but something prevented you. . . . Can I bathe my eyes in your room before I go?'

Kent led the way to it, and returned to the parlor till she rejoined him. Then they went slowly downstairs, and he put her into the hansom. She leaned forward, and gave him her hand.

'Don't be afraid of me,' she whispered again.

'God bless you!' he said, closing the doors.

CHAPTER XXIV.

CYNTHIA wrote to him to come to her.

The day was bright, and a promise of spring was in the air as he journeyed down. Some of its brightness seemed to tinge his mood, and he was conscious of a vague wonder at the pleasurable emotions that stirred him as the fields and hedgerows shot past.

Cynthia stood on the platform awaiting him, though he had not telegraphed the time of his arrival. He perceived her at once, and was momentarily a prey to misgivings. Her welcoming smile as they advanced toward each other dissipated his dread, but revived his embarrassment, and his reflection of it appeared to her pitiable.

'I knew,' she said frankly, 'that you would come by this train.'

She gave instructions to a porter about his luggage, and Kent passed out into Monmouth by her side. He learnt that her brother had come down to see her, and was now at the cottage. Cæsar was spending a fortnight's holiday with his parents.

'He was going back this evening, but I made him stay till to-morrow. Mrs. Evans found him a room a few doors off.'

He understood that it was to lessen the awkwardness of the first evening for him that she had detained her brother, and was grateful to her as he replied.

'You must know the place well by now?' he murmured, looking about him.

'Every inch, I think. It's so pretty. I'm sorry it isn't summer; you would see. We have a lot of artists then. I got great friends with two girls painting here in the autumn; we used to go to tea at each other's lodgings. I learnt a lot. . . . That's our house—the one at the corner. There's Mrs. Evans at the gate. She calls you "the master." She hopes the master will find her cooking good enough for him. For tea she has made some hot cakes specially in your honor."

As they drew nearer, a nurse approached wheeling a child. He heard that it was 'Humphrey,' and bent over the little fellow timidly. Cynthia hung about them, praying that the boy would not cry. She asked him who the gentleman was, and, having been repeatedly told that 'papa was coming,' he answered 'Papa,' whereat she triumphed and the man was pleased.

In the parlor, which struck Kent agreeably with its quiet, old-fashioned air, 'the Right Hand of McCullough' was perusing a financial paper. He put it aside to greet Kent cordially. His presence dominated the evening, and, in the knowledge that he was departing early next day, Kent even found him amusing, though that was not his aim. Ostensibly he was not taking a holiday, but had come to England on a mission, and his vague allusions to it were weighted by several names of European importance. Occasionally his attention wandered, and he lapsed into a brown study, obviously preoccupied by millions. For this he apologized, lest it had been unnoticed, and rallied Cynthia on the 'yellow-backs' which were visible on the bookshelf.

'I see a lot of yellow-backs,' he said, lifting a playful finger.

A novel, by a woman, of which *The Speaker* had written that 'its dialogue would move every literary artist to enthusiasm,' lay on the window-sill—Kent had already observed it with gratification—and Cæsar acknowledged that he had read it. He conceded that it possessed 'a superficial smartness.' 'Superficial' was his latest word, and when his discourse took a literary turn, the adjective recurred with all the damnable reiteration of 'our great country' in an American leaderette.

Kent's bedroom was furnished very plainly, but was exquisitely neat. His gaze rested with thankfulness on a large table, whose solidity assured one that it would not wobble. On it were a blotting-pad and an ink-stand, of whose construction the primary object had been that it should hold ink; a handful of early flowers were arranged in a china bowl. There was a knot in his throat as he contemplated these preparations—the more touching for their simplicity—and when he sat down, the table confirmed its assurance, and he found that the position afforded him a view of a corner of the garden.

It was here he worked.

By degrees the frankness of her manner became more spontaneous in Cynthia, and her husband's embarrassment in her society was sometimes forgotten. They were, as she had promised, the best of friends. Their rambles together had a charm which one associates with a honeymoon, but in which their own honeymoon had been lacking. In these rambles Kent was never bored; it appeared to him delightful to place himself in her hands, and be taken where 'she listed in the April twilight. To seek shelter from showers in strange quarters was adventurous; and milk had a piquancy drunk with Cynthia in farmyards. He signed the extension of the Streatham agreement with gladness.

The alteration in her impressed him still more strongly now that he had opportunities for studying it, and the gradual result of three years, presenting itself to him as the fruit of ten months, was startling. His wife had become a woman—in her tone, her bearing, in her comments, which often had a pungency, though they might not be brilliant. She was a woman in the composure with which she ignored their anomalous relations—a very fascinating woman withal, whose composure, while it won his admiration, disturbed him, too, as the weeks went by. It was in moments difficult to identify her new personality with the girl's whose love for him had been in such constant evidence. Among her other changes, had she grown to care for him less? He could not wonder if it were so.

Shortly after his arrival, Messrs. Kynaston had begun to send his proof-sheets, and in May 'The Eye of the Beholder' was published. In the walk they took after Cynthia had read it, she and Kent spoke of little else. It had amazed him to perceive how eager he was to hear her verdict, and at her first words, 'I'm proud of you,' the color rushed to his face. He would never have supposed that her approval could excite him so, or that her views would have such interest for him. When the criticisms commenced to come in, it was delicious, as they sat at breakfast, to open the yellow envelopes and devour the long slips with their heads bent together, and then, after he had paid a visit to the child, he would go up to his room, and wish the corner of the garden that he overlooked contained the bench.

Despite the seven rejections, and the opinion of Messrs. Cousins' reader that the construction rendered the novel hopeless, the reviews were magnificent. The more important the paper, the less qualified was the praise. The lighter periodicals were sometimes a little 'superior,' but the literary organs were earnest and cordial in their approbation, and no less an authority than **The Spectator** described the construction as 'masterly.' **The Saturday** repeated that Mr. Kent's style was admirable; and The Athenœum, **and** The Chronicle, **and** The Times, and every journal to which a novelist looks, described him as a realist of a high order.

Delusions die hard, and the bitter reviewer, rending the talented young author's book, is a companion myth to the sleepless editor poring indefatigably over illegible manuscripts in quest of new talent. As a matter of fact, it is only to his reviewers that the struggling literary man ever owes a 'thank you'; and Kent wrote with exultation and confidence under the stimulus of the encouragement he received. 'The Eye of the Beholder' did not sell in thousands—you may lead a donkey to good work, but you cannot make him read—but in a moderate degree it was a success even with the public, and composition had an irresistible attraction in consequence.

Nevertheless, the question whether Cynthia's attitude was not perhaps the one which had become most natural to her haunted Kent with growing persistency.

Had it been possible, he would have asked her. He found himself desirious of a little tenderness from the woman who had wearied him once—or the woman who had sprung from her. She was merciful; she was charming; she drew him toward her strongly, but she talked to him as if she were his sister. The suggestion of a honeymoon in their rambles now tantalized him by its illusiveness, and he was piqued by the feeling that their intercourse was devoid of even the incipient warmth of courtship.

It occurred to him that the book upon which he was engaged might be dedicated to her, and the idea pleased him vastly. It begot several other ideas which he indulged. Roses were transferred from a shop-window to Cynthia's bosom, and he sent to town for a story she had said she would like to read. Her surprise enchanted him, and he wished, as her gaze rested on him, that he could surprise her oftener. The thought of the evening to be passed beside her would come to him during the day, and, tantalizing or not, filled him with impatience to realize the picture again. Tea was no sooner finished than they put on their hats, and wandered where their humor led them, returning at sunset, and sometimes under the stars. Supper would be awaiting them, and afterward they sat and talked, or dreamed, by the open window, until, all too early, she gave him her hand and said 'Good-night.'

His heart followed her. Surely Kent comprehended that the feeling she awoke in him was more than admiration, more than pique, was something infinitely different from the calm affection into which his first fancy had subsided. He felt that the conditions she had imposed had aroused no ephemeral ardor, but had illumined in himself as vividly as in her a development which possession had left obscure. He knew he loved her—he loved her, and he was unworthy of her love. He could not speak—that was for her—but his eyes besought, and the woman read them. She made no sign. So speedily? Her pride forbade it. Her manner toward him remained unchanged, but tenderness tugged at her pride, and joy at what she read flooded her very soul.

She would be contemptible to condone so soon, she told herself. He would never know how he had made her suffer, never suspect how in minutes the unutterable recollection she had hidden for his sake had wrenched and tortured her while she talked to him so easily; she prayed that he never might know. But to yield at his first sigh, because he looked unhappy—how could she contemplate it?

Yet *was* his unhappiness her only temptation? She trembled. Was she despicable to long for his arms about her again . . .was it degraded to feel that even to-day——

In July Kent was lonelier than he had been hitherto. His wife could seldom contrive to accompany him when he went out, and the excursions were in any case curtailed. She seemed to care less for walking, and there were little aggravating things that demanded her attention, or to which, at least, she elected to give it. The child missed her when he woke at eight o'clock if she was not at home to run in to him; she wanted to practice on the wheezy piano; there was needlework she was compelled to do—always something.

On the first occasion Kent was merely disappointed, and returned early in low spirits; but after the third of his solitary expeditions, his misgivings oppressed him with double weight. She was indifferent; no other explanation was possible—she was indifferent, and no longer chose to mask it.

'You are always busy,' he told her at last. 'I miss you dreadfully, Cynthia. Is it so important that what you are doing should be gone on with to-night?'

'I should like to finish it to-night,' she said constrainedly—'yes. I'm sorry you miss me, but the girl is clumsy with her needle; one can't expect perfection.'

'Yesterday something else prevented you. You have only been with me once this week.'

'Surely more than that,' she said calmly; 'twice, I'm certain.'

'Once; you went with me on Tuesday. There is all day for the boy, Cynthia; you might spare me the evening.'

She bent lower over the pinafore, engrossed by it.

'It isn't only the boy, poor little chap! What a tyrant you'd make him out! Yesterday I didn't feel like going; I was up to my eyes in a book.'

Kent regarded her hungrily.

'I have very little claim on you I know, but when I first came—'

'Sh!' she said; 'never refer to your claim on me, please. Besides'—she smiled—'what a mountain out of a molehill. If I haven't been with you since Tuesday, we must have our walk together tomorrow.'

Kent found this very unsatisfactory. It was a concession, and he did not seek her society as a concession. The walk, as usual latterly, was brief, and neither had the air of enjoying it very much. They roamed through the dusty roads for the most part in silence, and for the rest with platitudes. He could not avoid seeing that her companionship was accorded reluctantly, and after their return, when she put out her hand in the stereotyped 'Good-night,' he resolved, as he remained ruminative and miserable, that he would not beg her to go with him any more.

He was not without a hope that, by refraining from the request, he might move her to gratitude; but his wife's avoidance of him did not diminish, and when August came, he questioned whether he ought not to leave her for awhile. The part she had allotted to herself had plainly proved more than she could sustain, and to relieve her of his presence temporarily might be the most considerate plan he could adopt. The notion repelled him violently. Though she was colder and ill at ease, she enchained him. He had very little, and that little he was loath to lose. To look at her across the room, unobserved, in their long pauses was not charged with regret only—the bitterness had an indefinable joy as well; he liked to note the effect of lamplight on her profile as she read, took pleasure in her grace when she moved. To spare her what distress he could, however, was his duty—yes, if she wished it, he would go. He debated, where he sat smoking by the window one evening, whether she would wish it if she knew how dear she had grown to him; whether, if he stammered to her something of his remorse——His pain had become almost intolerable.

The hour was very still. In the west, on the faint azure, some smears of flame color lingered—then, while he stared out, faded, and hung in the sky like curls of violet smoke. Over the myriad tints of green came the low whinny of a horse. His wife sat sewing by the table, and, turning, Kent watched the rhythmical movement of her hand, a passionate longing assailing him the while to free his tongue from the weight that hampered it, and cry to her he loved her, though she might not care to hear. He knocked the ashes from his pipe, and sauntered nearer.

'Aren't you going to smoke any more?' she said.

'Not now; I've been smoking all day.'

'You should try to write without.'

'I ought to—but I never could.'

He touched the muslin on her lap diffidently—it **was** on her lap.

'What are you making—another pinafore?'

'Yes. Do you think it's pretty?'

His hand lay close to her own, but she held the garment up to him, and he drew back.

'Very nice,' he said briefly.

It was not so easy to voice emotion as to feel it. A half-hour crept away; shadows filled the room, and a gray peace brooded over the grass outside. The tones deepened, and beyond a ridge of blackened boughs the moon swam up. He decided that he would speak after supper; but after supper, when she resumed her sewing, he felt it would be useless. He sat by the hearth, holding a paper that he did not read. Presently the landlady was heard slipping the bolt in the passage, and Cynthia pushed her basket from her, preparing to retire. With her change of position, a reel escaped, and rolled to the fender. Kent had not noticed where it fell, but he became conscious, with a tremor, that she was stooping by his side. In rising, it seemed to him that her figure brushed his arm as if with a caress. She had drawn apart from him before he could do more than wonder if it had been accidental, but now he watched her with a curious intentness. She wandered about the room a little aimlessly, righting a photograph, settling a flower in a glass upon the shelf. After she had gathered up her work, she hesitated, and sought some books—her hands were full when she had chosen them. He opened the door, and she moved toward it slowly.

As she passed out, her head was turned, and for a moment her gaze engulfed him. . . . Kent realized that she had gone without saying 'Goodnight.'

THE END

The Codes Of Hammurabi And Moses
W. W. Davies

QTY

The discovery of the Hammurabi Code is one of the greatest achievements of archaeology, and is of paramount interest, not only to the student of the Bible, but also to all those interested in ancient history...

Religion   **ISBN:** *1-59462-338-4*   **Pages:132**
MSRP $12.95

The Theory of Moral Sentiments
Adam Smith

QTY

This work from 1749. contains original theories of conscience amd moral judgment and it is the foundation for systemof morals.

Philosophy   **ISBN:** *1-59462-777-0*   **Pages:536**
MSRP $19.95

Jessica's First Prayer
Hesba Stretton

QTY

In a screened and secluded corner of one of the many railway-bridges which span the streets of London there could be seen a few years ago, from five o'clock every morning until half past eight, a tidily set-out coffee-stall, consisting of a trestle and board, upon which stood two large tin cans, with a small fire of charcoal burning under each so as to keep the coffee boiling during the early hours of the morning when the work-people were thronging into the city on their way to their daily toil...

Childrens   **ISBN:** *1-59462-373-2*   **Pages:84**
MSRP $9.95

My Life and Work
Henry Ford

QTY

Henry Ford revolutionized the world with his implementation of mass production for the Model T automobile. Gain valuable business insight into his life and work with his own auto-biography... "We have only started on our development of our country we have not as yet, with all our talk of wonderful progress, done more than scratch the surface. The progress has been wonderful enough but..."

Biographies/   **ISBN:** *1-59462-198-5*   **Pages:300**
MSRP $21.95

The Art of Cross-Examination
Francis Wellman

QTY

I presume it is the experience of every author, after his first book is published upon an important subject, to be almost overwhelmed with a wealth of ideas and illustrations which could readily have been included in his book, and which to his own mind, at least, seem to make a second edition inevitable. Such certainly was the case with me; and when the first edition had reached its sixth impression in five months, I rejoiced to learn that it seemed to my publishers that the book had met with a sufficiently favorable reception to justify a second and considerably enlarged edition. ...

Pages:412

Reference   ISBN: *1-59462-647-2*   *MSRP $19.95*

On the Duty of Civil Disobedience
Henry David Thoreau

QTY

Thoreau wrote his famous essay, On the Duty of Civil Disobedience, as a protest against an unjust but popular war and the immoral but popular institution of slave-owning. He did more than write—he declined to pay his taxes, and was hauled off to gaol in consequence. Who can say how much this refusal of his hastened the end of the war and of slavery ?

Law   ISBN: *1-59462-747-9*   **Pages:48**
MSRP $7.45

Dream Psychology Psychoanalysis for Beginners
Sigmund Freud

QTY

Sigmund Freud, born Sigismund Schlomo Freud (May 6, 1856 - September 23, 1939), was a Jewish-Austrian neurologist and psychiatrist who co-founded the psychoanalytic school of psychology. Freud is best known for his theories of the unconscious mind, especially involving the mechanism of repression; his redefinition of sexual desire as mobile and directed towards a wide variety of objects; and his therapeutic techniques, especially his understanding of transference in the therapeutic relationship and the presumed value of dreams as sources of insight into unconscious desires.

Pages:196

Psychology   ISBN: *1-59462-905-6*   *MSRP $15.45*

The Miracle of Right Thought
Orison Swett Marden

QTY

Believe with all of your heart that you will do what you were made to do. When the mind has once formed the habit of holding cheerful, happy, prosperous pictures, it will not be easy to form the opposite habit. It does not matter how improbable or how far away this realization may see, or how dark the prospects may be, if we visualize them as best we can, as vividly as possible, hold tenaciously to them and vigorously struggle to attain them, they will gradually become actualized, realized in the life. But a desire, a longing without endeavor, a yearning abandoned or held indifferently will vanish without realization.

Pages:360

Self Help   ISBN: *1-59462-644-8*   *MSRP $25.45*

QTY

The Rosicrucian Cosmo-Conception Mystic Christianity *by Max Heindel* ISBN: *1-59462-188-8* **$38.95**
The Rosicrucian Cosmo-conception is not dogmatic, neither does it appeal to any other authority than the reason of the student. It is: not controversial, but is: sent forth in the, hope that it may help to clear... New Age/Religion Pages 646

Abandonment To Divine Providence *by Jean-Pierre de Caussade* ISBN: *1-59462-228-0* **$25.95**
"The Rev. Jean Pierre de Caussade was one of the most remarkable spiritual writers of the Society of Jesus in France in the 18th Century. His death took place at Toulouse in 1751. His works have gone through many editions and have been republished... Inspirational/Religion Pages 400

Mental Chemistry *by Charles Haanel* ISBN: *1-59462-192-6* **$23.95**
Mental Chemistry allows the change of material conditions by combining and appropriately utilizing the power of the mind. Much like applied chemistry creates something new and unique out of careful combinations of chemicals the mastery of mental chemistry... New Age Pages 354

The Letters of Robert Browning and Elizabeth Barret Barrett 1845-1846 vol II ISBN: *1-59462-193-4* **$35.95**
by Robert Browning and Elizabeth Barrett Biographies Pages 596

Gleanings In Genesis (volume I) *by Arthur W. Pink* ISBN: *1-59462-130-6* **$27.45**
Appropriately has Genesis been termed "the seed plot of the Bible" for in it we have, in germ form, almost all of the great doctrines which are afterwards fully developed in the books of Scripture which follow... Religion/Inspirational Pages 420

The Master Key *by L. W. de Laurence* ISBN: *1-59462-001-6* **$30.95**
In no branch of human knowledge has there been a more lively increase of the spirit of research during the past few years than in the study of Psychology, Concentration and Mental Discipline. The requests for authentic lessons in Thought Control, Mental Discipline and... New Age/Business Pages 422

The Lesser Key Of Solomon Goetia *by L. W. de Laurence* ISBN: *1-59462-092-X* **$9.95**
This translation of the first book of the "Lernegton" which is now for the first time made accessible to students of Talismanic Magic was done, after careful collation and edition, from numerous Ancient Manuscripts in Hebrew, Latin, and French... New Age/Occult Pages 92

Rubaiyat Of Omar Khayyam *by Edward Fitzgerald* ISBN:*1-59462-332-5* **$13.95**
Edward Fitzgerald, whom the world has already learned, in spite of his own efforts to remain within the shadow of anonymity, to look upon as one of the rarest poets of the century, was born at Bredfield, in Suffolk, on the 31st of March, 1809. He was the third son of John Purcell... Music Pages 172

Ancient Law *by Henry Maine* ISBN: *1-59462-128-4* **$29.95**
The chief object of the following pages is to indicate some of the earliest ideas of mankind, as they are reflected in Ancient Law, and to point out the relation of those ideas to modern thought. Religion/History Pages 452

Far-Away Stories *by William J. Locke* ISBN: *1-59462-129-2* **$19.45**
"Good wine needs no bush, but a collection of mixed vintages does. And this book is just such a collection. Some of the stories I do not want to remain buried for ever in the museum files of dead magazine-numbers an author's not unpardonable vanity..." Fiction Pages 272

Life of David Crockett *by David Crockett* ISBN: *1-59462-250-7* **$27.45**
"Colonel David Crockett was one of the most remarkable men of the times in which he lived. Born in humble life, but gifted with a strong will, an indomitable courage, and unremitting perseverance... Biographies/New Age Pages 424

Lip-Reading *by Edward Nitchie* ISBN: *1-59462-206-X* **$25.95**
Edward B. Nitchie, founder of the New York School for the Hard of Hearing, now the Nitchie School of Lip-Reading, Inc, wrote "LIP-READING Principles and Practice". The development and perfecting of this meritorious work on lip-reading was an undertaking... How-to Pages 400

A Handbook of Suggestive Therapeutics, Applied Hypnotism, Psychic Science ISBN: *1-59462-214-0* **$24.95**
by Henry Munro Health/New Age/Health/Self-help Pages 376

A Doll's House: and Two Other Plays *by Henrik Ibsen* ISBN: *1-59462-112-8* **$19.95**
Henrik Ibsen created this classic when in revolutionary 1848 Rome. Introducing some striking concepts in playwriting for the realist genre, this play has been studied the world over. Fiction/Classics/Plays 308

The Light of Asia *by sir Edwin Arnold* ISBN: *1-59462-204-3* **$13.95**
In this poetic masterpiece, Edwin Arnold describes the life and teachings of Buddha. The man who was to become known as Buddha to the world was born as Prince Gautama of India but he rejected the worldly riches and abandoned the reigns of power when... Religion/History/Biographies Pages 170

The Complete Works of Guy de Maupassant *by Guy de Maupassant* ISBN: *1-59462-157-8* **$16.95**
"For days and days, nights and nights, I had dreamed of that first kiss which was to consecrate our engagement, and I knew not on what spot I should put my lips..." Fiction/Classics Pages 240

The Art of Cross-Examination *by Francis L. Wellman* ISBN: *1-59462-309-0* **$26.95**
Written by a renowned trial lawyer, Wellman imparts his experience and uses case studies to explain how to use psychology to extract desired information through questioning. How-to/Science/Reference Pages 408

Answered or Unanswered? *by Louisa Vaughan* ISBN: *1-59462-248-5* **$10.95**
Miracles of Faith in China Religion Pages 112

The Edinburgh Lectures on Mental Science (1909) *by Thomas* ISBN: *1-59462-008-3* **$11.95**
This book contains the substance of a course of lectures recently given by the writer in the Queen Street Hall, Edinburgh. Its purpose is to indicate the Natural Principles governing the relation between Mental Action and Material Conditions... New Age/Psychology Pages 148

Ayesha *by H. Rider Haggard* ISBN: *1-59462-301-5* **$24.95**
Verily and indeed it is the unexpected that happens! Probably if there was one person upon the earth from whom the Editor of this, and of a certain previous history, did not expect to hear again... Classics Pages 380

Ayala's Angel *by Anthony Trollope* ISBN: *1-59462-352-X* **$29.95**
The two girls were both pretty, but Lucy who was twenty-one who supposed to be simple and comparatively unattractive, whereas Ayala was credited, as her Bombwhat romantic name might show, with poetic charm and a taste for romance. Ayala when her father died was nineteen... Fiction Pages 484

The American Commonwealth *by James Bryce* ISBN: *1-59462-286-8* **$34.45**
An interpretation of American democratic political theory. It examines political mechanics and society from the perspective of Scotsman James Bryce Politics Pages 572

Stories of the Pilgrims *by Margaret P. Pumphrey* ISBN: *1-59462-116-0* **$17.95**
This book explores pilgrims religious oppression in England as well as their escape to Holland and eventual crossing to America on the Mayflower, and their early days in New England... History Pages 268

QTY

The Fasting Cure *by Sinclair Upton*   ISBN: *1-59462-222-1*   **$13.95**
In the Cosmopolitan Magazine for May, 1910, and in the Contemporary Review (London) for April, 1910, I published an article dealing with my experiences in fasting. I have written a great many magazine articles, but never one which attracted so much attention...   New Age/Self Help/Health Pages 164

Hebrew Astrology *by Sepharial*   ISBN: *1-59462-308-2*   **$13.45**
In these days of advanced thinking it is a matter of common observation that we have left many of the old landmarks behind and that we are now pressing forward to greater heights and to a wider horizon than that which represented the mind-content of our progenitors...   Astrology Pages 144

Thought Vibration or The Law of Attraction in the Thought World   ISBN: *1-59462-127-6*   **$12.95**
by William Walker Atkinson   Psychology/Religion Pages 144

Optimism *by Helen Keller*   ISBN: *1-59462-108-X*   **$15.95**
Helen Keller was blind, deaf, and mute since 19 months old, yet famously learned how to overcome these handicaps, communicate with the world, and spread her lectures promoting optimism. An inspiring read for everyone...   Biographies/Inspirational Pages 84

Sara Crewe *by Frances Burnett*   ISBN: *1-59462-360-0*   **$9.45**
In the first place, Miss Minchin lived in London. Her home was a large, dull, tall one, in a large, dull square, where all the houses were alike, and all the sparrows were alike, and where all the door-knockers made the same heavy sound...   Childrens/Classic Pages 88

The Autobiography of Benjamin Franklin *by Benjamin Franklin*   ISBN: *1-59462-135-7*   **$24.95**
The Autobiography of Benjamin Franklin has probably been more extensively read than any other American historical work, and no other book of its kind has had such ups and downs of fortune. Franklin lived for many years in England, where he was agent...   Biographies/History Pages 332

Name	
Email	
Telephone	
Address	
City, State ZIP	

☐ **Credit Card**   ☐ **Check / Money Order**

Credit Card Number	
Expiration Date	
Signature	

Please Mail to: Book Jungle
PO Box 2226
Champaign, IL 61825
or Fax to: 630-214-0564

ORDERING INFORMATION

web: *www.bookjungle.com*
email: *sales@bookjungle.com*
fax: *630-214-0564*
mail: *Book Jungle PO Box 2226 Champaign, IL 61825*
or PayPal *to sales@bookjungle.com*

Please contact us for bulk discounts

DIRECT-ORDER TERMS

**20% Discount if You Order
Two or More Books**
Free Domestic Shipping!
Accepted: Master Card, Visa,
Discover, American Express

www.ingramcontent.com/pod-product-compliance
Lightning Source LLC
Chambersburg PA
CBHW080729020726
47503CB00010B/2851